THE REMBRANDT
MURDER

THE REMBRANDT
MURDER

Henry James Forman

COACHWHIP PUBLICATIONS
GREENVILLE, OHIO

The Rembrandt Murder, by Henry James Forman
© 2025 Coachwhip Publications edition
Cover: Wallpaper © Phase4Photography; frame © Nina
    Malyna; 'Tartan Chief,' Ideogram

First published 1931
Henry James Forman, 1879-1966
CoachwhipBooks.com

ISBN 1-61646-625-1
ISBN-13 978-1-61646-625-1

1
A Great House

There was nothing Roland Ross, Professor of Criminology at King's College, envied King Solomon more heartily than the experience of having the demon Asmodeus lift for him the roofs of all houses. As a student of human nature and of the twists and peculiarities of the human mind, Ross felt that if he ever met Asmodeus, a little personally conducted jaunt over the roofs of New York would be the only favor he would suggest with any degree of urgency.

There was, for example, that magnificent house in Fifth avenue which he had visited twice or thrice, one of the most imposing of the metropolis. Its priceless furnishings, its pictures, bronzes, marbles and decorations, its matchless tapestries and rugs, diffused an air of opulence and luxury perhaps unique even in the richest city in the world.

Behind the house and continuous with it in Sixty-second street runs a one-story gallery built of the same gray stone, some seventy feet toward Madison Avenue. The gallery houses a collection of pictures variously estimated at from two to five million dollars. Surely, thought Ross, nothing but happiness should dwell in a house like that.

Besides, its owner, James Harding Goold, stood out in the history and economics of America as one of its richest citizens. His name, long prominent in the business and financial annals of the city, indeed, of the entire country, projected like a solid pier in lists of charitable givers and contributors, in boards of directors and civic enterprises. The high gods had very evidently conspired to exalt the fortunes of James H. Goold over those of his fellow mortals. Partly by inheritance, but more by his own skill and success, riches beyond the dizziest dreams had come to him easily and swiftly.

To Ross, however, a single glance had shown that the Goold household was not a happy one. To begin with, a childless home, notably if it be a rich one, seems, as under some Biblical curse, irrevocably marked for extinction. And had it not been for Lorna, Goold's orphaned niece living in the house, no laughter apparently would ever have been heard within its walls.

Ross, of course, knew the current reports and gossip. Current reports and gossip, however, seldom explain and sometimes they even mystify. Behind them all there is always some hidden profound cause of which surface facts are only conditions. He knew, for example, that for more than two years Mrs. Goold had been a bed-ridden invalid, a paralytic, unable to move her lower limbs; that, indeed, she had been an invalid for some time preceding her paralysis. Yet, had he been able to overhear some of the conversations between Mrs. Goold and her favorite nurse, Miss Baker, he might have concluded that the invalid herself was perhaps the happiest person in that household. She was resigned, yet she was cheerful. To Miss Baker she had more than once confessed that but for the devotion of her husband, his loyalty and fidelity, and her love for him, she might not have cared to go on living.

"But surely, Mrs. Goold," had protested Miss Baker, "you would not think of committing the terrible sin of suicide?"

Miss Baker, somewhat stout and fortyish, differed from most of her kind in that she was pious, God-fearing and a Bible-reader.

"No, Miss Baker," Mrs. Goold had assured her with her resigned wistful smile, "I could not possibly do that. No. I would simply have stopped living. But when I think of the devotion and kindness of that marvelous, that wonderful man—he, with his genius and his power!—and all this love and kindness he has given me. Always—always—ever since I have known him—" there were tears in her voice—"I am greatly blessed," she whispered huskily. "And nothing—nothing I can do for all his devotion and his loyalty, his perfect loyalty, except try to spare him every atom of pain and shock, is there?"

Miss Baker tried her best to smile sentimentally.

"You have been with me now—how long is it, Miss Baker?" went on the invalid.

"Over two years, Mrs. Goold."

"Oh, dear, it seems twenty—you know what I mean, Miss Baker—it's this condition, not you. You have always been so sweet to me. But do you remember any day since you've been here, when he didn't come in to see me, if he was at home? Or when his fresh flowers haven't arrived? Even when he's away, out of the country, those sweet re-membrances never fail, do they?"

"No indeed, Mrs. Goold." Miss Baker rose somewhat restlessly for one of her build, and proceeded to lower a window-shade half an inch. Mrs. Goold was a vastly wealthy patient and she, Miss Baker, knew, she hoped, her place and the position to which it had pleased God to call her. But at moments like this she was visited by a rebel-lious impatience in her warring members. It was all very well for this bed-ridden wife, shut away from the world in a sick-room, to be obsessed with the idea that her husband

was an Angel. Common report, however, declared otherwise, and what was more, Miss Baker felt certain common
report was right.

Her calling and her proclivities had given her no mean
insight into whited sepulchres, and if ever there was a
whited sepulchre, that, to her mind, was James Goold.
Wherever there was smoke, there was sure to be fire. And
where people whispered so much of Goold's ways, his
women and his wickedness, there was sure to be some
truth in it.

"Of course," she went on bravely, somewhat heavily,
"everyone knows how devoted Mr. Goold is to you."

Everyone knew, too, felt Miss Baker, that the best thing
a body could do was to foster this ingrained belief of the
poor paralytic woman in the perfect love and integrity
of that husband. In her Bible-quoting mind, however,
was running the verse from Paul's Epistle to the Romans,
which she knew so well:

"The wages of sin is death."

Wasn't there the story of that woman, Sheila Something, only quite recently? And weren't there others before
that? Some day some one of these women, or some one
connected with them, would topple this Colossus off the
pedestal upon which his afflicted wife had fondly placed
him. There would be a great scandal—or something.

Whether Goold was the sinner repute gave him credit
for will presently emerge. But that, in any case, he was
none the happier, the picture of him sitting alone in his
gallery, getting the news over the radio, playing solitaire
by the hour, or brooding with corrugated forehead should
at least suggest.

Whether he loved his wife as much as she very evidently
believed is a question that may perhaps best be answered
by the fact that for some time past his mind had been
centered upon a woman—a woman so beautiful, and one

whom he had loved so passionately, that her passing out of his life had left it seemingly empty, but actually a prey to the most intense and aching jealousy. Goold was what is called a strong man. The chief difference between a Goold and a weaker man is that a Goold is capable of concealing his suffering—which is probably the more acute for that very reason. He could conceal it from all those about him, he felt certain, with the possible exception of his niece. Lorna, however, young girl though she was, had been of late peculiarly tender and affectionate with him. The bond between them was a close one. And if Lorna knew of the ache in his heart she never betrayed it. Lorna, he often reflected, was like a daughter with the wisdom of a mother.

His wife, naturally, had to be spared in every possible way. Goold was not the type of man to speak of his business worries to his wife, not even when she had been hale. Her grave invalidism naturally protected her now against the betrayal of so much as the shadow of worry. Though he himself had always been rich, even before his fortune had become colossal, he had married a poor girl because he had loved her. If his heart had later strayed, no one who knew would have dreamed of conveying such knowledge to his wife.

Besides, her own pride, her pride in him, in his towering capacity and ability, would have indignantly repudiated the slightest maculation on his fame had she heard of it.

But even had Ross known all of these things, as some of them he did know by current rumor, he would still have been deeply interested in the underlying cause, the *causa causans,* the inner mystery behind all the facts and appearances.

As events came about he was destined to discover the only thing worth discovering—the truth.

2
Roland Ross

"Detective stories," said Professor Ross in his vibrant, genial voice, "detective and mystery tales form the natural literature of the machine age. In a way that is inevitable. Life itself today has so many more thrills than were dreamed of half a century ago, that the usual forms of literature, the work-a-day novels of sentiment, of observation or even of psychology can hardly compete with it. Mind, I don't condemn the species. It is said to bring entertainment to the jaded and rest to the weary. I simply state the fact. As a matter of reality, however, there are no mysteries. I repeat, there are no mysteries. There is only lack of knowledge.

"Sir Arthur Conan Doyle has achieved perhaps more than any other criminological fictionist because he has shown that there is no such thing as a master mind in crime, provided there is an acute mind in detection resolved to ferret him out. Every criminal, no matter how astute, always has his special stigmata and leaves his own peculiar traces on his crime.

"This is a course in Criminal Anthropology. Crime is a serious obstacle to civilization, and society cannot tolerate an increase and must work for a decrease in crime. At least a secondary object of this course is to help to reduce it. In a way, this course is a laboratory in scientific understanding of criminals, but not, mind you, in making Lecoqs and Dupins out of you. With these fabulous creatures of superhuman attributes and some of their less vital descendants in the current fiction we simply have nothing to do.

"These lectures may possibly help you to understand the criminal type of human being, to get some notion of his physical, mental and psychic make-up. But, let me add by the way, that if there is any one thing the generous citizens and alumni of King's College had no thought of in endowing this chair, it was to increase the volume of detective fiction, already immense. Though I gather," he went on in another tone, at once whimsical and endearing, "that most of them read it passionately—and, I am free to admit, so do I.

"Next time, then," he returned to his professional manner, "we should begin our consideration of criminal types, and I suggest that you read the first thirty pages of Hooton's text." He nodded, with a smile, his usual signal for dismissal and the class, an odd assortment of the serious and the frivolous types of students, broke up and drifted out of the room.

It was three o'clock in the afternoon. Ross's work for the day was over. His cheerful air as he left the lecture room, Philosophy 707, and with firm, brisk step descended the stairs softly humming to himself, showed clearly that neither his professional dignity nor his duties weighed upon him more heavily than upon the youngest of his students.

Lorna Storey and Jimmie Trumbull, two of these students, left Philosophy Hall together, as had been their custom now for several days.

With her violet eyes, her perfect clothes and even more perfect complexion, Lorna was unquestionably the most attractive co-ed on the campus. She was twenty-two. Unlike many of her contemporaries, she had a serious interest in anthropology, that is, in human beings. Her decision to continue postgraduate work and enroll in Ross's course came simultaneously after her first meeting with Ross at her uncle's house. To her a knowledge of human nature was the supreme knowledge worth pursuing and Ross the most adequate professor of the subject she had ever met.

Jimmie Trumbull, however, though nearly three years older than Lorna, was far more desultory in his choice. Thoughtful parents having left him an income sufficient not to make a plunge into bond selling immediately oblig-atory, he fancied that a year of graduate work at King's after his small New England college, and certain courses wisely selected by himself, might better fit him for the adventure of Life.

On registration day he had happened to overhear the one girl who took his eye saying that she was about to reg-ister for Ross's course in Criminal Anthropology. Instant-ly Jimmie felt that of all the stores of learning available at King's, nothing could possibly be more conducive to his own future success in life than that very course. And thus, well-watered by adroit attentions, such as taking the seat next to hers, enquiring the names of text books and generally making himself agreeable, his acquaintance with Lorna grew with the usual modern rapidity. She, upon her part, discovered in Jimmie certain traits of simple loyalty, kindliness and a warm ingenuousness that appealed to her.

"I see clearly what we've absolutely got to have, Lorna," Jimmie began as they sauntered down the stairs. "First thing we want is a good murder. Then we'll go to work on it, solve it and hand in our report as a thesis to Ross and get an A on the course. Could anything be easier?"

"Don't be gruesome, James. But do you know, that man Ross puts ideas into my head?"

"Criminal!" cried James, lighting a cigarette. "And your uncle a trustee, too! What do you suppose they do to a professor who goes and puts ideas into people's heads?"

"Don't be so humorous on an empty stomach, Jimmie dear. It's unhygienic. I suggest only five wisecracks a day—one after each meal."

"Five! When did you ever see me eat five meals a day, woman?"

"Don't be so passionate, darling. I know how the subject of meals stirs you."

Jimmie's whole-souled laughter sounded better than any of his repartee.

"You are a brilliant conversationalist, Jimmie," Lorna glanced at him kindly. "But let us leave this airy piffle, shall we?" They were crossing the street to where Lorna's wine-colored roadster was parked. "Would you feel like running out to Bronx Park, and possibly beyond, to see the leaves turning? I'd adore it if you'd come, James."

"To the ends of the world, with you, my lass! But how is it you are not going home, Lorna?"

"Well, to tell you the truth, home isn't a very pleasant place for me just now. Uncle Jim has been pretty gloomy since his return from Europe and I don't much blame him, either."

"How come?" queried James.

"Well, with my aunt the way she is—a paralytic, there isn't much fun at home. Besides—oh, well,—perhaps I'll take you home to dinner, Jimmie. Your bright childish prattle and cunning ways might brighten him up, if he's there."

"Great, Lorna, great! But imagine me," he cloaked his very genuine modesty with a boisterous laugh, "imagine me cheering up James H. Goold—who has everything in the world!"

"Don't be a sap, Jimmie," said Lorna sweetly. "He has money—yes, but there are some things—" and she paused.

"Oh, well," stammered the boy, "I don't mean—what I meant was—well, you know—" Jimmie was at his best when he was inarticulate.

"Yes, I know, of course," she interposed quickly to lessen his embarrassment. "Let's go. Would you drive, Jimmie?"

He would and did—picking his way through the uptown traffic along Riverside Drive into Broadway and thence into Fordham Road on the way to the Park.

A brooding silence seemed to have settled upon Lorna and the young man realized that it was more than the mere desire not to disturb him while driving in heavy traffic. Something was troubling her. She appeared positively smaller as she shrank back in her corner.

"Did you notice," he began as soon as they entered the Park, "Ross still sometimes smiles when anyone calls him Professor?"

Lorna nodded.

"He's a master of Arts of neither university, as somebody said about somebody," grinned Jimmie.

"Exactly—as Dempsey snobbishly said about Gene Tunney," Lorna smiled faintly at Jimmie's uncertain erudition. "He's not long on degrees, if that's what you mean. My uncle told me all about him. He was a natural student, crazy about all kinds of knowledge. But his way of getting it was his own. I think he shipped as a sailor before the mast out of San Francisco when he was barely eighteen. Then he came back and tried college again for a while. Since then he's been everywhere and seen everything. Do you know, Jimmie, that he's herded sheep in Australia, served in the Philippine police, written books on anthropology, spent years in China, Siberia and Europe and the rest of the world and that he writes scrumptious light verse? And don't you love that funny little squeak in his voice when he's excited about anything?"

"Look here, little girl," protested the young man, half seriously, "if you don't look out you'll be falling in love with him—see if you don't!"

"A lot of good that would do me! As though every woman in the class wasn't in love with him already! He doesn't even see us. I am afraid, James, that is where Ross differs from you. He's not susceptible. Look at those leaves on that maple! Did you ever see such gorgeous reds? Aren't they heavenly!"

"Yeah," said James, whose artistic perception was rudimentary. "Yeah, they certainly are great." His mind of the one-track variety, was still running on Ross.

"Old King's," he went on, "certainly did a good job getting a bird like Ross in among the dry sticks of its faculty. 'People, people, human beings—their desires, their passions and their motives—that's what ought to interest you.' Remember how often he gets that off, Lorna?"

"Yes," said Lorna pensively. "He makes us feel as though we were just out of the kindergarten. Yet nobody wants to miss a word he's said."

"I went to lunch with old Smith the other day, you know—the History Prof.—at the Faculty Club. Did I tell you, Lorna? And those old birds gathered around Ross with their cigars and fired questions at him like a lot of machine guns. I can't even remember the questions," he laughed. "About dialects of North Siberia; something about the Kulu gods of the Himalayas; the population of Bukovina; the snails of Tahiti; the economic life of the Mongols, and the mating habits of the Trobriand Islanders, wherever they are. Those are only a few—all I can remember—and Ross answered them all. And besides that he has a theory that every criminal should have his ductless glands examined and that in ninety-nine per cent of 'em they'd be found defective. Can you beat it?"

"Shan't try to, Jimmie," Lorna returned almost drowsily, as though her thoughts were far away. "And only last week my uncle told me that Police Commissioner Wells has made Ross a sort of consultant to the Detective Bureau—a dollar-a-year man—to help fight the crime wave."

"Gee! That about caps it, doesn't it?" exclaimed James.

"Not to gild the lily, it about does, Jimmiekins. But don't let's talk about Professor Ross any more, please. Let's park here. I want to sit still and think a while. Then we'll go home. Mind?"

Jimmie, the soul of amiability, did not mind at all.

3
In Quest of Trouble

The subject of the young people's conversation that afternoon, Roland Ross, for all his wide and miscellaneous knowledge, admitted to himself that he was baffled—floored. The encyclopedic quizzes by his colleagues at the Faculty Club were child's play to what presently confronted him.

He had walked ten city blocks down Fifth Avenue through the crisp autumn twilight before he realized that he was in the Seventies and on his way to James Goold, bent upon the most singular mission he had ever been foolhardy enough to undertake.

"Just what am I going to say to Goold," he asked himself, "and how say it? Goold is a man of the world, of course, and one ought to be able to talk straight to him, but what man, simple or complex, would tolerate a stranger's mixing up in his innermost private affairs? If the man doesn't brain me he will have an excellent right to kick me out. And no one would applaud him more than I. Looks to me as though my absurd promise is destined to end my connection with the august society of scholars known as King's College. Phew! The thinking mind revolts at this incredible piece of folly I have let myself in for. Better leave the problem simmering in the brain until the solution leaps out on the spur of the moment.

"The subconscious!—blessed subconscious! What would we do if psychology had never discovered that! . . . James Goold! If only it were anybody but Goold! What a mess—what a mess! Why did I make that promise?—Only because it is so difficult to fulfill! Oh, vainest of the vain—Roland Ross! But for every problem there is said to be a solution."

And resolutely he kept on with unhurried steps down the avenue. He walked past Sixty-second street as far as the Plaza, turned back upon his tracks and finally found himself in front of the massive side entrance to the Goold mansion, the gallery door in East Sixty-second Street.

Self-possessed though Ross ordinarily was, and calm even in the face of danger, he had never before, he knew, experienced so strange a thrill as when he approached the door to press the bell button. But suddenly he paused in the act of lifting his hand. The heavy black metal door was not only unlocked, it was ajar some six or seven inches away from the jamb. That was odd. Was it an accident, or had Goold done it in anticipation of his visit in order to eliminate servants? Unlikely. Goold might have done that for a woman, but not for Professor Ross. However, Ross remembered that this was only the door of the vestibule.

He was aware of voices, at once rollicking and languid voices, in the well-known intonations of the negro. What could that be? Two negroes were warmly discussing the technical points of a prizefight, determining in their ingenuous way precisely how to achieve a foul. That was a radio instrument going, of course.

There was an inner door and presumably an inner bell.

His astonishment was great when, as he pushed the heavy door open and found himself in the shallow vestibule to see the inner door likewise ajar to the same extent of about five or six inches. There was, moreover, no bell in the vestibule and no light. That was singular.

The radio voices were now louder, more clamant and raucous.

The only thing he could do now was to step back out-side and ring the door-bell. He pressed the button firm-ly and waited, a slight perspiration, notwithstanding his self-possession, suddenly making him feel his clothes against his body.

No one answered his ring. Thirty seconds is a long time to wait at a door when one is keyed up. Ross waited a good sixty seconds and still no one came. The massive limestone of the gallery appeared to him gray and cold and forbid-ding. No light was showing in the oblong one-story struc-ture with its row of barred windows higher than normal from the ground. Always this house and particularly this queue that was the gallery had given the appearance of being close and guarded. Now, to Ross's heightened ner-vous reactions, it presented a picture almost sinister. Why were the doors ajar to a gallery that housed more than two million dollars' worth of pictures! Still no answer.

Resolutely he pushed open the outer door, and then the inner. If there was any meaning in all this curious negli-gence in so well-ordered a house, he would learn what it was, come what might.

He was standing within the gallery. It was dusk. James Goold's great teakwood desk and chair stood in the centre of the upper portion of the gallery almost opposite the door.

James Goold himself was sitting in the chair, his chin resting upon his breast in a pose of lassitude. Seemingly he had gone to sleep in his chair.

At his left was standing a radio instrument housed in a dark, handsomely carved console of teakwood matching his desk. He had been obviously listening to something over the radio, perhaps the stock market prices, and fallen asleep. That was possibly why the servant had not turned on any lights. Awkward. That failed to explain, however, the open doors and the lack of response to the bell. Should he waken Goold? A man roused from a nap was very apt to be irritable. Goold was a big man, of course, still no one with a request, a request of the magnitude Ross felt himself burdened with, desired to approach an irritable man.

Yet here he, Ross, was, by appointment!

Never before in all his experience of life had Ross found himself in so embarrassing a situation.

What was the best way of making his presence known, of awakening Goold, and yet not impair his good humor? Should he call a servant or go back to the door and slam it hard enough to awaken the sleeper? Softly Ross approached the desk a little nearer. He stood now perhaps four feet from Goold. By this time his eyes had grown more accustomed to the dusk.

He had all but decided to sink quietly into the comfortable upholstered chair that stood beside Goold's desk and wait until Goold wakened or someone came into the room when, on a sudden, he was startled by something queer in Goold's attitude. Impulsively yet carefully he bent down to look at Goold's eyes. They were not closed. They were open wide and staring glassily at the edge of his desk. Was the man in a drunken stupor? At almost the same instant Ross's hand touched the right hand of Goold hanging limply over the arm of the chair.

A faint tremor of chill passed through Ross. The hand of Goold was cold. Quickly he touched the man's right temple with the tips of his fingers. There was no pulse in it.

Goold was dead!

4

In the Gallery

Goold was dead!

Very simple, but to Ross the discovery of this fact, the man to whom he talked over the telephone scarcely an hour earlier, who was instinct with life, the modulations of whose voice were still sounding in his ears, was at once stunning and numbing. It sent a cold trickle of perspiration all over his body, and instinctively he gasped for the breath of life.

And why was this damnable radio going! The drawling voices in the negro dialect had given way to the crash of a jazz band in some hotel tea room, and the wail of the saxophone on a sudden sent its derisively lugubrious chord round the atmosphere of the dead man. There was to Ross something at once uncanny and revolting about this combination of life's incongruities, and he stood for a second or two moveless, rooted, as in face of a problem never before encountered in his varied existence.

How had the man come by this sudden death? Was it one of those abrupt strokes or heart disease that so often lay low in a twinkling some of our busiest, most important men in the turmoil and pressure of present-day existence?

He must summon help—a doctor, servants,—marvels of resuscitation were being done these days. Simultaneously with this thought—and for that he blamed himself—there flashed through his mind the notion that, if those letters he had come to talk about were lying here visibly before him, he could take them then and there and abstract that much evil from the world. He dismissed this bare reflection swiftly, having long since accepted the workings of the human mind for what they are.

He reverted to the idea of help. That damned radio! One of Goold's mitigations of his solitude. Solitary even in death! He must turn it off; he made a movement toward the instrument. Then suddenly he paused: Wiser perhaps not to touch anything, before one knew . . . somehow the active radio irresistibly seemed to suggest violence. Suppose this death of Goold's was not due to natural causes?

Then, all at once, his own position there flashed upon him. If only he had been properly admitted by a servant! But what was the use? He had not been properly admitted. To any idiot his presence there was, to say the least, suspect. But, would that have made any difference? At once the power of his own mind began to override the non-essentials. Standing as he would have been on the stoop before two doors ajar, anyone finding him there with Goold dead inside would have suspected him at least as much as he would be suspected now.

With a sudden resolve characteristic of him Ross moved to the door, found the switch beside it and turned on the lights.

The flashing on of the lights, by their suddenness making the room brighter than it actually was, seemed to centre them upon Goold's body and desk. Irresistibly Ross moved toward the body, surveyed it intently—and then he knew the cause of Goold's death.

At the back of the dead man's head was a bullet wound about an inch above the collar. The bullet had entered the cerebellum and had not re-emerged. A trickle of blood, now clotted, had run down his collar. The hair was slightly singed and blackened. The pistol must have been held close. Death had doubtless been instantaneous.

"So," Ross murmured to himself, "that's the music we have to face." In the face of crime, however, he instantly forgot himself and his own peculiar position there. Upon one corner of the desk at Goold's right was a block set in with a cluster of four ivory push buttons. They were unmarked. Which was he to press to summon help? He had no desire to alarm the house as yet. He wanted merely to call a servant. The bell nearest at hand would probably do that. Ross pressed it and waited.

The illumination that flooded the room, less garish and softer now that he was accustomed to it, lighted up that carefully arranged collection of pictures for which this gallery was noted; from the heavy oils of the Renaissance, through the lighter shades and pastels of the eighteenth century, the Greuzes and the Corots, through the Impressionists and post-impressionists. Near by was even a Renoir, a Cezanne and a single Gauguin. Facing Goold some fifteen feet away upon a marble pedestal was a lovely copy of the irresistible "Dancing Faun," of Pompeii.

"Man makes himself a paradise," passed through Ross's mind, "but forgets to leave his passions outside. Passions have no place in paradise."

A tall scholarly-faced butler appeared in the doorway which led to the house behind Goold's desk. Oddly, he gave Ross the impression of the president of a small New England college thinking of endowments.

He halted for the fraction of a second, surprised at the flood of light, but his face betrayed no sign of surprise.

"Did you ring, sir?" he asked as he moved toward Goold.

"It was I who rang," answered Ross, checking him with a gesture. "I have just come here by appointment made with Mr. Goold over the telephone about an hour ago. The outer door was ajar and as I stepped into the vestibule I found the inner door also open. I stepped back to the bell and rang it, but there was no answer. So I walked in—thinking the doors might have been left open for me, though I could not guess why. I found Mr. Goold sitting here, asleep, I thought at first, so I switched on the lights. And then I saw that he was—dead. So I pressed this bell on his desk."

A tremor seemed to pass over the tall, slender body of the butler and his blanched features went whiter.

"Dead, sir? You are sure, sir? Why, it can't be—" and at once, seemingly, with his long stride, he was bending over his employer's chair, and then recoiling slightly as he perceived the wound.

"Good Lord, sir! This is terrible, sir! What's to be done?" And instinctively he made a movement to shut off the radio.

"No, no!" Ross stopped him. "We had better not touch any more things than we can help before the investigation. Better call the family physician, I should say, and then we must call the police."

"The police, sir?" he repeated as though finding that extremely unpleasant to his sensibilities.

"Yes, of course. It's a matter for them now rather than for any doctor. What's your name, by the way?"

"Cross, sir."

"Thank you, Cross. I am Professor Roland Ross, of King's College."

"I know it, sir. You were here once before—about four months ago."

"Quite correct, Cross. With a memory and an eye like that, you ought to be extremely helpful. Now, better call your medico."

The butler approached the telephone instrument resting on the left-hand corner of Goold's desk.

"I suggest," said Ross, "that you cover your hand with a handkerchief as you handle the instrument. Someone other than Mr. Goold might have touched that 'phone."

With the responsive intelligence that seemed characteristic of him, Cross spread a clean linen handkerchief over his palm and, taking up the French 'phone, he called for Dr. Humphreys and left word, asking him to please come to the Goold gallery at once.

"Shall I call the police now, sir?" he turned to Ross.

"Yes—no—wait a minute. Come to think of it, I am a sort of policeman myself. I'd almost forgotten. A week ago Commissioner Wells appointed me a consultant to the Detective Bureau. Perhaps I'd better—"

Ross paused. Cross, for all his control, betrayed an expression of uncertainty, not to say suspicion.

"You are thinking," said Ross, "that you know so little of me, you'd rather not take the responsibility of accepting my word too far—is that it?"

"I—er—well, you see, sir, since you put it that way, I am only a servant. I mean to say—"

"Quite correct," interrupted Ross. "And that being the case, go ahead and get the Varsity Club and see if you can get Mr. Roderick Wells, the Police Commissioner. He is generally there about this time. That is where I first met him. You can't go higher than the Police Commissioner himself in reporting a crime, can you?"

The butler bowed and turned again to the instrument.

Ross, in the meantime, was bending over Goold's chair, scrutinizing the back of the dead man's head. Obviously the weapon had not been of great calibre or more of the skull would have been crushed, also the bullet would doubtless have re-emerged. As it is, it was probably stopped by the bony structure of the skull or was merely embodied in the brain. A post mortem would settle that. "A .32, I should say," he murmured to himself.

Cross, upon receiving a busy signal, stood silent for a moment, the instrument still held to his ear, seemingly in absolute control of himself, but with a hot glitter of excitement burning in his eyes. Guardedly he was taking stock of the stranger who had intruded so curiously into this appalling tragedy.

With his ruddy complexion, his close-cropped reddish moustache, his longish nose and wide-set, gray-green eyes, Ross appeared to the butler vastly different from any professor or any police officer he had ever seen. He seemed to the butler at once genial and intent, preoccupied and yet almost playful in his concentration. Did this man, wondered Cross, realize the immensity of the tragedy? Yet there was something steel-like in the gray eyes that aroused Cross's respect.

Ross glanced up into the scrutinizing eyes of the servant and smiled faintly.

"No, Cross," he murmured, "I couldn't have done quite that. At least, I hope I'd face a man before killing him. The wound, as you see, is in the back of the skull."

The butler, evidently surprised that his unformed thought should have been so plainly read, seemed confused and was about to say something. The radio had suddenly paused of itself and there was an instant's hush over the room in keeping with the atmosphere.

"Yes, Plaza, miss—that's it." The operator was now speaking to Cross, to the butler's evident relief. "Is Mr. Roderick Wells there?" He spoke into the instrument. "Yes, Police Commissioner Wells. . . . Yes, please . . . Thank you. They have gone to call him, sir," he turned to Ross. "Would you like to speak to him, sir?"

"Perhaps I'd better," said Ross, taking the receiver, still protected from contact. Almost immediately he heard the voice of Wells at the other end.

"Commissioner," he began in a low tone, "this is Ross—Roland Ross . . . Yes. I am speaking from the house of James Goold. Something very serious has happened here. I came here by appointment . . . Yes, yes, with Goold himself. Made an hour ago over the 'phone. Now he's—dead . . . Yes, found him so . . . Oh, yes, decidedly . . . I should say it was murder beyond a doubt . . . I agree. But hadn't you better jump over here for a minute before we do anything else? . . . Good! Please come to the gallery door in East Sixty-second Street . . . No—no one beside the butler. He's right here with me. He will let you in.

"Well," Ross replaced the instrument upon its stand and returned Cross's handkerchief. "That is that. One thing we do know, at any rate—nearly the exact time of death. It must have been within a few minutes of my telephone conversation with him. I 'phoned, let me see, it was a quarter to six when I was talking with him. I looked at my watch because of the appointment. When I came in and touched him he was barely cold. He must have been shot almost immediately after I put down the receiver, say, somewhere between five forty-five and six. Tell me, Cross, who made up this household besides Mr. Goold, his wife and Miss Storey?"

"No one but the servants, sir."

"Are there many of them in the house?" inquired Ross, more with the air of making conversation than of cross-examining the butler.

"Altogether there are six of us," the butler answered with his customary air of guarded reticence.

"That's quite a number," murmured Ross as if to himself. "No other man besides yourself in the house?"

"No, sir. The others are all female."

At this point both of them were startled to see a tall, somewhat portly man, with a medical kit-bag in his left hand, entering the room. His round, smooth-shaven face had about it that air of urbanity under pressure, peculiar to the successful medical practitioner.

"Dr. Humphreys," Cross murmured the name as if to himself.

"Well, well, what's happened?" The physician glanced from one to the other of them and then at the sunken figure of the master of the house. "Mr. Goold?" he went on, astonished. "I thought his heart was sound as a bell. Not hurt, is he?" and he moved toward the desk, opening his kit-bag which he placed in the chair beside it.

"Shot," said Ross quietly. "Back of the head above the collar."

"Good Lord!" cried the doctor, "you mean—murdered?" And he surveyed Ross with a mixture of urbanity, curiosity and horror.

"It does look so, doctor."

The physician now bent over the back of Goold's chair, peering at the wound and pressing his thumb against the bony structure about it.

Ross, in the meanwhile, turned to the butler. "Those doors are still open," he murmured.

Cross, as if recalled to himself, moved quietly to the door and closed the outer and then the inner one. Then, as though checked by a sudden afterthought, he examined a small electric switch against the wall in the gallery nearest the door. He peered at it for an instant and then came back with a look of more than normal gravity to Ross.

"The switch has been set, sir, to shut off the current for the bell."

Ross lifted his eyebrows. "Better not touch it," he murmured, "until they come."

Dr. Humphreys, in the meanwhile, had gone through the procedure of feeling for a pulse in the temple, peering into the dead man's eyes, flexing the joints and so on.

"Dead about an hour, I should say," he shook his head sadly. "James Goold—a superman! I should like to make a more extensive examination. I suppose the police have been notified?"

"Coming any minute," put in Ross. "At least, the Commissioner is. I telephoned him first."

"How did it happen?" queried Dr. Humphreys.

"Ah," said Ross, "when we learn that!—I came here by appointment and found him—like this."

It was Dr. Humphreys' turn to lift an astonished eyebrow. At this moment the squeak of a taxicab brake penetrated into the stillness of the room and Ross said:

"That must be the Commissioner." The voices, the solemnity, the movements, all had by now assumed the slow rhythm of dissolving matter—of the dead.

Automatically but without haste Cross moved to the door.

5
Police Commissioner Wells

A moment later Commissioner Wells, stocky, well-built, with all the febrile energy of the business man, bustled into the room.

Wells was the newest of the rapidly changing police commissioners of New York, appointed by a mayor who enjoyed the prestige of well-known names in his administration. Wells, as the chief executive of a large wholesale business, had achieved prominence and much publicity by constant and restless participation in civic enterprises.

It is part of our civil logic that a man who knew much about the export business must infallibly know much about crime and the means of reducing it. By consequence, Roderick Wells, who was noted for his speeches at the Chamber of Commerce and on certain civic occasions, found himself at the head of the greatest criminal investigation organization in America.

"Good evening, gentlemen," he glanced at the three men in the room, and then addressed himself to Ross. "Well, well, professor—this is quite a beginning for your career as a consultant to the Department. What is it—plain murder?"

"Murder, beyond any doubt," Ross nodded slowly and pointed to the back of Goold's head. "Have you met Dr. Humphreys, by the way?"

The Commissioner shook hands with the physician and said: "I presume you have made an examination?"

"Only a cursory one, Commissioner, an examination seems hardly necessary." And he indicated the back of Goold's head.

Wells took out a pocket torch shaped like a fountain pen and flashed a thin beam of light over Goold's collar.

"Yes, I see," he nodded, "bullet wound. No weapon, I suppose?"

"We have made no search as yet," said Ross. "But I imagine not."

At this moment the intermittent radio broke forth again, and Wells turned a questioning look upon the others. "This been going all the time?" he asked.

"We have not shut it off until the arrival of the police," said Ross, "but now you are here, I think we may safely dispense with this accompaniment," and protected by his handkerchief, he carefully turned off the instrument.

"You found him this way, Professor?" Wells asked.

Briefly Ross gave him an account of his arrival there, the open doors, and the manner in which he had found Goold's body. He also mentioned his newest discovery— that the switch controlling the door bell had been shut off.

"The switch!" exclaimed Wells. "I didn't believe there was one in a modern house. Must have been some whim of Goold's to enable him to control the bells."

Ross nodded but said nothing.

"Is there anything further for me to do?" put in Dr. Humphreys blandly with the quiet importance of a busy physician.

"Oh, yes, doctor. Can't let you go like this—you made the first examination. I have telephoned my people at headquarters from the club before I started. They ought to arrive here any minute. They may want to ask you a question or two. You haven't disturbed him in any way, have you?" he pointed toward Goold.

Dr. Humphreys shook his head moodily. He did not like his own wishes to be overridden in this roughshod manner.

"Well, well," continued the commissioner, "nothing much for us to do until they come though, in the meanwhile, I suppose we can look around a bit. No sign of a struggle, I take it."

"Nothing at all," Ross shook his head. "You see no marks of any disturbance, do you, Cross?"

"No, sir," said the butler.

Ross walked a few paces eastward toward the back of the room, glancing at the pictures, then suddenly he paused in the middle of the room, gazing in astonishment at the rear wall of the gallery. This was the wall farthest away from them and the least illuminated.

"A great collection of pictures here, isn't there, professor?" remarked Wells conversationally.

"Do you see the central picture on that far wall, Commissioner?" demanded Ross over his shoulder.

"You mean the frame?"

"Yes, I mean the frame. The empty frame. The last time I was here that frame was occupied by a priceless picture—Rembrandt's 'Tartar Chieftain.'"

"By gad!" cried Wells. "You—what is your name?" he snapped at the mute butler, standing aloof like a guardian of an outraged privacy. "When did you last see the picture in that frame?"

Cross moved a step or two nearer as if to confirm his vision.

"This afternoon, sir, it was still there."

"You can swear to that?"

"Absolutely, sir."

A slight tremor in his voice now betrayed his emotion.

Wells turned from him to Ross with a faint smile of amazement.

"If that's the case," he said with great distinctness, "then half the work of the police has been done for them. The fellow who took that picture is the same who murdered Goold. Eh, Professor?"

Ross did not immediately reply. Finally he drew a step nearer and said:

"Possibly, possibly, Commissioner, but—don't let us be rash in our conclusions. That's the cardinal sin in any investigation."

"But doesn't it stand to reason, Ross?" demanded Wells hotly. "A picture worth anywhere from a quarter of a million up was here this afternoon. Gone now—nobody knows how. Owner murdered. What could be simpler, eh?"

"Quite so, I know," Ross agreed pleasantly. "Seems obvious. Still, the first law of criminal investigation is 'thou shalt not jump to conclusions.'"

"Oh, well, Ross, now you are being the professor. All very well in the classroom. But this is the real thing, isn't it? Any roundsman—the cop on the beat, could see a thing like that."

Ross smiled. "That's just it. The cop on the beat is not universally accounted an expert in criminology."

"Oh, well, have it your own way," growled Wells. "It seems self-evident to me. The bunch from headquarters will be here any minute. Let's see what they think."

"In that case," said Ross, turning to the butler, "better run over in your mind all the people who have been here this afternoon. They'll be sure to ask you that."

"Yes, sir," said the butler.

"Seriously," began Wells again, approaching Ross with a perplexed brow and lowering his tone as though for personal consultation, "seriously, now, Professor, doesn't the thing seem pretty open and shut—I mean that the fellow who took the picture is the fellow who killed Goold?"

"Well," said Ross, "as I said, it was a possibility. But not, I should say, very probable. Consider: Goold looks like an able-bodied man, doesn't he? And we know he was one. We have agreed there was no sign of struggle or disturbance of any kind. Of course, the assailant might have come from behind—in fact, must have come from behind. But, at the same time, Goold might have been shot in any one of a dozen different ways that have nothing to do with the missing of the picture."

"And the radio instrument, you say, was going when you came in?"

"Yes, Commissioner, and intermittently ever since until you ordered it shut off."

"Your coming in the way you did," said Wells, with a furrow of perplexity between his brows, "that's another point that will need explaining to the men."

"Perhaps they will arrest me as a starter?" smiled Ross.

"I don't mean that—but you know how they reason—you haven't told me, have you, why you were coming to see Goold?"

"No, Commissioner, I haven't. You know, he was one of the donors of the endowment for my chair. I could make a reason, I suppose. And Goold being dead, you couldn't disprove it, but I'd rather not. Take my word for it that if it should prove to have a necessary bearing on the case, I shall certainly give it to you."

Wells nodded gloomily, none too well pleased with this answer.

The brakes of motor cars were now suddenly audible outside and Cross was moving to the door.

"That must be Callahan and his men," said the Commissioner. "Now we must get down to business. This will make a terrible noise in the town. The newspapers!—the reporters will be upon us before we know it. And when they come, I have got to watch my step, what I say to them."

The door opened and admitted Inspector Callahan, followed by half a dozen other men from Police Headquarters.

6
The Scene of the Crime

The honorific greetings of the men as they approached Wells, their chief, and the formal introduction of Ross to the others, with the exception of Callahan, whom he already knew, were in the routine of the occasion. The gravity of all these police officials, however, was marked. This was no gang murder. Goold had been a rich and powerful citizen of New York and he had been mysteriously murdered. The newspapers would ring with it—the entire big inchoate city would resound with the crime. The public would demand results. Above all, it would demand a victim. Publicity beyond reckoning lay in success, and promotion was certain. But ignominy and disgrace were inevitable in the event of failure. This was not one of those crimes that would be speedily forgotten.

"I called Dr. Bly, the medical examiner," said Inspector Callahan in a low voice, "asked him to come up here hotfoot."

"Well, of course," said the Commissioner, "though I am afraid we know all he can tell us. Professor Ross talked with Goold on the telephone—when was it, Ross?—five forty-five, you said?"

Callahan glanced at his watch, "And it's seven twenty-five now."

"Dr. Humphreys, here, who made a brief examination when he arrived," said the Commissioner, "concluded Goold had been dead about an hour. And you arrived at about seven wasn't it, doctor?"

Dr. Humphreys nodded.

"That fixes the death pretty much about six o'clock."

Inspector Callahan, tall, well-built and straight, glanced at Dr. Humphreys and said nothing. He had been in the police department for thirty years, had risen from a roundsman, and he somewhat resented any outside opinions. His closely buttoned double-breasted coat seemed characteristically to shut in all police secrets in a police bosom.

"Dr. Bly ought to be here any minute," he finally uttered, as though Dr. Bly's examinations alone could possibly be official.

"By the way," asked the Commissioner irrelevantly, "do the reporters know anything about this business?"

"Their lookout saw us jump in the car," said Callahan. "Nothing on the blotter, as yet, but they'll know soon enough. Can't keep a thing like that from them, Commissioner."

"No, I suppose every doorman, watchman and telephone operator at headquarters works for the reporters as a tipster. Remind me to look into that, Callahan."

Ross looked at the two men inscrutably, as though wondering why they considered all that important in the investigation of a major crime.

"Well, anyway, Callahan, we had better get busy," snapped the Commissioner as though recalling what they were all there for.

Approaching the chair in which the dead man was slumped, Callahan peered at the wound for a moment and then, straightening up, said:

"Well, hadn't we better wait till Doc Bly comes? Then we can move the body and not be cramped."

"Have you anything to suggest, Ross?" Wells turned to his new aid, whom the others were almost pointedly ignoring.

"Just about what the Inspector here says," was the diplomatic answer, "except perhaps this: Miss Storey is doubtless wondering why her Uncle doesn't come in for dinner. And Mrs. Goold, an invalid, will also have to be told the sad news. Why wouldn't this be the time for Dr. Humphreys to break the news to the family?"

"A good idea!" declared Wells, "eh, Inspector?" Callahan nodded. "Are you the family physician Dr. Humphreys?"

"I am," answered the doctor.

"You have been treating Mrs. Goold?"

"For a good many years."

"Fine. Then you are the logical man to break the news. I don't envy you the job, but those things have to be done. Can Mrs. Goold stand the shock, do you think?"

The doctor shrugged his shoulders. "I suppose she'll have to. She suffers from a spastic paralysis of the lower limbs. Organically she is sound enough. Must this be done now?"

"I'm afraid so," said Ross. "This will be a long investigation. I'm surprised that already no one has tried to find out what is going on here."

"Yes," said Wells with finality. "I'm afraid you're elected, Doctor."

"We'd better say nothing to the servants just yet," put in Callahan. "We'll have to question them ourselves."

"Yes, keep it very private, as long as we can," agreed Wells. "Just Mrs. Goold and the niece."

Dr. Humphreys with a deprecating air of resolution moved to the door leading into the house. Cross was about to open it for him.

"Here, you," Callahan stopped him. "I want you here. Dr. Humphreys will have to get along by himself."

"I wasn't leaving, sir," said the butler and the hot glitter returned for a moment to his eyes.

The routine men took this as their opportunity for exposing some four or five plates to their accompanying flares which for a few moments filled the long room with their smoke. Wells blinked as he stood impatiently by and, no sooner had they finished, than he turned to Callahan and said:

"Well, so that's over. Now let's get down to business. Do you realize, Callahan, that a picture worth a quarter of a million or so was in that frame back there this afternoon, and that it's gone now?"

"Is that so, Commissioner!" exclaimed Callahan, eager to be impressed. "Well, if that's the case, that ought to make it easy for us. If that picture was taken by the guy I think took it, we ought to lay our hands on him in twenty-four hours."

The Commissioner's eyes gleamed.

"All I can say is, the men who solve this case won't lose by it. I want results, but you'll find I'm a square shooter when I get them. What are you smiling at, Professor?" he turned upon Ross.

"Not smiling, Commissioner. I was only thinking—if the thief is the type who picked that particular picture, the most valuable in the collection, he is no ordinary thief."

"Yes," went on Wells as though his own thought had been expressed. "And remember, Callahan, he committed murder to get it. Pretty desperate criminal, I'd say. No easy type. But if you get him, Inspector, yours will be the glory."

Callahan smiled suavely.

"Potosi!" he snapped, turning to the thronging men behind him. "Your job. Better get busy. Ought to be prints on that frame back there."

The finger-print expert and one of the other detectives detached themselves from the group and walked briskly to the rear of the gallery. Potosi was known to be one of the foremost experts in the country, and possibly in the world. For twenty-two years he had been the authority on finger-prints to the department, and had studied the systems in use at Scotland Yard, in France, in Italy, in Germany and in Argentina. He was, besides, a very shrewd Italian-American, and it was said that more than one gang of criminals had offered a reward in their world for his death. He went about his work with the air of a virtuoso, in the most complete and meticulous absorption.

"There must be plenty of other finger-prints about the place," suggested Wells.

"Sure," said Callahan, "we'll get all there is, Commissioner."

One of the detectives standing at a window near the door and peering out to the street from time to time behind the shade, suddenly announced:

"There's Doc Bly, Chief, I guess. Will I open the door for him?"

Callahan nodded succinctly and Dr. Rufus Bly, a middle-aged man with graying hair, smooth-shaven and sallow, entered hurriedly, and then smiled mechanically as he looked at the thronging men.

"Good evening, gentlemen," he said. "I came as quickly as I could. Is this—" he nodded at what remained of James Goold in the chair—"the body?"

Without waiting for an answer, he deposited his bag on the floor beside the chair, his hat on Goold's shimmering desk, and proceeded rapidly with the examination. With a flashlight he peered at the wound in the back of Goold's head.

"Now," he said, "let's lay him down—right here on the floor."

Callahan's men proceeded to lift the body out of the chair and to lay it flat on the floor.

Notwithstanding all his experience, Ross turned away for an instant. He had no fear of, or qualms about, death. He had seen it in many forms. But the indignity of a police investigation over a corpse was unpleasant to him whenever he saw it.

"Hardly any rigor as yet," murmured Dr. Bly. "Well," he looked up, "you gentlemen certainly lost no time. He hasn't been dead three hours, certainly not more than that. A gun shot wound, pistol bullet, doubtless, lodged somewhere in the skull. Death, I would say, was instantaneous, about two hours ago—two and a half, perhaps."

"Yes," put in Wells impatiently, "we have fixed the time of death. The family doctor was called when the body was discovered. He must have been shot sometime between five forty-five and six."

Dr. Bly nodded and rose from his kneeling position.

"As to the bullet, the calibre of the gun, and so on, only an autopsy would disclose that," he said.

"Would you say," the voice of Ross broke the momentary silence, "that there was anything remarkable about the face, Dr. Bly?"

"The face? It's a strong face. But the deceased was a very able man. Everybody knows that."

"That's not exactly what I mean, Doctor. The expression of the features—do you notice anything strange about them—unusual?"

"You mean the look of—sort of surprise? Nothing strange about that. Any of us would look surprised if we suddenly got a bullet in the back of the head."

"But you said death was instantaneous, I think?"

"Sure I did. But considering that fright is one of our basic instincts, as any freshman studying psychology will tell you, the noise and the shock of a pistol shot could set those facial nerves working, and the muscles, too, at practically the same instant. Nothing to surprise us in his surprise. You a doctor, sir?"

"No, no, I'm not," murmured Ross. "But to me it seemed that that look of surprise, or amazement, I should say, set those features slightly before the shot, possibly a fraction of a second before, rather than a result of the shot."

The politician doctor shrugged his shoulders.

"You may be right—possibly. He may have got a flash he was about to be murdered."

"Professor Ross is one of the consultants of our department," put in Wells sententiously.

"I see, I see," responded Bly indifferently.

"Would you say, Doctor," pressed Ross, "that the expression was one of terror or rather of amazement?"

Bly gazed down at the features for a moment, his lips puckering in an effort of judgment.

"Surprise," he stuck to his word; "yes, I'd say surprise. Not terror. No, hardly. But, as I said, the difference is slight."

"Well, well," broke in Wells, "is there anything else?"

"Nothing here," said the medical examiner. "The rest is a matter for the autopsy."

"Then the body can be moved, I take it," said Wells impatiently.

"Oh, yes, Commissioner," pronounced Bly. "I haven't had my supper yet," he added, and began to gather up his kit and his hat. "That's all, I think, unless you want me for something else."

Both Wells and Callahan shook their heads and the medical examiner moved toward the door.

"All very well to say move the body," grumbled Wells when the detective at the door closed it behind Bly. "Question is, where are we to move it to, just now?"

Ross glanced about the room. Before the large Gothic fireplace in the middle of the north wall stood a long heavily upholstered davenport.

"Over there, I should say—where it will not be obtrusive when you have the people of the house in to be questioned."

"Oh, your idea is to have them in here," queried Wells.

"Sure, Commissioner," interposed Callahan respectfully. "One by one. That's the best way. Don't want each one to hear what the others say." And he stole a covert glance at Ross.

With a gesture, he ordered his men to place Goold's body upon the davenport. For some reason this action brought a visible spasm of pain to the hitherto almost impassive features of Cross, the dead man's butler.

"Potosi!" Callahan called to his expert who was squatting on the floor over the frame with flashlight, brushes and powder. "How are you getting on down there?"

"All right, Inspector, we have got some prints here."

"Well, plenty more around here, Potosi, when you get through. There's the desk and this radio instrument, I want you to be extra careful about."

"Very good, Inspector," Potosi called back, "I'll be there directly."

"Did I tell you," said the Commissioner, "that that radio was going full blast when the body was discovered?"

"Shouldn't wonder," nodded Callahan. "Probably started by the murderer to cover his movements. Now," he went on, "we have got to have the help in here to question them. And since you're here," he turned to Cross, "we might as well begin with you. Or, do you want to question this man?" he turned deferentially toward his superior.

"No, no, Callahan," said Wells, "you go ahead, but let's move along."

"Wouldn't this be a good time to look into that desk?" suggested Ross, still thinking of Sheila's letters.

"Just going to do that," said Callahan, and putting his handkerchief round the handle, he opened the drawer on the right. It seemed empty and clean, so far as one could see. He drew it out further. At the very back of it was a small package of .32 cartridges. Only a few had been removed, not more than half a dozen.

"Well, this tells us something," snapped the Commissioner, looking to Ross for interpretation.

"A .32," Callahan's eyes glistened. "Sure it tells us something."

"Yes," said Ross thoughtfully. "It tells us something, but—not much. It tells us that there was in all likelihood a pistol here, though we have no idea when it was removed. It tells us its calibre and probably its make. But, it might have been here an hour or a year ago. Cross," he turned to the butler, "did Mr. Goold keep a pistol in his drawer—do you know?"

"No, sir, I don't know. This desk was generally kept locked by Mr. Goold and no one else had any keys to it that I know of."

"There you are, Commissioner. Whatever this has to tell us will be told later. Let us open the middle drawer."

Wells nodded and Callahan slowly drew out the shallow middle drawer as far as he could. Nothing there but stationery, paper, envelopes, a cheque book.

"Doesn't seem to get us anywhere," muttered Wells.

At this moment the door leading from the gallery to the house burst open and a beautiful girl, her face tear-stained and wrung with anguish, rushed in, and then paused with her back against the door, facing the roomful of men.

7
Questions

Wildly she looked about from one to the other of the men until her tear-blinded eyes lighted upon Ross, and she all but stumbled toward him.

"Oh, Professor Ross, where is he?—where is Uncle Jim? I saw him only a little while ago—alive and well—and now—oh, it can't be true!"

She clutched at Ross's arm as one fearful of the answer he would give.

Ross took her hand and held it in both of his own.

"I am deeply sorry, Miss Storey," he murmured in a voice that thrilled her with its kindness. "Come sit down in this chair. I won't say a lot of platitudes to you. I know how you feel. You saw him a little while ago, you said?"

"Yes," she cried with a great sob, "only about two hours ago. I just ran in here for a moment to say 'hello.' He was sitting in this chair, fussing with that radio instrument. He smiled—I told him I was bringing Jimmie Trumbull to dinner."

She endeavored to blot her tears with a tiny handkerchief.

"And the first you knew was when Dr. Humphreys told you?"

"Yes," she sobbed, "just now."

"And your aunt, he has told her?"

She nodded, covering her eyes.

"How did she take it?"

"Terribly. Dr. Humphreys is giving her sedatives."

Ross nodded sadly.

"And what did you do, Miss Storey, just after—after you saw your uncle?"

"Oh, I just ran out again," she was still sobbing. "You see, I had my car outside. Jimmie Trumbull was in it, waiting. I drove the car over to the garage at Sixty-third and Lexington and then we walked home."

"By home you mean here, Miss?" demanded Callahan, bent upon getting into action.

"Yes, of course," she said. "This is my home."

"You're his niece, aren't you? You don't live with your parents?"

"My parents are both dead," she breathed.

"How long have you lived here, Miss Storey?" put in Wells, not unkindly.

"Eleven years."

"Any other children, are there?" queried Callahan.

"No. They never had any children of their own."

"You were like the daughter of the house, is that it?" interposed Wells.

"Uncle Jim certainly has always treated me like a daughter," and a sob stifled her voice.

"And your aunt, did she also treat you like a daughter?"

"Yes, of course."

For a moment the police were silent. Ross then approached her chair more closely and in a gentle voice asked her:

"Could you, Miss Storey, fix exactly the time when you saw your uncle and talked with him?"

"I think so, Professor Ross. At least, I'll try. After we left your classroom, Jimmie Trumbull and I, we drove out to Bronx Park for a little while. Then we drove back and came here. It must have been about half past five, or perhaps a very little later."

"How many minutes would you say?"

"Well, I only talked to him for a few moments. I just asked him whether he was dining at home, and how he was and whether there was anything I could do for him. I told him I was bringing Jimmie to dinner. All that couldn't have taken more than a couple of minutes."

"You say, Miss Storey," began Callahan weightily, "you asked him how he was and whether there was anything you could do for him?"

She nodded.

"He wasn't sick or anything like that, your uncle, was he?"

"Oh, no. Not sick."

"What was it, then made you ask those questions?"

"Oh, nothing. He didn't look very happy. That's all."

Callahan nodded.

"And did he say he was dining at home?" asked Ross.

"Oh, yes, Professor Ross, and he said he was glad to have Jimmie dine here. But what I had meant to say was that when I got to the garage and left the car, I looked at the clock in the garage office and saw it was a quarter to six."

"A quarter to six," repeated Ross. "Could it have taken you more than five minutes to drive to the garage?"

"No, I don't see how it could."

"Good. That fixes the time when you talked to your uncle at somewhere between five thirty-five and five-forty, doesn't it?"

"I should think so, but I couldn't swear to fractions of minutes or even minutes."

"I see, of course not. Now, when did you return to the house?"

"Oh, in about twenty minutes, I should say, certainly not more than twenty-five. We just strolled along, Jimmie and I. We stopped to look in a bookseller's window on Madison avenue, and also into a toy shop. We didn't hurry."

"And you entered the house by the front door," asked Wells, "on Fifth avenue, that is?"

"Of course," she said. "Only Uncle Jim used the gallery door. He's the only one who had a key to it."

"And after you came in?" Ross took up the interrogatory in his gentlest and most conversational tone.

"We went straight up to my sitting-room. We got out some reference books to look up something in your lecture. We looked at Hooton's text, as you told us to. And we were just talking—waiting till dinner time."

"When you came in to speak to your uncle," Callahan asked her, "you didn't see anybody leaving this here gallery, did you, Miss Storey?"

"Not a soul."

"Didn't get the idea there had been anybody here just before you or that anybody was expected, did you?"

"No," she shook her head. "Besides, my uncle was receiving people here all the time. He transacted much of his business here. Uncle Jim was not communicative about his affairs—his business."

"Well, that'll be all now, Miss Storey." Callahan released her. "I guess you'll want to go to your own room, and I wouldn't say anything to any of the others about the questions, or anything, if I were you."

Lorna nodded, rose, and somewhat unsteadily moved to the door. Ross, walking beside her, opened the door for her.

"Oh, Professor Ross," she implored, "won't you stay after the others go? I do so want—I want you to—" she could not finish.

"Certainly, Miss Storey," Ross reassured her. "I shall stay as long as I can be of any use."

She nodded gratefully and disappeared through the door.

"Now," said Callahan, with seeming relief, "I want to ask you some questions, Cross—is that your name?"

"Yes, sir," said the butler.

"And we don't wany any more interruptions. So will one of you stand against that door." He nodded toward his men.

One of the detectives moved over and leaned his back against the door leading to the house.

"Care to sit down, Cross?" Callahan asked him.

"No, sir, thank you. I prefer to stand."

"Well, will you tell us, then, just what were your movements and what you did between five o'clock this afternoon and the time when you saw Mr. Goold dead in his chair at this desk? By the way, what time was it you did see him dead in his chair?"

"It was about five minutes to seven, sir."

"Very good. Now go ahead from five o'clock on."

"Yes, sir. May I go back a little earlier than five o'clock, sir?"

"All right," said Callahan, "where do you want to begin?"

"I should like to start at four-thirty, sir."

"Very good, go on."

"At four-thirty I came into this room without being called. I knew Mr. Goold was in and I came to inquire whether he wanted any refreshments, tea or a drink of any sort."

"And Mr. Goold was here alone?"

"Yes, sir, he was, but not alone. There was—a lady with him."

"You know this lady?"

"Yes, sir."

"Tell us who she is."

"Must I tell that?"

"You certainly must!" Callahan all but crunched the words with his teeth.

Cross, however, glanced toward Ross and perceiving something of encouragement, answered briefly: "She was Mrs. Cullen Forbes, sir."

Wells's eyebrows lifted eagerly and Callahan moved a step nearer to the butler. Before, however, either of them had a chance to put a question, Ross quickly interposed:

"She was just leaving or just arriving, which?"

"Just leaving, sir. In fact, I opened the door for her."

"What was her condition?" quickly thrust in Callahan—"I mean, did it look just a friendly call, or what?"

"I couldn't say," said Cross slowly. "My impression was she had been crying."

"Crying!" repeated Wells. "Did you see her crying?"

"She was wiping her eyes with a handkerchief, sir."

Some of the others smiled fleetingly.

"Did you hear her say anything at all to Mr. Goold?" Callahan returned to the attack.

"Er—yes, sir. I heard her say, 'Jim, you'll be sorry for treating me like this.'"

Wells and Callahan exchanged glances full at once of meaning and amazement. Upon looking at Ross, however, they perceived an expression impassive, almost bored.

"Just when did she say those words to Mr. Goold, Cross?" Callahan asked him with slow emphasis.

"Just as I opened this inner door. She had risen from the chair beside the desk, sir. She was wiping her eyes and those were the words she said."

"Then what happened?" asked Ross.

"Mr. Goold said, 'This lady is leaving,' and I opened the door for her and let her out."

"And did you notice the time?" pursued Ross.

"I should say it was about four-thirty, sir."

Ross nodded: "Now if you will be so good as to answer the Inspector's question and tell us all your movements directly after that."

"Almost directly after the lady left I opened the door for a person who gave his name as Patrick Steele. He said he wanted to see Mr. Goold. I left him outside and told him I would see if Mr. Goold was at home."

"Well, well," put in Wells impatiently. "Did Mr. Goold see him or did he not?"

"Yes, sir, he did."

"For how long?"

"For about eight or ten minutes, sir. Not more."

"That brings us to about four-forty, more or less," murmured Ross.

"Now, who is this Patrick Steele, do you know?" demanded Callahan.

It appeared that Patrick Steele was a jockey who had been in Goold's employ and had been discharged. He had come to sue for re-employment.

"Do you know why he had been discharged?" demanded Callahan.

"I had a notion, sir, he wasn't quite honest," the butler answered in his clear, precise intonation. "He had ridden Mr. Goold's horses for some time but for something that happened in the Kentucky Derby—Mr. Goold had an entry there—Steele was dismissed."

"Do you know whether Mr. Goold took him back?" queried Wells.

"I believe not, sir."

"What makes you believe that?" asked Callahan.

Cross hesitated perceptibly.

"You happened to overhear part of the conversation, isn't that it?" suggested Ross quietly.

"Yes, sir, that was partly it, but I saw the man's face when he was leaving. He appeared very angry."

"Burke!" Callahan called to one of his men. "Make a note of that. I want that jock, Patrick Steele, brought into the office."

"All right, Chief," murmured the subordinate.

"You are helping us a great deal," the Commissioner put in, and Ross added:

"As we knew you would."

"Now, Cross," said the Commissioner, "we'll go on with your story."

"I'd gone back to my pantry. I had not been there two minutes before I heard the gallery bell—the door bell, that is. As I went through to open it, Mr. Goold said: 'Cross,' he said, 'I'm not in to anybody unless—use your judgment—understand?'

"'Yes, sir,' I said, and went to the door. The gentleman at the door was Mr. Cullen Forbes."

"Cullen Forbes!" exclaimed Wells in astonishment. "Did you let him in?"

"No, sir—that is, not at first. I was about to say, 'Not at home,' but I recollected Mr. Goold telling me to use my judgment. Mr. Cullen Forbes is a very important man, as you know, sir. I said I'd see if Mr. Goold was in, but Mr. Forbes, he said, 'Don't talk rubbish, Cross. I know Mr. Goold is in. I only want to see him for five minutes.' And Mr. Goold must have heard Mr. Forbes's voice for he came to the door and said, 'Come in, Cullen'—very quietly he spoke. Nothing for me to do then, of course, but to let him in."

"Were the two men great friends?" asked Callahan.

"Mr. Forbes has been coming to see Mr. Goold ever since I can remember," answered the butler.

"How did they appear this last time you saw them?" Ross put in almost casually—"wholly friendly?"

"Now that you speak of it, there was something between them—a sort of tension, you might call it."

"And what did you do about it?" demanded Callahan abruptly.

"I? Nothing, sir. It wasn't my place to do anything about it."

"Did you go back to your pantry?" Ross led him gently.

"Yes, sir, I did. But I didn't stay there more than a minute or two. I happened to be passing the door leading to the gallery, when I heard Mr. Forbes talking very loud. I heard him say, 'Jim, you know how I feel about this. I want those letters. Give them to me and I promise to burn them there in your fireplace without looking at them. Refuse and you know me well enough to know what will happen.'"

Ross's heart missed a beat, but neither Callahan nor Wells perceived anything unusual about his expression. They were too excited by what they had just heard and were exchanging glances full of meaning.

"Go on," urged Wells, "go on—don't omit anything."

"I couldn't quite hear what Mr. Goold answered, sir. He must have been walking up and down the room and at the moment turned away from the door. But I did hear what Mr. Forbes said in reply."

"What was that?" from Callahan.

"He said, 'Think twice before you refuse, Jim. I want those letters before tomorrow morning. They can't be farther away than a deposit box. Personally I don't believe they are as far. For your own sake, for all our sakes, I ask you to give them to me. You're too big a man to go in for that kind of thing, and I don't mean to let you. I am going now. Tomorrow morning at ten o'clock I'll meet you here or anywhere you say and take those letters.'"

The butler paused, wiping his moist forehead with an immaculate handkerchief. In all his life as a servant he had never been called upon to expose so much of the privacy of his masters. It was one of the great crises of his life, and for a man in a critical situation, his poise evoked the admiration of all, but particularly of Ross.

"What happened next?" Callahan now addressed him almost with respect.

"Mr. Goold must have let Mr. Forbes out himself. Leastways he didn't call me. I heard the outer door close. Then I heard Mr. Goold walking up and down the room."

"No other visitors?" Ross now asked him.

"No, sir, none that I know of until—" and he paused, perplexed.

"Until you saw me here?" put in Ross.

"Yes, sir."

Wells glanced away for an instant, then turning to Callahan, said casually, "Did I tell you, Inspector, that Professor Ross had an appointment here with

Goold, and when he arrived at the house, at this gallery, that is, at about ten minutes to seven, both doors were ajar and when he walked in, he found Goold sitting at this desk—dead?"

"Oh, is that it, Commissioner?" said Callahan with a sudden gleam of heightened interest in his eyes. "I didn't quite know. I see now."

"The bell didn't ring," put in Ross in an easy explanatory tone, "and the first thing I did when I walked in was to switch on the lights and to ring one of these bells on the desk, which brought Cross into the room." The little squeak on the word "Cross" was the only sign of Ross's excitement.

"Oh," said Callahan, as one who was now at length greatly enlightened, "that is how it was. That makes it a little clearer in my mind. Now," he addressed the butler more briskly, "now tell us all the rest. All that occupied you from the time you knew Cullen Forbes had gone to the time you came in and found Professor Ross here."

8

The Glazier

The fact that Callahan assumed the sly alert air of a cat, as soon as he heard that Ross was the first to discover the body, and that he had come in to the gallery in a rather unusual manner, left Ross comparatively undisturbed.

But that other glaring fact, that Cullen Forbes knew of the existence of certain letters and had demanded them from Goold; that his wife, Sheila also desired them, and that she was unaware of her husband's knowledge—that brought in a complication, the gravity of which could not fail to impress Ross profoundly. All his faculties were now engaged in watching Callahan's line of inquiry, of noting every detail of this examination and its drift. His own position in the circumstances sank to insignificance compared to the unfavorable light in which it placed Cullen Forbes and his wife.

"The rest—that is not so easy, sir," the butler went on. "The work of a man in my position is made up of a lot of little things one cannot always remember very clearly."

"You just damn well have got to remember," growled Callahan, showing his teeth as a concession to good humor.

"It won't be difficult, if you just give yourself time to reflect," Ross encouraged him.

"I went down into the basement a little after five," pursued Cross with an upward gaze in an effort to recall his movements. "I opened the wine room and took the two bottles of claret I was going to warm for this evening. I also looked at the furnace, for the furnace man was out for the afternoon. Then I stopped at the room, a sort of lumber room, in which I keep some of my things down there. Then, one of the maids came down to look for me—to ask me a question."

Callahan endeavored to hide a grin, and Ross, for the first time, disapproved of the butler's statement. That phrase, "to ask me a question," betrayed an uneasiness which hitherto Cross had been too shrewd to show even a sign of.

"Then," continued Cross, "just as she left and I was ready to return upstairs with the bottles, a funny thing occurred. A golf ball came crashing through a pane of glass in one of the basement windows. The windows are barred, but some boy, I fancy, had been playing on the pavement and his ball broke the pane."

"Did you have a light on in the basement at the time?" Ross asked him.

"Yes, sir, certainly—but not in my room."

"Where was the light as regards the broken window?" Callahan at this point appeared displeased at what he evidently deemed irrelevant interruptions.

"The light, I should say, was just about opposite the broken window."

Ross nodded.

"Go on," urged Wells.

"Well, I left the bottles on the floor of my room and ran out to see if I could catch the person who broke the window."

"The basement door is on Sixty-second Street?" queried Ross, seemingly impervious to the disapproval of Callahan.

"Yes, sir. But I couldn't see a soul. No one even passing by at the moment. I looked up and down and turned the corner at Fifth Avenue. But no one likely to have thrown the ball was in sight. But as I was going back to the basement door I happened to catch sight of a chap with a crate on the back—the kind glaziers sometimes carry. A foreign chap, he looked, with a dark brown beard, a bit stooping he was, lost in thought, you might say. He didn't seem to notice anything as he came shuffling along toward me. His lips were moving as though he might be praying. And when he came nearer I saw that it was actually a glazier's crate he had on his back.

"'Can you put in a pane?' I asked him.

"'Glass?' says he.

"'What else?' says I.

"'Yes,' says he.

"He didn't seem to speak much English. He came along with me into the basement, however, and went to work on the window. I watched him for a bit. Seemed to know his business, he did. Then, let me see, then I heard my pantry bell ringing. I told him I'd be back in a jiffy, though I doubt whether he understood me, and ran upstairs. Mrs. Goold's nurse was in the pantry—Miss Baker, that was. She said Mrs. Goold wanted me to make her some eggnog. That, if I may say so," he added with the first smile that evening, "is a sort of speciality of mine.

"Well, there was nothing for me to do but to make the eggnog. It didn't take more than a few minutes—eight or ten. Then I ran downstairs again. The man had not yet finished. He cracked the first pane and had to put in a second. I was sorry for him. But I told him he must hurry up. I stood by while he worked, not wishing to leave him alone, and as soon as he finished I gave him half a dollar and sent him off. That was about all, sir," he turned to Ross, "until you rang for me."

"That was about all!" almost roared Callahan in a rage of irony. "You should be ashamed of yourself," he glowered at Cross. "Can't you see that glazier is pretty near certainly the man who killed Mr. Goold?"

"Him—that man, sir?" exclaimed Cross contemptuously. "Oh, no, sir! I could swear—" then he paused as though the weight of the possibility suddenly overcame him. "But how could I have thought such a thing? I could almost swear he hadn't moved from the spot he was working at."

"Never mind that," returned Callahan in some disgust. "Would you know him if you saw him?"

"Oh, certainly sir."

"What nationality do you think he was?"

"Nationality?"

"Yes, was he a Jew, an Italian, a Polack, a Hunkie—or what?"

"I don't believe I can say, sir. He wasn't a Jew, I should say, nor yet an Italian, sir. Might have been a Pole, or something like that."

"You say he had a dark beard?"

"Yes, sir, a dark brown beard. Rather long, a bit flowing, you might say."

"Gimme all you can about him," demanded Callahan. "Describe him, give me a picture of him."

"Well, I can't say as to the color of his eyes except that they weren't blue. Brown, most likely. His mouth was pretty much covered by his beard and moustache. Not very tidy, he was. He appeared sallow like. The nose was a bit flat and thick. He wore an old brown overcoat. I can't say what he wore underneath. He wore a rather dilapidated brown derby hat. I'd know him anywhere."

Ross nodded to encourage the excellent description as well as to counteract Callahan's anger.

"When you came up to make that eggnog," he said, "you used the stairs nearest the kitchen?"

"Yes, sir," said the butler, "they lead right into my pantry."

"Just so," said Ross. "And you also returned to the basement by the same stairway?"

"Yes, sir."

"Very well. Now that means there is another stairway from the basement to the house, doesn't it?"

The butler looked somewhat surprised.

"Oh, certainly, sir. Didn't I say so? There's a stairway that comes up just outside this door that leads from the gallery to the house."

"No, you didn't say so," barked Callahan, "and that's as important as anything you have omitted."

"I haven't omitted anything I could think of, sir," Cross defended himself.

"What sort of accent should you say that glazier had in his speech?" asked Ross, and Callahan appeared hurt at what evidently seemed to him an irrelevant deflection of the inquiry. Ross, however, who had the faculty of not perceiving things he did not wish to perceive, went on, "I mean was it a French accent, a Jewish accent, or what sort?"

"I couldn't say, sir. It was foreign, I know that. Not French, though, I should say, and not what I'd call Jewish. It was strange to me, sir. Besides, we talked mostly by signs and gestures, the man being foreign."

"Burke!" snapped Callahan. "I want a line-up of all the east side or west side glaziers we can lay hands on tomorrow at the office—especially those answering this description—get me?"

"I get you, Inspector," responded Burke.

"Well, and the first thing you did when you came up and found the Professor here, and Mr. Goold dead, was, what?"

"I called Dr. Humphreys, sir, at Professor Ross's suggestion."

"All right," said Callahan, "that's all we want from you for the present."

"One moment," put in Ross. "Two more questions. Are you sure, Cross, your making of the eggnog did not take more than eight or ten minutes?"

"Not more than ten, at the outside, sir."

"Did you hear any sound—anything like a shot, or loud report, while you were in the pantry making eggnog and talking to Miss Baker?"

Cross was silent for a moment.

"Er—no, sir," he answered finally. "Not what you would call heard. The nurse was chatting along, and she laughed at something—she's a very nice woman—besides, the cars and trucks passing outside all the time, one often hears the exhausts backfiring—one pays no attention. You get used to them and it's as though you don't hear them."

"All right, for the present," said Callahan. "We may want you again. Meanwhile you go back into the house, round up the servants and tell them that Mr. Goold has been shot, and that they'll have to be questioned. But mind, don't tell them anything else. I'll send a man with you, who will stay with the servants. You better go back to your pantry."

"Before we leave the house," said Ross, to no one in particular, "we shall want to see that basement."

"Yes, sir," said the butler, as though realizing that in Ross he had his only friend in the room.

"You go along now," Callahan dismissed him and with a nod ordered one of his men to accompany Cross as he passed through the door with an audible sigh of relief.

"One moment," Ross stopped him in the doorway. "Just one thing: What makes you sure, Cross, that that picture that's missing was there this afternoon?"

"Oh, that, sir. One of the light bulbs over it had burned out. I remembered noticing it last evening. And this afternoon before Mr. Goold came home I put in a new bulb. The picture was certainly there, sir. By the way," he added, the consciousness of the major domo all at once returning upon him, "shall I bring you gentlemen something to eat, sandwiches or something?"

"If you can swing it, sure," Callahan responded promptly. "I don't see where my men are going to get any supper tonight. And a sandwich and a cup of coffee or something wouldn't hurt any of us."

Ross nodded to the butler. Wells said nothing. To him this phase of criminal investigation was still entirely new. Cross walked out behind the detective and closed the door.

9
Amalie

The door had no sooner closed upon Cross and his accompanying detective than it opened again and Dr. Humphreys emerged, still immaculate, but having the air of a
man who had put in twelve or fifteen hours at hard labor.
He gazed at the roomful of men and nodded briefly toward
the Commissioner.

"Well," said Wells conversationally, "I hope your patient is not in too bad a state?"

Dr. Humphreys lifted his eyes ceilingward as though to
warn him that the less said about that the better:

"You can imagine, an invalid lady, bed-ridden, unable
to move her lower limbs for two years, is not very robust,
when it comes to standing shocks. The hardest job I have
ever had in all my practice. I have given her an opiate and
left the night nurse in charge. I believe she will sleep now,
but I shall certainly look in early tomorrow, if I am not
called sooner."

"A very good thing for us you were at hand," said Wells.

"Yes," nodded Humphreys. "The very atmosphere of
this house at this time is sufficient to affect unfavorably
even a hale person."

"But there's no reason why we can't question the nurses,
is there?" inquired Callahan.

"None that I know of," answered the doctor. "Though someone ought to remain near Mrs. Goold if the nurse is called away from her."

"Thank you very much, Dr. Humphreys," from Wells. "In case we should want you further, we shall know where to find you, I presume. We shall let you know about the inquest."

Dr. Humphreys, with evident relief, bade the others good night and left the house with every sign of alacrity.

"Well, that's that and that brings us to the help. Now, I wonder, whom we had better tackle next. That maid who went down into the basement to ask the butler her question—" he could not conceal something of a grin.

"If I may suggest," observed Ross, "the young man with Miss Storey, Mr. Trumbull, since he waited in the car outside, possibly he might have seen something."

"A good idea, Professor," agreed Callahan. "Rooney," he turned to one of his men, "go in there and bring along this Mr. Trumbull."

Jimmie Trumbull, visibly excited, yet obviously endeavoring to appear calm and nonchalant, faced the group of police officials with a perceptible tremor in his knees. At once eager and shy, he fixed his eyes on Professor Ross who was now one of the police investigators, and dimly there struggled in his mind the hope that the professor would say:

"Mr. Trumbull, the police authorities would be very glad if you, with your sharp insight and deep acumen, would join us in this important investigation."

Not only, however, did Professor Ross say nothing of the sort, merely smiling in his direction, but Wells, and Callahan in particular, made him feel rather as though he were a small boy, and their questions seemed to him of the most elementary and perfunctory. Almost he would have liked to encourage them by saying:

"Gentlemen, better let me in on this. I have long been a student of crime, and I feel sure I could render you a great deal of valuable assistance."

Nothing of this, however, came within miles of getting itself spoken. He told them that he had waited in the car, he repeated Lorna's account of the trip to the garage and the walk back, and the subsequent session in her sitting-room, during which time he knew nothing whatever of what had happened in the gallery. He was dismissed with what seemed to him great brevity, with only Ross's kindly admonition:

"Better stay near Miss Storey if possible, Mr. Trumbull. She needs some friend near her."

"Yes, sir. Anything at all I can do—"

"That'll be all for the present," the insensitive Callahan interrupted sharply. And Jimmie, flushing and abashed, vanished through the door under Callahan's hard smile.

"Now," said Callahan, "there's the maid. That will be a job. Better say goodbye to any thoughts of supper, boys," he addressed his men ostensibly, but actually the world in general and himself in particular, somewhat plaintively. At this moment, however, the door opened and Cross appeared with a tray of cups and a silver urn of steaming coffee, and behind him a trim, slender French maid, bearing another tray—sandwiches. Her snapping brown eyes surveyed the assembled men in a swift unabashed appraisal, and somewhere deep within her she seemed to smile, though no feature of hers showed the slightest diminution of composure.

"Well, I'm not so hot as a prophet," grinned Callahan, his eyes fixed upon the food.

And the Commissioner said, "Thank you, Cross. That's very good of you."

"If there's anything else I can do, sir," murmured Cross.

Callahan spoke up. "Is this the young woman who came down to the basement to ask you a question?"

"Yes, sir," answered Cross in an even tone.

"All right," said Callahan, "then she may as well remain here and we'll go on with the examination."

Seemingly undisturbed by this, Cross poured out the coffee and he and the maid passed it about, together with the sandwiches, among the men. When he had finished, he returned the trays to the desk and quietly, without haste, left the room.

The men from headquarters fell upon the food like castaways, to the evident satisfaction of the maid who could not resist smiling at their appetite. Smiling was evidently easy for this young woman. It was noticeable that neither Wells nor Ross partook of any food, though each of them took a few sips of coffee. The invisible line of breeding that lay between Ross and Wells on the one hand, and the police officials on the other, made it seemingly impossible for the two men to eat the while Goold still lay on the davenport covered with a rug, but just as natural for the others to eat with the gusto of guests at a wake.

"Now," began Callahan, after he had satisfied the foremost sharp pangs of his hunger, "would you mind telling us your name?"

It was impossible for this girl to make a movement, to turn her head, or to glance at an interlocutor without a certain coquetry, a gesture or an air intensively feminine and challenging.

"My name is Amalie Dubois," she answered, as though she was conferring the first of many favors.

"Where were you, do you remember, between five and six this afternoon?"

"Oh, in a lot of places." Her smile still held and her enunciation betrayed a trace of French accent.

"Tell me every place you were in and the time you were there, as nearly as you can fix it in each case."

"Oh, well," she threw a dramatic glance up to the ceiling. "How can I do that, Monsieur? I am here, there, everywhere. I don't sit with my hands in my lap. I am maid."

"You are maid, very good," went on Callahan. "But it isn't so long ago, is it, that you can't remember where you were during that hour? Only some three or four hours ago. Now, then, please tell us where you were at, say, five o'clock exactly?"

"May I sit down, Monsieur?"

Callahan rose from his chair beside the desk, none too well pleased to cede it, and invited her with a gesture almost of mockery to take his place. Amalie, however, saw nothing discrepant in this procedure, took the chair, and glanced up into Callahan's eyes above her with the faint smile, at once appreciative and impersonal, of a lady for whom a total stranger had performed a slight courtesy.

"At five o'clock," she said, "I was in my room."

"In your room—good. Then where were you at five minutes past five?"

"Leaving my room."

"To go where?"

"Where? Down the stairs, of course."

"Where downstairs?"

Amalie paused and seemed to hesitate. Callahan fixed his eyes narrowly upon her. To Ross this attempt to frighten the girl, even though she did not appear as one easily frightened, seemed absurd.

"Was that when you went to the basement?" he suggested. And he perceived that the color in Amalie's cheeks had risen slightly.

"Yes, sir," she answered with no change of tone, however.

"Why the basement?" demanded Callahan.

"I had some business there," she retorted with the first note of impatience.

"What business?" pressed Callahan. Again Amalie seemed to hesitate.

"Let me help you," put in Ross, ignoring the glare from Callahan's eyes at his interference. "You were going down to the basement, Amalie, to see Cross. You had arranged to meet him there about that time. Isn't that true?"

The girl darted an angry glance at him but because of something gentle and humorous and sympathetic in his eyes, she could not help smiling faintly.

"Isn't that true, Amalie?" repeated Ross.

"Yes, sir," she answered, glancing away with a La Gioconda smile.

Callahan, as though admitting tacitly that Ross was getting better results, nodded to him as a signal that he might continue the questions.

"Yes," repeated Ross. "Now, Amalie, be sure that we have no desire to pry into your private affairs. We do not care to know how often you meet Cross nor the reasons for the meetings. All we wish to know is what happened this afternoon when you were in the basement with Cross. I mean, everything that you heard, or saw, or even thought, to the smallest detail. Is that clear to you?"

"Yes, sir," she answered, her confidence growing more firm.

"Good. Now, how did you get down to the basement from this floor—will you tell us, please?"

"By the stairway. There are two; one right outside this door. It is like the stairway from the butler's pantry. It also goes to the basement."

"And you used the stairway near this door, of course?"

She nodded and looked intently at this man who seemed to divine her movements.

"Did you hear anything or see anything as you passed this door between the house and the gallery? I don't mean that you listened behind the door, but you might have overheard something in passing."

"I didn't hear or see a thing," she answered.

"Now, where in the basement did you meet Cross?"

"I had to tell him something," she began, for the first time irrelevant and obviously self-conscious.

"We only want to know where this happened, Amalie," Ross gently reminded her.

"There's a room there next to the wine cellar where Mr. Cross, he keeps things of his own, odds and ends, silver polish, cloths, a number of things. Also his trunk. It's a kind of junk room."

"It was in that room, then? Was there anybody else in the basement at that time?"

"I am not sure. The basement is large."

"You went straight from these stairs to Cross's junk room? He was in there, I take it?"

"Yes, sir."

"How long did it take you to tell him whatever you had to tell him, Amalie?"

"Perhaps fifteen minutes—perhaps a few moments longer."

"Could it have been as much as twenty-five or thirty minutes?"

"It could have been, though I don't think it was."

"We shall have a look at that junk room presently. How far should you say the room is from the bottom of the stairs?"

"Not far," she reflected, "perhaps twenty feet."

"Now, think carefully before answering this question: Who left the room first to go upstairs, Cross or you?"

Miss Dubois, however, was very positive in her answer:

"Cross, he left the room first, but I went upstairs first."

"How did that happen?"

"Well, someone, he threw a golf ball through the window and Mr. Cross, he was disturbed by the noise and he ran out of the room to see, and anyway, our interview was over, so I go upstairs."

"And you came up the same stairway, nearest the gallery door?"

"Yes, sir. Then I went—"

"Yes, I know, you went straight to your room, isn't that it? Now, during the time you were in your room after you came up, did you hear any noises of any sort, anything like a shot or explosion?"

"No, sir."

"That's all, Amalie, and thank you—unless these other gentlemen have any questions. You have been very good."

"No questions," said Callahan gruffly. "Now you go straight to your room and don't you talk to anybody."

The girl glanced defiantly at him and with a firm quick step left the gallery.

"How did you happen to think, Professor Ross, that that girl went down to meet Cross in the basement by appointment?"

Ross smiled. "Oh, that was nothing but a little chance shot, Inspector. If it worked, I thought, that might give us a slight advantage. As it happened, it did work."

"Yes, yes," interjected Wells impatiently, "but what on earth does that tell us? Are we interested in the amours of a pack of servants?"

"No, we are not, Commissioner," admitted Ross, "but we are trying to fix the whereabouts of every person in the house at the time of the murder, so far as we can. And salient, important facts unfortunately, Commissioner, only come out by hard digging."

Wells said nothing but Callahan nodded a reluctant affirmation.

The servants who followed contributed very little. The cook, a Mrs. Shearer, a trim matron with graying hair, who appeared in her white smock like some scientist's laboratory assistant, answered calmly, crisply and succinctly. She had been in her kitchen at that time in the afternoon occupied with the preparation for dinner. She had heard nothing unusual; she had seen no one or anything outside her own orbit. Exactly the same was true of the girl, Linda Holweg, assisting her, a Swedish damsel with flaxen hair.

Of the two remaining maids, Harriet O'Malley and Bessie Brown, only the latter had anything to say. For the half hour between five-thirty and six the maids were usually in their rooms, either changing their clothes, or in other ways preparing for their evening duties. Bessie Brown, however, declared that at about a quarter to six, she couldn't be sure of the exact minute, she had happened to leave her room which was nearest the stairway, to cross to Harriet's room to borrow some pins. In the hallway below she saw a nurse walking softly along the corridor.

"Did you recognize which of the nurses it was?" Ross asked her.

She had not, though she supposed it was Miss Baker. Neither was the nurse carrying anything in her hands, so far as she could remember. Wasn't particularly interested.

"Were the nurse's movements in any way stealthy or suggestive of secrecy?" Ross asked her.

Bessie Brown thought not. Nurses always moved quiet-like. And as her observation and her fixing of the time appeared anything but precise, it seemed obvious that she may have observed Miss Baker at that time on her way to or from the butler's pantry in connection with the famous eggnog.

"Well, that about finishes the lot of them," observed Callahan wearily, "with the exception of those nurses."

10

An Angry Nurse

When Miss Baker came into the room she was in street dress and there was a forbidding gleam about the eye-glasses she wore. She glanced at the men assembled in the gallery as upon so many inquisitors bent upon disturbing her routine and upon annihilating her peace of mind. Before anyone had time to ask her a question, she began in *medias res,* as though merely continuing a long train of argument that had already been going on inside her.

"As I'm a day nurse, I don't really see how I'm going to get my sleep and be fit for the next day's work if I'm kept up here to all hours."

"There are times, Miss Baker," Commissioner Wells attempted to mollify her, "when we none of us are exactly in a position to consult our own convenience. We are all somewhat in your position."

The expression about Miss Baker's mouth conveyed that this particular line of reasoning interested her not at all. The irrelevancy of her next remark conclusively proved it.

"Yes, I know," she admitted almost sullenly. "But nurses are supposed to tend the sick, and I should think some allowance would be made."

"True," said Wells, interested in this impermeable type of mentality, notwithstanding his annoyance. "But we are investigating a death. And according to your kind of reasoning, that is one step more important."

Miss Baker said nothing, but took the chair offered her, without thanks, and smoothed out her dress with fingers that conveyed her displeasure better, evidently, than any other words she could further trust herself to utter.

"Miss Baker," began Callahan heavily, as if determined to ignore this trivial rebellion, "have you been long a nurse in this house?"

"Going on three years," she answered, "two years last June."

"Mrs. Goold has been an invalid all that time?"

"A paralytic—has to be handled like a helpless baby."

"You are in a position, then, to tell us something about the relations of Mr. and Mrs. Goold, and also their relations to other people," put in Ross.

"If you mean was he nice to her, I will say he was. And very attentive, too. But if you want me to say that he was a saint—well, it's not for me to talk scandal. I'm a nurse in the house. And nurses have to keep things to themselves just as a doctor has."

"Now, just what do you mean by that, Miss Baker?" and by this time even Callahan had ceased to be annoyed by Ross's interventions because he had finally realized that they usually led to a point.

"What I mean by that?" repeated Miss Baker in some disdain. "I haven't said anything but what everybody knows. I guess Mr. Goold led his own life. If you mean was there any open scandal, you know as well as I do that there wasn't. I guess the newspapers of this city would take care to protect the name of a man like Mr. Goold when they mightn't be so kind to poorer people."

"Did you," Ross smiled at the ruffled woman encouragingly, "did you ever perceive any signs of scandal even though it wasn't open?"

"No, I can't exactly say I did. I only saw Mr. Goold when he came up to the sickroom, and I will say he came up at least once every day. I don't see how he could help but do that, seeing that his wife is a helpless cripple and she simply worships him."

"All right, all right," broke in Callahan, "now we've got that straight, will you tell us exactly what you did between half past five and six o'clock."

"My duty, my regular duties as a nurse." Then, evidently realizing that she might expedite her release by answering the questions as put, she continued:

"Well, I don't know exactly what I was doing at half past five, but I do know that at about a quarter to six Mrs. Goold called me and asked me to go down to the pantry and get her some eggnog. She didn't have it every day but some days she felt weaker than others and she needed it. And that butler, Cross, being an English butler and used to making it, he always made it up for her. It wasn't that he did anything special, or that I couldn't have done myself, but just that he put a drop of sherry into it and it kind of picked the poor lady up."

"And about how long a time did you spend down there in that butler's pantry getting that eggnog?" asked Callahan.

"Not more than a few minutes. I couldn't say to the second, but just about as long as it took Cross to get the ingredients together and to mix it up and to let it stand for a few minutes and then to shake it again and to pour it out."

"Should you say," put in Ross, "that the whole thing, your going and your waiting and your coming back, might have taken as much as fifteen minutes?"

"I don't exactly see how it could take as long as that but I wouldn't swear that it didn't. It might have done."

"Did you stop for a chat at all with Mr. Cross?" Ross put in half negligently.

"Well, a person has to say a civil word at least to a person working in the same house."

"So that eighteen or twenty minutes consumed is not an impossibility, Miss Baker?"

"I wouldn't swear to the time," she answered stiffly.

Ross nodded bright encouragement to her.

"Now, one question," he added almost cajolingly. "You said a little while ago that Mrs. Goold called you. Weren't you in her room at the time? In other words, where were you when she called you?"

"Where? In the little dressing-room, of course. That's the little room next to hers where the night nurse rests at night when Mrs. Goold is sleeping, or where either of us sometimes sits when she's resting. It isn't as though even a sick person didn't want to be alone sometimes, if only for a few minutes."

"Did you during the day often leave Mrs. Goold alone in this way?"

"No, indeed. I know my duties too well. Only when Mr. Goold, or sometimes Miss Lorna, came in to see her. Or, when she just asked to be alone."

"And how was it this afternoon—did someone come in to see her?"

"Oh, no. She was reading. I guess that may seem strange to all you gentlemen, but Mrs. Goold is a very wonderful woman, crippled though she is. She asked for her Bible, and I guess she wanted to read or meditate alone. If that poor woman didn't get the comfort she does from her Bible, I guess she wouldn't be alive today."

Callahan looked at Ross in a surprise slightly tinged with annoyance, for here was a line of questioning that could obviously lead nowhere, and yet, late as it was, Ross, presuming upon his honorary position, was delving into trifles of no importance. Ross perceived his glance and looked at once both amused and humbled. "Only one question more," he added, somewhat as a naughty boy does one more naughty thing when he has been reproved, just to assert his independence. "I am sure, Miss Baker, that a woman of high principles like yours would never have spied upon Mrs. Goold in the silence of her prayers and meditation?"

"Certainly not, sir," snapped Miss Baker.

"Miss Baker," Wells suddenly interposed, "tell me this, please: Once you got that glass or cup of eggnog from Cross, did you go directly back to Mrs. Goold's room?"

"Where else would I go?" was the indignant reply.

Then suddenly anyone who was watching her closely, as Ross was doing, could perceive a shade of pallor sweeping over the nurse's face.

"One thing more, then: What were your reasons for hostility, or antagonism, we might say, against Mr. Goold?"

Miss Baker glared at him and then glanced angrily down at her hands, which were shaking in her lap.

"Antagonism? Hostility? I didn't say any such thing! But I guess everybody knows the kind of a life he led, with his poor wife lying crippled up there, unable to move her limbs. But suppose I did feel that way? I know my place! I hardly ever spoke to him unless he spoke to me first, and that wasn't often. I guess a person can have opinions without making themselves disagreeable."

For some reason the Commissioner had succeeded in distinctly agitating Miss Baker.

Callahan, however, realizing that this line of inquiry led him nowhere, seized upon the interval of relaxation in the questioning to say:

"You didn't hear a shot or an explosion while you were waiting for that eggnog, or carrying it to Mrs. Goold's room, did you?"

Almost before Miss Baker could supply a negative, he went on, "Very good, Miss Baker. That's all we shall want from you just now. And if you don't sleep on the premises, I would like you to stay here tonight. I don't want any people to leave this house tonight. Now, I reckon this man Cross, or whoever has charge of those things, will be able to put you up."

"But I have engagements," she protested. "It isn't as though I haven't a home of my own."

"So have we," Callahan retorted even more peremptorily. "That's about all, Miss Baker. Now, if you'll go and relieve the night nurse for long enough to have her come here to speak to us for a few moments, we'll thank you."

Miss Baker's anger, as she all but stamped out of the room, brought a weary smile to the men, but otherwise made no impression.

A pounding on the outside door which caused one of Callahan's men to open it brought him back in a minute with an urgent message from the newspaper men to the effect that they could not wait any longer, that their papers would soon be going to press. They had sent a flash of Goold's death almost three hours earlier and now they wanted the story.

"Tell them," said the Commissioner, "that in about five minutes I shall come out to them and we will go down to Headquarters where they will have the entire story. Tell them I'm sorry but I can't receive them here, and as Mrs. Goold is an invalid, there is no one in the family to receive them."

Whether this message satisfied the newspaper men or not, it somewhat speeded the action of the police, and particularly of the Commissioner, whose very position depended upon newspaper publicity.

"What's left now, Callahan?" he asked. "Aren't we about through?"

"There's that other nurse, the night nurse. Can't be much to her for she came in after it all happened, I guess. We ought to be able to dispose of her in a jiffy."

"All right, all right, let's get it done."

The night nurse, Miss Kelly, who was a blonde with large blue eyes, made a distinctly favorable impression upon Callahan's assistants. Miss Kelly was one of those young women who looked their best with men's eyes upon them. Her starchy white seemed to set off her golden bobbed hair and baby blue eyes to perfection. She smiled easily and was easy to smile at.

In answer to the somewhat hurried questions of Callahan she said precisely what was expected of her, that she had been a little late, that she had come in after seven, and that the first thing she heard was this terrible news about Mr. Goold. That since then she had been occupied with her duties in attending upon her patient.

"Then you know nothing more than you have gathered since you came into the house this evening?" asked Callahan.

She declared that she did not. Whereupon Ross, who seemed bound upon doing the wrong thing, and to disregard the fact that the newspaper men were impatiently waiting upon the Commissioner, gently asked this pretty nurse:

"Then you have no knowledge at all, Miss Kelly, that might help us in our investigation of Mr. Goold's tragic death?"

"Well, no, sir—no. Not what you would call knowledge."

"Call it by what name you like, Miss Kelly," he encouraged her. "But won't you tell us just what is on your mind?"

"Well, it isn't anything, really. But for the past two or three months, I've had a feeling that something queer was going on in this house."

Callahan's face hardened and he was about to speak brusquely to her, when Ross checked him with an almost imperceptible gesture and then continued in a half encouraging, half indolent tone:

"Now, just give us in the best way you can some idea of what this thing was, and why queer, and so on—you know, just exactly as you would talk to a friend over a cup of tea."

"It's very hard," said Miss Kelly, smiling and puckering her pretty forehead. "But I have had a feeling as though there was something going on here that you couldn't exactly lay your hands on, but that was something mysterious— like a terrible—that something was going to happen."

"Just what gave you this idea? What little or big things, what happenings or incidents?" Ross smiled gently as he bent toward her.

Miss Kelly's blue eyes rested confidingly upon Ross's face and she smiled.

"It's just—some people say I'm psychic. I wasn't thinking of that, but it's just been a feeling that something strange was taking place in the house lately and that something was going to happen. It isn't any particular occurrence, as you might say, but just a feeling on my part. Sometimes when I dozed off in the little room next to Mrs. Goold's, I'd wake up suddenly and I'd be all in a quiver about it. I thought first it was dreams, but it's happened again and again, and I would shudder, kind of. Though I can't tell you exactly what it is."

"Then that's all you base it on?" Callahan this time insisted upon breaking in. "Just what you felt when you waked up from a snooze?"

Miss Kelly flushed. "Well, I said I couldn't exactly describe it. But since you gentlemen asked me—"

Callahan's expression conveyed to all, including Miss Kelly, how trifling to him was the value of her testimony.

"Young lady," he began with a sort of brisk ponderousness, "do you ever go to fortune tellers, astrologers, seances, and those things?"

"Why—why—" Miss Kelly bridled for a moment with a hurt expression, "I guess every woman has her fortune told sometime. But as to seances, no. I never took any stock in those."

Callahan nodded wearily and added:

"Then all you have is this feeling that you can't name, is that it?"

Miss Kelly nodded, evidently disappointed that after giving her best this brusque man was inclined to award her so little credit for it.

"Ever hear any noises during the night that you thought suspicious?" Ross asked her

"No, sir, I can't say I did."

"Then just this one little question, Miss Kelly," Ross concluded suavely. "Do you know or are you aware of any enemies of Mr. Goold or Mrs. Goold?"

"Well, I can't say that," Miss Kelly seemed to be visibly regaining her composure under Ross's gentle leading. "But I have for some time had a feeling that there was a lot of hatred around the house. It's just as though it was all over me—I can't exactly explain."

"Did you have the feeling that the hatred was here in the house?" queried Wells.

"Well, it's as though it was all around. I'm sorry, that's all I can say."

"Very well, that winds it up," put in Callahan hastily, as though fearing to be bothered by any more questions. But to Ross, somehow, the vague answers of this vague young woman seemed to give a certain modicum of food for thought.

"I've never yet had a murder case," declared Callahan, once the nurse had left the room, "that there wasn't some half-wit full of astrology and spooks and fortune telling, who knew by hindsight that something terrible was going

to happen. Kind of a surprise to find a nurse of that calibre in this place. Now, Commissioner," he turned to his
superior, "I guess that winds us up here. I'll keep two or
three men here and I'll send over for the—remains. Best
thing I can do is to get back to the office."

11
"An Arrest Will Shortly Follow"

"Potosi!" Callahan called to the finger-print expert who was working on a small table with his lenses in the rear of the room. "You got anything yet?"

"Yes, sir," was the answer, "but we'd better go down to the office to develop these. And I think we'd better take this frame down to the office, too."

"Well, well," murmured Wells, looking at his watch, "it seems we've done about all we could for the present, haven't we? Is there any reason why we need remain here?"

"No reason why you should, Commissioner," from Callahan. "Somebody ought to satisfy those newspaper vultures out there; and I guess you'll want something to eat. We'll mop up here quick as we can and I'll be down at the office in a little while."

"Then," said the Commissioner, "I might as well go."

Callahan nodded obsequiously as he turned to a subordinate and made a gesture, ordering the door to be opened for his superior. Whereupon the most energetic and the least experienced police commissioner New York ever had put on his excellently cut light overcoat and his soft gray hat and took his leave with these sacrificial words:

"Any time day or night you can call me on this. I'll be waiting to hear news—real news. I'll call up Burton, the District Attorney, and tell him about it. As for you men, the sky is the limit. But this is a murder that has got to be solved. There has simply got to be an arrest. If I break every man in the department, someone must be brought to trial for this. Goodnight, everybody."

"Well, now," Callahan all but grunted with relief as soon as the door closed behind the Commissioner. "Now we'd better get busy." His remaining subordinates snickered covertly. "I can just hear the Commissioner telling the newspaper men the whole sad story and winding up with, 'An arrest will shortly follow.' First thing, now," he went on more soberly, "is to get this body moved where it belongs."

He took up the telephone and gave instructions for the removal of Goold's remains to the mortuary, and then gazed about with the searching eye of a Napoleon surveying the terrain of a battle. But for some reason ideas did not seem to flash very rapidly upon his brain, and his eyes grew smaller and duller as he stood there in silent perplexity.

"Professor," he finally blurted out, "don't you think if we put that butler on the grill again, we'll get something out of him?"

"What's on your mind, Inspector?" Ross mildly inquired.

"Well, I kinda don't like his looks. Strikes me he knows a hell of a lot more than he admits. Shouldn't wonder if in the end we pin the whole shebang on him."

"There, Inspector, I must differ with you. He seems to me the most useful witness we have had. He has given us more real information than anybody else. Would you want to ruin a first-rate source of information?"

"You don't think there's a chance at all, at all, of his being the fellow we want?"

"Frankly, Inspector, I don't."

Potosi and his assistant now left the gallery, and there remained but Sergeant Burke and two other detectives, besides Callahan.

"All right, Professor," Callahan began again, as though he had thought the matter over. "Suppose I play along with you, what would you do next?"

"I would certainly recall Cross, but not for the purpose of grilling him. I would merely ask him to take us through the basement and show us the lay-out, and treat him very pleasantly. In fact, as he is a sensitive man, and intelligent, and we want all we can get out of him, I would show him every courtesy and consideration."

"Well, you may be right, at that," Callahan sighed with heavy resignation. "But I can't see—why, I've got what almost amounts to a hunch about this butler. I'm going to keep him watched, anyway. Still, you've got the reputation of knowing a lot about crime, Professor."

Ross laughed quietly.

"Oh, come, come, Inspector, it isn't a matter of what I know or what you know. It's a matter of trying to discover the murderer of Goold. It's a puzzling case. You've had a lot of experience, Inspector. But I will tell you one thing that I have learned in my own. The more puzzling the case, the more certainly we must guard ourselves from guessing. I start from the assumption that I don't know a thing and work from there on. What do you say to looking over the basement, Inspector?"

"All right, all right," drawled Callahan. "Only the crime was committed up here, not in the basement. Still, get that butler bird," he addressed himself to Burke.

"You're right, Inspector," said Ross. "The crime was committed up here, but we may have to go farther than the basement before we find the criminal. For some reason, criminals have a habit of not staying on the scene of their crimes."

With his usual calm poise, Cross, when summoned, conducted Ross, Callahan and Burke to the basement. Geographically, at least, the statements of both the maid,

Amalie, and the butler were borne out with a fair degree of accuracy. The party descended by the stairway nearest the gallery door, examined Cross's lumber room, measured the distances, and for some time Ross looked carefully, not at the pane the glazier had actually put in but with a pocket lens at the bits of broken glass beneath the window.

Callahan, watching him, could hardly contain his impatience. Now that the Police Commissioner had gone, Callahan, supreme, was very different from what he had been under the eye of his superior. He was more argumentative, more impatient, possibly even less brilliant—in short, he was himself.

"Now, what the heck, Professor," he broke out, "is all this peering at bits of broken glass going to tell you?"

Ross smiled abstractedly.

"Not much, possibly, but that glazier was a fairly long time putting in a simple pane of glass. You remember he conveyed to Cross that he had cracked the first pane he tried. If I could feel sure that he cracked it purposely to prolong his sojourn in the basement, we should have some grounds to suspect him, wouldn't you think so?"

"I get you, Professor. Well, in that case, what do you make of it?"

Ross held up a strip of broken glass.

"You see this edge? The diamond that cut this glass was exceptionally good. The glass itself is of a fair make. No reason why it should crack in cutting that I can see."

Callahan grunted.

"Now, that kind of stuff, Professor, is what drives me woozy. That's what they do in books. But no real detective has ever solved a real crime by any of that boloney. If we round up that glazier tomorrow, we'll damn soon know whether he's the murderer or not. What can some bits of broken glass tell us that don't even carry a finger-print?"

"Well, have it your own way, Inspector," laughed Ross. "So long as you don't grudge me mine." And Ross put the bit of glass in an envelope, which he returned to his pocket.

"I hardly think, sir," Cross for the first time took it upon himself to speak without being questioned, "that glazier was likely to have committed that sort of crime. He appeared, if I may say so, a most defenceless immigrant."

"Defenceless nothing," growled Callahan. "He's got to be found if we can find him."

"Yes," said Ross, "I suppose he must. Now," he added with that curiously indolent-seeming irrelevance which so annoyed Callahan, "there's one little experiment I'd like to make. Mr. Burke here has doubtless no more familiarity with this basement than I have myself. I wish, Inspector, you would request him to go up these stairs as swiftly and softly as he can, enter the gallery, spend, say, two minutes there—that's about as long as it would take, I should judge, to cut a picture from its frame—and get back here to this window pane. You see, I want to time him to see how long it would take. Does that meet with your approval, Inspector?"

"Sure it does. Check, Burke."

Callahan and Ross took out their watches. "Now on your way, Burke," ordered Callahan, his eyes fixed upon the dial.

Swiftly, guardedly, yet clumsily, too, with considerable histrionic ability, Burke made his way to the stairs, glanced about him cautiously, crept up as quickly as he could, yet exercising great care against unnecessary noises, and disappeared above the line of vision. The two minutes and some twenty seconds consumed by Burke in this act of disappearance seemed to the time keepers longer than their silence indicated. Yet the total time that elapsed for Burke's excursion was slightly over four and a half minutes.

"I get you, Professor," nodded Callahan, pocketing his watch. "That glazier bird had plenty of time to get the picture. You said," he turned to Cross, "you were gone eight or ten minutes to make that shot of eggnog. Then that glazier had time to commit the murder and to steal two pictures if he had to. I get you."

"Exactly," said Ross, "that gives us at least something to start on. Cross," he now addressed the butler, "let me ask you this. You have been in Mr. Goold's service—how long?"

"Seven years, sir."

"Seven years. Do you know of any enemies Mr. Goold had—enemies whose names leap to your mind at the mere mention of the word?"

"No—sir—I can't say."

"You hesitated somewhat at the negative, didn't you?"

"Yes, I did, sir. Because it occurred to me that a man like Mr. Goold must have had enemies. He was a strong man. But I can't possibly think of enemies who would stoop to murder."

"Stoop or rise—you can't think of a soul in Mr. Goold's acquaintances you would suspect in these circumstances?"

"No, sir—not even—" he hesitated, then uttered firmly, "not even Mr. Cullen Forbes."

"You haven't had a feeling," Callahan began, "like one of those nurses, that there was something queer about the house, that something mysterious and terrible was going to happen?"

"No, sir, I can't say I have. Though this isn't exactly what you might call a gay household, with sickness in it and all that."

"Well, then, I'm through here for this evening," nodded Callahan, leading the way to the stairs. "As soon as the body goes, we are through here for the present. There will be a man left on duty at every outside door. You better tell the other servants, Cross, to stay in until we tell them they can go out. Don't want to make it hard, but it will be easier for you, too—keep a lot of bothering people out."

"Very good, sir," said Cross.

"You won't mind," said Ross, "if I stay on here for a few moments. Both Miss Storey and Mr. Trumbull are students of mine. Just as well that some friend of theirs, some older person, have a talk with them, particularly with Miss Storey."

"All right, Professor—go as far as you like. Only let me in on anything good that you get. I guess the Commissioner," he added with a grim smile, "will expect us to deliver the murderer to him tomorrow morning, all dressed and ready for shipment."

"Hardly," laughed Ross. "He can't be as unreasonable as all that, he being an experienced business man."

"They have come for the body," one of the plainclothes men informed Callahan as he opened the gallery door.

"O.K.," said Callahan. "Then you fellows can go and eat. How many doors are there to this house?" he turned to Cross. "Three? All right. I want a man to stay at every door. Phone to the office, Burke, to send up some of the night men. I want tab kept on everyone coming and going. The servants are not going out of the house until further orders. You stay here, Burke, until the men come."

"All right, Chief," said Burke, and wearily he picked up the telephone.

Ross then asked Cross to announce him to Miss Lorna Storey.

"Now, the first thing we do, Burke," Callahan lowered his tone, though they were alone, "is to cover that Cullen Forbes outfit—get me?"

Burke nodded impressively.

"There," went on Callahan, "is our best lead to may-be the biggest case and the biggest story we were ever up against. Suppose it was Forbes or his wife who killed

Goold, get me? Could anything bigger happen in our big burg?"

"I sent a man out on that nearly an hour ago," said Burke with great satisfaction, "about the time the Commissioner left."

"Good work," Callahan gazed at his sergeant with profound respect. "Though how the Commissioner will react to this I can't say. You can bet he'll keep the Forbeses out of the papers long as he can. Forbes is a big guy in this town. And that Professor isn't any too keen to have 'em involved, you could see that, couldn't you? Oh, it's going to be a sweet mess, take my word for it, Burke."

Burke did.

12

Lorna Turns Watson

By the time Ross arrived in Lorna's sitting room she was already composed, and though her face still bore traces of grief, she greeted him with a smile very sad, but wholly charming and eagerly friendly.

Jimmie Trumbull who had been sprawling in a chair leaped up to greet the professor, his admiration for whom had increased tremendously.

"Oh, Professor Ross," began Lorna, "do you think they will find him—the criminal?"

"Frankly, I don't know, Miss Storey. The discovery of any criminal becomes almost a problem in mathematics. You would like to see the criminal found, I take it?"

"Oh, yes!" she cried. "Who wouldn't? It seems such a dastardly thing to kill a man like Uncle Jim for the sake of a mere object like a picture. People who would do that ought to be exterminated."

"Well, well. I understand how you feel. But we must remember, we don't yet know the murder was committed for the sake of the picture. That reminds me, there was some trouble about that picture, wasn't there—some law-suit brought by the seller of it against your uncle?"

"Oh, yes. But that was more than two years ago."

"Would you mind telling me just what the circumstances were? I was, I believe, abroad at the time and I remember it only very faintly."

"It was very simple, Professor Ross. Prince Peter Erzer-off met Uncle Jim in Paris after the war. He was naturally in great need of money; he'd lost all his Russian property in the Revolution, and he offered to sell some of his pictures including the Tartar Chieftain, by Rembrandt. Uncle Jim was not interested in the others, but he bought the Rembrandt.

"Well, about three years ago Erzeroff came to this country and claimed that the picture had not actually been sold, but only pledged for a loan of the sum Uncle Jim had given him. Uncle Jim told him he remembered no such arrangement and refused. Erzeroff brought suit again him, but he lost and the picture remained here—till today."

"Erzeroff," put in Jimmie Trumbull, "was one of the fellows implicated in the murder of that Russian monk Rasputin, just before the Revolution, wasn't he?"

"Why that's true!" cried Lorna. "I never thought of that. Do you think, Professor Ross, he might have—"

"I don't know—I don't know—" Ross murmured half absently. "Do you happen to know whether Erzeroff is in this country now?"

"No, I don't," she was thinking hard as she spoke, "I wonder whether we couldn't find out? I suppose the police could."

"I presume they could," said Ross. "But quite frankly, and between ourselves, I'd much prefer that we find out all we can for ourselves. They work in a different manner—a little too abruptly, for me."

"Couldn't we," suggested Jimmie, "find out by writing to the State Department at Washington? He's a foreigner and all that. His passport must be registered—or something?"

"Writing is no good," said Ross—"in this case, and in most others for that matter."

"What would you suggest then, Professor Ross?"

Ross was silent for a space, lost in thought.

"I wonder," he began, "if my suggestion will interest you? Suppose you two join me in working upon this case. You are both students in Criminology. It will involve absence from lectures, but field work is even more important."

Lorna and Jimmie leaped from their chairs in the eagerness of their excitement. A case to work on!—It was tragic that so soon after expressing an idle wish, it had come home to her so terribly. Nevertheless, she braced herself.

"Only send us, Professor Ross," she said, "and see whether we shall go! Wouldn't you, Jimmie!"

"Wouldn't I!" echoed James. "Just try me!"

"Very well. Then we might as well begin at once. Your idea of asking the State Department as to the whereabouts of Erzeroff is not at all a bad one, Trumbull. There are other ways, but that would make the least noise just now. What would you say to hopping the midnight train to Washington, getting your stuff and landing here again by tomorrow evening!"

"Can do!" cried Jimmie. "Only I hope nothing important will happen while I am away. What had I better say to them in Washington, by the way?"

"Oh, the truth," smiled Ross—"the varnished truth. You want to see Erzeroff on an urgent matter of business."

"And you think they'll tell me?"

"Ah, that depends on your adroitness and address."

Jimmie looked grave. He was, in his way, not immodest, and he disliked to have so much depend upon his own adroitness and address. Nevertheless:

"I'll go," he said, "and if the information can be got, I'll get it."

"That," smiled Ross, "is the only possible attitude in a difficult world."

"Then," said Jimmie, importantly rising, "I'd better go now and make my arrangements."

"Jimmie! but you'll have something to eat?" protested Lorna.

"Not tonight, thanks, Lorna," he answered, bravely stilling the pangs of hunger. "I'll pick up something on the way."

"Bravo!" Ross tapped him on the shoulder. "Knights-errant of old used to vow to forego bathing, or sleeping soft, or something of that sort, until their quest was accomplished. A little hunger won't hurt us. Good luck, Trumbull. Let me hear the minute you return."

When Jimmie had left, Ross remained silent for a moment, surveying in his mind all that had gone before.

"Miss Storey,"—he began.

"Oh, I wish you would call me Lorna, Professor Ross," she broke in. "This seems hardly the time for ceremony."

"Very well, thank you. Lorna, then—will you tell me what you know about your uncle's—friendship with Mrs. Cullen Forbes?"

If he expected Lorna to blush and to hesitate, he found himself mistaken in the generation.

"Sheila? Oh, it was more than a friendship, Professor Ross. It was a real affair. Why, Uncle Jim was always having affairs, ever since I can remember. You know a girl knows these things by instinct. I was eleven years old when my parents died and I came to live here. Uncle Jim had too much vitality to be monogamous. Besides, Aunt Julia—" and at this point she paused.

"She didn't care for him?" suggested Ross.

"Oh, yes, she did in her way, I suppose. But it was a queer way—at least it seemed so to me. She adored him. She was both possessive, and yet somehow aloof. She was so proud, she would never see a fault in anything that was her own, or at least she pretended not to see any. I suppose it was just sort of Victorian, but I don't know. Her nature, I imagine. Anyway, when she was paralyzed and took to her bed, I was terribly sorry for her, but relieved on Uncle Jim's account. At least she stopped watching him, listening at doors and extension telephones and so on. She really seemed more at peace than she'd ever been before. Poor Aunt Julia," and the girl's lips quivered. "She is heartbroken now."

"I see," Ross nodded sympathetically. "And her case is quite hopeless?"

"I think so, Professor Ross, from what her doctors say. She remains paralyzed from the waist down. One doctor advised her to be psychoanalyzed. This she has always refused."

"And her mind—is that in any way affected?"

"No, I don't think so. Not that Aunt Julia ever had much mind, poor dear. But she seems to live in a world of her own, reading fiction and the Bible, or just gazing before her with a sort of fixed smile. Uncle Jim used to come in to see her every day—" with a gesture she indicated that she could not speak of it any more. "You'll stay and have a bite with me, won't you, Professor Ross?" she suddenly asked irrelevantly. "You won't mind our having it up here, will you. Somehow I can't go downstairs now."

"I shall be delighted," agreed Ross.

Lorna rang a bell. The maid Dubois appeared and demurely answered, "Yes, Miss Storey," when the order for supper was given her.

"Let me ask you an unpleasant question," Ross all but whispered, knowing that a maid such as this French girl would not hesitate to listen at the door before departing. "Your uncle was not the man, I feel sure, to go in for affairs with the maids, was he? Some men do, you know."

"Oh, no, Professor Ross. I am absolutely positive about that. He was too proud—and terribly particular. Beauty or brains or both, or great charm—those appealed to him. Uncle Jim's flames were never common."

"Forgive me," said Ross gently. "But in a case like this, you see, every possibility, even the remotest, has to be faced."

"I understand perfectly," returned the girl with the smile of a touching sadness hovering upon her lips. "We are not angels, any of us, are we? Too bad, isn't it?"

"I wonder what I should be doing, if we were," speculated Ross. "Certainly not about to eat supper with you."

"Oh, there are so many other things," laughed Lorna softly. "We'd probably be picking asphodels and turning them into wreaths or something for each other's necks."

"Oh," said Ross, "in that case I am willing to try the angelic state—for a season or so."

Lorna blushed faintly and called out, "Come in!" in response to a knock at the door. Cross and the maid Dubois, bearing trays of food entered the room.

Imperturbable and calm as was his wont, Cross moved about the room with the tranquility and dignity of a man whom no shock could conceivably disturb, shedding an aura of calm about him. It was no wonder the maid could not resist following him with her eyes. For one of her mercurial temperament a man like Cross was like a tower.

"Hence, Britannia rules the waves—and the Colonies," remarked Ross as the two servants left the room. And Lorna, who followed his train of thought accurately, added as a rider:

"And why France does not."

Ross rose for a moment, went to the window and peered behind the shade to the street below. A small crowd had gathered upon the opposite pavement and a patrolman was moving it on. The extra papers with the mere announcement of Goold's death were already being cried and drawing idlers to the scene of the tragedy.

"It's a great comfort your being here," said Lorna. "I am dying to know," she went on, "just how you came into this, Professor Ross. Though I am so glad you are in it, that I've been afraid to ask."

"It's simple enough, Lorna. About a month ago when Wells became Police Commissioner, we met at the Varsity Club and he asked me whether as a matter of civic duty, I would be willing to act as an occasional consultant to his department of Criminal Investigation. I agreed of course, and promptly Wells proceeded to forget all about me. Then circumstances which I had better explain to you brought me into the present case.

"A moment ago we spoke of Sheila Forbes. She is an old friend of mine, Lorna. But when I first knew her she was Sheila Langdon, a golden-haired child of ten, with the sun in her hair and laughter in her baby-blue eyes, who used to romp about me when I was about sixteen. Our families were neighbors at Sausolito. She certainly was beautiful as a child—as beautiful as she is now as a woman—an adorable creature. But she married the wrong man."

"She was a Mrs. Brice, wasn't she?"

"Yes—Truxton Brice, a profligate and a drunkard. That was the last I'd heard of her. You can then imagine my astonishment when a beautiful young woman came into my office up at King's a few weeks ago and informed me she was Sheila Langdon."

"You hadn't seen her since childhood?"

"Not in twenty years. She'd read in the papers of my appointment and came to renew old friendship, she said. She was now Sheila Forbes, married to one of the rich men of New York. It was only this afternoon that I called on her for the first time—and at her urgent request."

"Oh!" Lorna gasped. "Today—this afternoon! It sounds like some terrible romance!"

"Yes," smiled Ross. "Romance is the common fare of daily life. That's why the less sophisticated public is so constantly hungry for it. Well, to put it briefly, she told

me with the utmost candor of her former intimacy with
your uncle—which is no surprise to you—of her quarrel
with him and of her marriage during his absence to Cullen
Forbes—in quite the modern fashion."

"Oh, do you think so, Professor Ross? It sounds quite
ancient to me—almost like something in Homer. Modern
people are not so messy about their love affairs."

Ross smiled: "I am no authority, Lorna, as you see, being an academic bachelor. It had merely struck me as quick
work on the part of Sheila."

"Quick—yes," murmured Lorna—"and rather superfi-
cial—don't you think?"

"Well, here's the point: She seems wildly, passionately
in love with her husband!"

"Then what is—?"

"The trouble?" supplied Ross. "That's difficult to tell
you. However, you're a straighter thinker than most wom-
en I have met, so here goes: It appears that your uncle
had a bundle of letters from Sheila, and one or two other
keepsakes, photographs and the like. According to Sheila
your uncle, violently jealous and hurt when he came back
and found her married to Forbes, had threatened to convey them singly and at intervals, as darts, to infuriate his
successful rival—Forbes!"

"Uncle Jim!—oh, how terrible!" Lorna shuddered.
"Poor, dear Uncle Jim! Victorians never grow up, do they?
But then, if Cullen Forbes knew of the affair, would those
letters and things have surprised him—even if poor Uncle
Jim had really done such a thing?"

"Ah, precisely what I suggested. Sheila, however, was
convinced that both men being strong, both were dangerous. That James Goold might have carried out what he'd
threatened, and that Forbes, notwithstanding his knowledge, might react violently and precipitate tragedy. Forbes
evidently knows of the letters, as appeared tonight; but

Sheila may not know he knows. Also, she fondly believes her husband does not know that her relations with Mr. Goold were any nearer than mere friendship.

"In any case, the little commission she had charged me with this afternoon was to see your uncle, to intercede for her and to beg for the return of those letters—without telling me she had already appealed in vain!"

"And you agreed to do it, Professor Ross?" almost groaned Lorna.

"Yes. Surprising as is the whole business, nothing surprises me more than the fact that I agreed. Some ancient instinct, I imagine, possibly paternal. She was so tearful and appealing and pathetic. I telephoned from her very apartment for an appointment and got it. I came before seven—to find—what you already know."

"How extraordinary!" breathed Lorna. "In that case, I wonder they didn't suspect you, Professor Ross?"

"Well, to be quite candid, I believe they do suspect me a little. In any case, I think Callahan does. The farther away they get from the real murderer, the nearer Callahan will approach, as he would put it, to pinning it on me."

"How terrible!" cried Lorna. "But then the real"—with an effort she brought out the hateful word—"murderer must positively be found, mustn't he?"

"Positively!" smiled Ross, "and something tells me we shall succeed. But we simply must go about it our own way. And that is why I want you two, Trumbull and yourself, to assist me."

"How marvelous! We'll be your slaves, Professor Ross, your Watsons, your Baker Street irregulars—anything to help. I know I can answer for Jimmie. Can't you give me something to do right away?"

"Not tonight," laughed Ross. "Except this. Have you by any chance clippings bearing upon that suit of Prince Erzeroff's against your uncle?"

"No, I'm sorry, I haven't. But couldn't I find some somehow?"

"Your uncle's lawyers would doubtless have a complete record of the case. But we don't need all that. The newspaper accounts are all we want. Suppose you go over to the Times office tomorrow and consult their index. Buy the papers of the days in question if you can. Otherwise, let us get photostat reproductions of the items."

"I'll be there as soon as the place is open tomorrow morning."

"Good. Now I want you to assist me in another matter."

"Anything, Professor Ross."

"Will you please select the most powerful flashlight in the house and come down with me to the gallery. The detectives have been there all evening. Now I want to make a thorough examination of the room in my own way."

Eagerly Lorna disappeared into her bedroom.

"Here is one," she held out a long-polished cylinder as she reappeared, "that's a perfect peach, a regular little searchlight."

How keenly soever youth feels tragedy, it is able, fortunately for itself, to shift the burden of its oppression so much more easily than older persons, that pain has no time to bite in too deeply. Lorna, acutely conscious of her loss, was still young enough to convert the force of it into an intense eagerness for immediate activity on her dead benefactor's behalf.

Together they descended the stairs and made their way to the door leading to the gallery. A single electric bulb was glowing in a side bracket; the room appeared calm, tranquil, peaceful as though no tragedy had occurred there within a few hours, or indeed at any time.

Lorna paused and looked about for an instant. Then she uttered a profound sigh. Her lips quivered.

"And he'll never be here again!" she all but whispered. Tears glistened in her eyes.

"I know, I know," Ross murmured kindly. "But we must not surrender to the grim finale that awaits us. Every life ends in a tragedy, you know. For every death, even the most peaceful, is tragic. Now, the first place I should like to look at is the space around this desk."

Lorna flashed her powerful white light at the base of the desk and swung it slowly back and forth. The polished floor, even after the many feet that had trodden it, disclosed nothing.

He then took the light from her and flashed it evenly along the base of the walls, examining the length of the floor under the pictures minutely. The hard polished surface yielded nothing whatever.

Beneath the space, however, where the Tartar Chieftain had hung, he crouched down upon his knees and asked Lorna to hold the light as he took out his pocket lens.

"Grit from the shoes of the detectives," he murmured, "particles from the frame and paint, dashes of powder they used for getting their finger-prints. That thief would have had to walk in a bed of clay to leave any distinguishable traces. But here—here is the imprint of the nail of a heavy boot. You see? It barely shows on this hard wood. Here is another. But I don't think these are from the detectives' shoes. They hardly wear makes so crude. We can take it for granted these dents in the floor were made by the man who took the picture."

He continued examining closely every square inch of the surface.

"Hello!" he exclaimed suddenly under his breath. "What's this?"

Close to the wall Lorna saw some tiny brown seeds, about the size of dried tomato seeds—three of them were lying close together. To these Ross was pointing.

"Well, well this is something," he murmured, swinging the flashlight slowly back and forth. "Let us see if there are any more of them."

"Here is another," whispered Lorna, the excitement of the quest possessing her as though the seeds were nothing less than nuggets.

"Four!" said Ross. "I think there ought to be more. Let us make a wider circle and draw inward. Ah," he caught his breath as he moved nearer swinging the light concentrically toward the wall, "here are two more, one crushed by somebody's heel. That makes six. There's probably another here somewhere. Seven, you know—lucky number. Perhaps we'll find it, but it doesn't matter."

"But what does it mean, Professor Ross?" demanded Lorna, her excitement suddenly suspended by the realization of her ignorance. "What do these tomato seeds signify?"

"They are not tomato seeds," Ross, still on his knees straightened up, holding the six brown grains on the palm of his open hand. "They are the seeds of a poisonous plant that looks a little like a thistle, called datura."

"Are you trying to mystify your poor Watson?"

"Not at all," he laughed. "Certain criminals sometimes use these seeds, scatter them on the scene of their crime as a sort of talisman—for good luck, good luck to themselves, that is. They believe that will obviate detection. Gypsies sometimes use them, and Eastern Europeans, and particularly Asiatics."

"How terribly exciting!" cried Lorna.

"Well, well," said Ross, "we shall see what news Trumbull brings as to Erzeroff's whereabouts. In the meantime perhaps we had better say nothing about this particular find."

The outer door of the gallery suddenly opened and a plain-clothes man entered the room.

"Thought I saw some people moving about," he announced pleasantly. "We were told to keep an eye on this room from the outside."

"Yes," said Ross. "I am Professor Ross. I took part in the first investigations. And this is Miss Storey, a niece of Mr. Goold's; she lives in the house."

"I see," said the plain-clothes man. "Just looking around, were you?"

"Just that," said Ross.

"Yeh—well, I don't know whether the Chief wants anybody to be snoopin' round until he gets back here tomorrow, see?"

"I see," nodded Ross. "In that case perhaps I'd better go home. You see, I only stayed because I am a friend of Miss Storey's and the shock to her—you understand—"

"Sure," said the man. "I get you. And as the Chief left you here, I guess it's all right. But, see, my orders—"

"Exactly," said Ross. "I'll see you tomorrow afternoon then," he turned to Lorna. "And meanwhile if there's anything I can do let me know."

The guard appeared much relieved when Ross, in his presence, said good-night to Lorna, took his hat and left the house.

As he walked briskly up Fifth Avenue expanding his lungs avid for the cool fresh air his mind revolved swiftly about the events of the evening and he smiled faintly to himself.

"I wonder," he reflected, "if the murderer is as far off, or as alien, as Mr. Inspector Callahan thinks he is."

13
Cullen Forbes Disappears

Upon entering his rooms, Ross made himself comfortable in a dressing gown and slippers and took up the first book that came to hand in order to switch off his mind, if only for a few minutes, from the many disturbing details of the shocking experience the last few hours had brought him. For however calm and coolly reasoning he appeared before others, he was profoundly moved by the tragic death of Goold and the seemingly inevitable scandalous publicity in which that soft beautiful creature, Sheila Forbes, was now involved.

So Sheila had been to see Goold that very same afternoon just before she had played hostess to himself!

"The more one learns about women," he reflected musingly, "the more one fails to understand them. Now, if Sheila could tell me so much, why on earth did she not tell me that she had just been seeing Goold, making the same request of him she had urged me to make, and had already failed? Why did she not tell me that her husband already knew about the letters? But, I remember, of course, that does not follow. He probably knew without her knowing that he knew. They are in a bad fix, those two."

The pages he was turning were those of Wilhelm Stekel's "Peculiarities of Behavior."

"Now why am I reading this book," he asked himself, as his eyes scanned the headings, Instinct, Impulse, the Sexual Roots of Cleptomania, and so on, "when what ought to preoccupy me is that glazier of Cross's?"

He remembered the envelope with the six little brown seeds and he went to his coat to look at them again. Before he had time to reach his cupboard the telephone bell rang.

"Now, what do you think of this, Professor,"—the voice of Wells at the other end—"Callahan has just informed me that Cullen Forbes and his wife have both left home suddenly—according to the servants, for an unknown destination!" His voice thrilled with suppressed rage.

"Do you want them so badly, then?" Ross heard himself asking the question merely to recover from the impact of that intelligence.

"Do we want them!" Wells uttered a bitter laugh at the other end of the wire. "In view of that butler's information, wouldn't you say they were highly material witnesses to our case?"

It would have been absurd to deny that.

"In that case," Ross spoke almost unconcernedly, "your men can doubtless find out what train they left by and to what destination."

"Sounds simple, doesn't it," said Wells bitterly, "but it appears they haven't left by any train. Forbes had a yacht in the Sound. It seems they went aboard early this evening and slipped away. Does it occur to you, Professor, that except for the mere announcement of Goold's death, nothing of the case will be public until the morning papers get on the street—about midnight? How did they know it was time to disappear? Do you see, Professor? It's a terrible thing, but I wouldn't stop at anything to get the right person."

"For innocent people they were certainly very foolish to do a thing like that," Ross murmured in a tone as matter-of-fact as he could make it.

"If innocent—yes," Wells retorted with bitter meaning. "They give it a very ugly look—if you ask me."

"Oh, come, Commissioner. You can't mean seriously that they, either of them, are responsible—but then, it's simple enough. Send them a radio requesting their immediate return. Your name and title will show them at once the gravity of the summons. I feel sure they'll return immediately."

"Well, maybe," snapped the Commissioner. "That is exactly what I mean to do, however."

"Only—I shouldn't make any of this public, Commissioner—don't you agree with me?"

"Oh, I suppose so," grumbled Wells. In his mind's eye he saw the text of his peremptory message in a box upon the front pages of the newspapers, the importance of the addressee and the sensational implications of the message itself, in view of the signature beneath it, "Roderic Wells, Police Commissioner."

"Now what do you make of it all, Ross? Have you any ideas?"

"Ideas is hardly the word, Commissioner. Some fragments of notions. I want to think it all over. But I promise you to turn over anything and everything of the slightest value."

"Good!" cried Wells in a sort of dreary exasperation. "Now I've got the District Attorney on my hands. He wants to know how you, a stranger, were in on this from the start and he has only just heard of it."

Ross smiled ruefully at the telephone. He was on the point of saying, "Well, I wish I weren't in on it—at least not as matters stand." But what he said was:

"I trust you to handle him, Commissioner."

"See you tomorrow," Wells's voice was clipped off by the fall of the receiver upon its rest.

Ross selected a pipe from a rack, filled it with Cotton mixture and lighting it, sank back with a profound sigh into the embrace of his chair.

"This mess!" he thought. "If the so-called stream of consciousness were not rather a sort of spring freshet, or a Mississippi flood, I might have some chance of thinking this business out."

Sheila Forbes—well, of course, she was out of it. Had he not drunk tea with her after she had come from Goold, and afterwards talked to Goold over the telephone in her very presence?

As to her husband, Cullen Forbes, that was less certain. True, Forbes had made an appointment, in blank, as it were, to meet Goold the next morning and to receive those precious letters of Sheila's. But it was not beyond the bounds of possibility for Forbes to have come back, to have seen Sheila coming out and to have become mad with jealousy; to have either let himself in with a key secretly in his possession, to have corrupted Cross to leave the doors open, or to have been let in by Goold and to have shot Goold at the first opportunity—possibly rifling the desk directly after and then letting himself out without closing the door. Possible, but extremely improbable.

Once, however, Forbes knew that Goold had been shot, his visit, certain to come out, would lead to questions which even a brave man might well shrink from. So he absconded. Foolish, but explicable.

Sheila being innocent, and her husband in all probability equally innocent, who then shot Goold? Callahan, almost as a matter of routine, would suspect the butler. But why should Cross kill his master? Absurd! He had an excellent place, even an enviable one. What post so enviable nowadays as that of a trusted butler in a rich man's house? To buy merely the comforts of modern living, so many and so necessary, hurries busy men to their graves.

As to the luxuries, only the rich can indulge in them and a very few of the immoral. Cross was obviously too intelligent a man not to realize this. That is one reason so many butlers appear so superior. Lacking the gift of money-making they prefer to serve rather than to struggle.

The glazier then: Ross did not often allow himself to be the prey of intuitions. Too often so-called intuitions had their origin in trifling forgotten impressions and muzzey-mindedness. Still, somehow he felt a strong intuitive certainty that the glazier was not responsible for the murder. But for all that, the glazier must infallibly be found.

With a sigh he rose and approached the window; motors were passing below. One or two stars were visible in the patch of night-sky directly over the tunnel of his street. The world was wagging on as though no important homicide had ever happened in New York, least of all that night.

He pulled down the shade, and with great deliberation, in order to reduce his thoughts to a slower rhythm, went through his habitual going-to-bed ceremony and extinguished the lights.

As he had a class at King's the next morning at ten, he had barely time to scan the contents of the newspapers bearing upon the murder of James Goold. The *American* carried a streaming headline clear across the front page and even the *Times* carried a three-column head.

The dead man's numerous interests and benefactions were enumerated, and comments upon the loss of so important a citizen as Goold were quoted from many sources, business, educational, philanthropic.

The city was stirred as it had not been for a long time over a murder. Not only did the newspapers lament the slaying of so eminent a citizen as Goold, but precisely in a case where the public desires details most, complained the *World*, the new police commissioner elects to publish least. Here in any case, was a murder in which all the public unanimously and imperiously demanded vengeance. The *American* alone referred to the fact that the late James Goold and Cullen Forbes were both friends, business colleagues and often rivals, and that recently Forbes had married Mrs. Sheila Brice, a "friend and protegee" of Goold's. The report added that neither Mr. nor Mrs. Forbes were in town.

"That reporter," thought Ross, "smells a rat. He has said all he dares to say for the moment. But this is where the trouble begins."

All the accounts carried the information that Police Commissioner Wells in person was at the scene of the crime within less than one hour of its commission. That though the mystery of the murder seems baffling, the Commissioner as well as Inspector Callahan, Chief of the Detective Bureau, energetically pushing the investigation, promise an early arrest. Ross's name was happily not mentioned, and nothing was said as to the theft of the Rembrandt. Callahan and Wells had evidently decided to withhold this part of the story from the public, a course which Ross wholeheartedly approved.

At quarter past eleven he was called to the telephone at the Faculty Club.

Lorna from a booth in the *Times* Building was telling him she had found the items bearing upon the suit of Erzeroff against Goold and that she would have photostat copies of the vital portions of the story by that evening, or not later than the following morning.

"Do the reports indicate any address of the plaintiff?" queried Ross.

"No. I don't remember that they do. I think I should have noted it if they had. But I can make sure."

"Very well. But as they probably do not, do you want to do any more today, Lorna?"

"Of course, I do—if you'll only tell me what."

"The plaintiff being a foreigner, the trial was, I take it, in the Federal Courts. Anyway, make sure of which court; and after you do, would you go down to the court in question, see the clerk, and get the original bill of complaint. From that, please note down carefully every address, the plaintiff's, his lawyers', and any others there may be. After that, I would suggest that you go home and rest."

"May I come to see you at your rooms?" suggested Lorna unself-consciously.

"On no account," he answered quickly. "I shall call you during the day. You will probably have no occasion for calling me."

"Oh, all right," Lorna, chilled, answered somewhat stiffly.

Ross, understanding the alteration in her tone at once, added *sotto voce:*

"It's not Mrs. Grundy that bothers me, Lorna. It's something quite different. Do you understand?"

Whether she understood or not that he meant he might be watched, he could not tell.

"Good bye then," she said and hung up the receiver.

Ross, notwithstanding his long practice in detachment, found it somewhat difficult to read students' papers in Criminal Anthropology. In face of the circumstances attending the Goold murder with which accident had succeeded in so closely connecting him, his mind found the papers more criminal than anthropological. Indeed he could hardly make head or tail of them.

By twelve o'clock just when he had told the waiter the sort of chop he intended to eat, he was called to the telephone—this time by Callahan.

"Ah, Mohammed himself," murmured Ross, "or is it the mountain?"

"Look here, Professor," the raucous voice of Callahan began abruptly. "I've got every damn walking glazier in New York, pretty near, lined up here at Headquarters. And I've got that butler, Cross, here, too. He doesn't recognize his man in any of 'em."

"How many have you there, Inspector?"

"About sixty—and they belong to nearly all nationalities. Would you care to rush down here and take a look at 'em before I turn 'em loose?"

"I can come, of course, Inspector. But it would be entirely useless. If Cross can't find the right man among them, it is certain I couldn't. Besides if Cross's glazier committed the crime or any part of it, that glazier is certainly not in your line-up."

"H'm! I get you!" growled Callahan at the other end. "'Course, I've sent out a general alarm, but hell, I can't ask for the arrest of every glazier in the United States, can I?"

"No," agreed Ross. "Besides, if the glazier is the criminal, he's in all probability not a glazier except for that one occasion."

"Sure," agreed Callahan dejectedly. "Well, there you are. I guess I'll turn those scarecrows loose, and that's all there is to it. Question is, what's the next move? I guess you've seen the papers?"

"I have," said Ross, "but I wouldn't let that disturb me, Inspector."

"Easy for you," grumbled Callahan. "You're not on the City pay roll."

"I may have some suggestion to make before long," Ross endeavored to make his voice soothing to this man who was impudent enough to show his hostility and yet to seek his advice.

"Yeh," said Callahan. "All right. Thanks. If you see the right guy up there at the College give me a ring, Professor. I'll appreciate it." And he put down his receiver.

At four o'clock Wells called Ross up at his rooms to say that thus far no response had come from Cullen Forbes.

"Looks dashed ugly for him," added Wells. "But I have asked the Coast Guard and the Navy, if they spot that boat to turn it back to New York—to arrest the owner if necessary."

"Arrest?" repeated Ross with a note of deep regret in his voice.

"Certainly!" snapped Wells—"material witnesses. They ought to answer when I call them back. This is not a game of hide-and-go-seek, you know."

"No—no," admitted Ross. "I suppose it's inevitable." And he realized that Sheila's scandal was now also inevitable, with all its attendant publicity and ugliness. Impossible to see how he could save her. She would be lucky if her husband were not actually tried and convicted for the murder.

"I may have something to suggest to you by tomorrow, Commissioner," he spoke almost automatically.

"Well, for God's sake, don't hold out on us if you have anything, Ross," Wells almost pleadingly returned and the conversation ended.

A little after six Jimmie called up from the Pennsylvania Station.

"May I come right up and see you, Professor Ross?"

"Certainly, Trumbull. You got what you went after?"

"Yes, sir—I think so."

"Good lad. Then my suggestion is that you go straight up to Lorna Storey's. I will meet you there and we can all talk it over together."

"Right-o!" said Jimmie. "Shall I wait for you before going in?"

"N-no! but, if you can avoid hurrying, it would be pleasant if we arrive at the door at about the same time. I shall be in a checker taxi, of which there is a stand near my building."

"I get you, Professor Ross."

Ross smiled to himself and wondered why more young people didn't take up detective work as a hobby. Still acutely conscious of the mystery underlying all life, the young intelligence is naturally disappointed at the masses of plain people that encompass it in our machine-made, regimented existence. The ferreting even of crime mysteries seems somehow to console and to restore the equilibrium.

"But if it comes to that," he thought, "I am a young idiot myself."

He hailed a checkered taxi and noted with a fatalistic shrug that a man in a derby hat hailed another.

"Can this be meant for me?" Ross murmured to himself, and he all but waved to the taxi behind in sheer good humor.

14

Ross Moves on His Own

"Hang it, Trumbull," Ross shook hands with the boy who was approaching the door of the Goold house with elaborate casualness, "can't go on calling you Trumbull. You are a sleuth after my own heart. And if you've got the information we want, my gratitude alone makes us intimates. Henceforth you are Jimmie." He glanced at Callahan's man lounging a little distance from the door.

"Thanks a lot, Professor Ross," Jimmie flushed to his ears. "That's exactly what I'd like to be to you." And he pressed the bell.

"And another thing," said Ross. "You're not exactly slopping over with your information. I like that."

"Well, I—you said," stammered the youth, "we'll talk it over together—with Lorna."

"Exactly. That's what I mean. Obedience is the first law of the novice in all brotherhoods."

The door was opened by Cross, imperturbable as ever, calm, pale, courteous.

"Miss Storey is waiting for you in her sitting room, sir."

"Very good, Cross. And by the way," went on Ross, "I heard you could make nothing of that assortment of poor glaziers, Inspector Callahan exhibited to you this morning."

"No, sir. None of them was the man I employed."

"No. But look here, Cross. I've been thinking it over. Suppose I suggested to you that the man you had in was a Russian, would your subconscious, or your impression, or intuition, or whatever it is, revolt instantly against the suggestion?"

Cross paused for a moment before replying.

"No, sir, it would not revolt, if I may say so. My experience of that class is limited. I have seen a number of Russian gentlemen in England and on the Continent, but not many poor persons. All the same, sir, that is just what this man probably was. Without feeling absolutely certain, I think you have hit it, sir."

"Thank you, Cross. That's encouraging." When the butler was about to lead the way, Jimmie told him he knew the location of Miss Storey's apartments perfectly, and swiftly walked up the stairs with Ross following.

Lorna greeted them warmly. "How dear of you both!" she exclaimed, taking a hand of each. "From now on I am an old-fashioned girl. One man to lean on is wonderful. Two is perfectly heavenly."

"And she calls herself old-fashioned!" Jimmie turned to Ross.

"Rank polyandry I call it," laughed Ross.

"You mean Pollyanna," smiled Lorna. "I am simply bursting with gladness that you are both here near me again."

"We are flattered," murmured Ross, "are we not, James? Now suppose you tell us all that you gleaned in Washington."

"Well, I was in luck," began Jimmie simply, turning about like a dog, before he sank into a comfortable chair. "I was at the passport division office before it opened. You see, I had nothing else to do in Washington. When the clerks began to arrive about a quarter to ten, they all passed me as I sat there near the doorman—an awfully nice darky. Well, one of those clerks proved to be a former schoolmate of mine named Billings. He was so glad to see me that he found out for me all I wanted to know in about half an hour—which I can tell you, is speedy for a Washington government office.

"The low down on our stuff is this: The last time Erzeroff applied for an extension of his permit to remain in the country was about five months ago. The extension was good for six months. The address the bird gave at that time was a hotel at San Diego, California. Since then the department has heard nothing from him or about him. But this is just about the time they would begin automatically to check up on him, so that he shouldn't outstay his permission. Of course, you see five months is a long time. He may have gone back to Europe in that time—or he may be getting ready to leave. Billings promised to let me know. But it may take immigration officers a week or even longer to check up on it. That is the heck of it. Question is, can we wait that long?"

"I can answer that question, Jimmie," said Ross. "We cannot wait that long. We haven't that much time to lose. I dislike to bring in too many agencies into this thing, but in order not to waste time, we can get some private agency here to have their people on the coast look up for us confidentially the present whereabouts of Prince Erzeroff, checking from his last address. Jimmie," he went on, "it looks as though you are elected. You are free, white and twenty-one. You are not related to the deceased, as Lorna is, and you are not likely to be shadowed by the police. I move that you get in touch with Burns, or Dougherty, or Pinkerton, or any national agency you like, and arrange to get that bit of information. Lorna will pay the bill, won't you, Lorna?"

"Of course," she responded eagerly. "But then what? What shall we do after we get it?"

"Ah, then I have a diabolical plot which you two will have to help me carry out. If that tartar prince is still in our midst, we shall have to learn a lot about him, about his goings and his comings, his friends and his enemies, so as to make sure whether at least the theft of the Rembrandt is in any way connected with him. There is a lot of work for at least one of you, and possibly both. If it should involve absences from Anthropology 9, your endeavors will make excellent field work. I shall mark you on it for the course. As a late ex-President would have put it, do our minds march together on this line?"

"They do," all but shouted the young people in unison. "But which of us is going," demanded Lorna, "Jimmie or me?"

"Circumstances will decide that, Lorna. But there may be reason for both of you going, though I confess I don't like to be left alone in New York."

"Both of your Watsons gone!" cried Lorna. "Oh, Jimmie, you'll have to stay here near Professor Ross!"

"Listen to the girl!" protested Jimmie. "Where do you get that stuff, Lorna? Isn't a woman's place in the home? Ask anybody!"

"Now, now!" put in Ross. "Perfect Watsons don't argue, you know. They obey when the time comes. Can they leave their practice for a week, or a month?—Can they not! Can they stay behind in utter neglect and desuetude for months, until Sherlock gives a sign?—They can, and they do!"

By this time someone had evidently managed to report that Ross was at the Goold house. For presently the telephone rang and Lorna was elaborately asked by Callahan whether she knew where Professor Ross could be reached. She told him Professor Ross was right here and handed over the telephone receiver.

"Look here, Professor," began Callahan plaintively, "we are up a tree about the glazier. I thought he would be in our hands by now, but we can't lay hands on him. Have you any suggestions?"

"None at the moment," answered Ross sympathetically, "but as soon as I have I shall turn them over to you. Have you any news, Inspector?"

"Well, no!" and the words sounded like a curse. "No answer yet from Forbes. I've got that jockey locked up here because he had a gun on him; but if you ask me, he is too far poisoned by bad hootch to have the nerve to kill anything. I'm keeping him jugged for a while, though. Let's see—anything else? Oh, the autopsy—they found the bullet. It's the same as the cartridges in the desk. No news in that."

"No—no news in that," repeated Ross half absently.

"I'll see you at the inquest tomorrow," Callahan added heavily, and hung up the receiver.

"Closer than a brother!" murmured Ross. "Callahan dislikes to lose sight of me."

"How filthy of him!" exclaimed Lorna.

"Well, he is a policeman," said Ross. "Allowances must be made. Besides when all is said and done, you know, I was the first one—to find your uncle." He went on quickly, out of consideration for Lorna:

"As to who is going in search of Erzeroff, we shall perhaps better be able to determine that tomorrow, or even the next day—as soon as we hear from the agency. You, Lorna, will have certain formalities to face that may keep you here. So in any case Jimmie can hold himself ready. It will probably take forty-eight hours before we hear from the agency people. James, have you enough money in the bank to give the agency its retainer—say a hundred or two hundred dollars? This checking on Erzeroff is a small job, you know."

"Certainly, sir. Anything up to three thousand."

"You are rich, James. Well and good. Then suppose you find your way to the agency you select and begin doing business. The hour need not trouble you. A good agency is open day and night. Make the best bargain you can for the information you want."

Jimmie began importantly to turn the leaves of the telephone book. In some connection he had heard of the Bennington Agency and he was seeking its number as a starter.

"You are not going to call them from here, are you, Jimmie?" cautioned Lorna.

"Catch me!" said James grandly. "Think I am an amateur? I've got it, Bennington. They sound good to me, without frills. Now, I'll go out and call them."

"Oh, if I could only do something!" cried Lorna. "If there is anything I hate more than another, it is waiting around."

"Youth," murmured Ross.

"You are the youngest of the three of us, Professor Ross. Only you have too many brains to fidget."

"You have more poise than most, Lorna."

"Oh, Professor Ross, won't you tell me," she began quickly, "what's on your mind? I know I'm stupid, but you must be working toward something—sending Jimmie about. Couldn't you tell poor Watson a little?"

"Oh, it's not as mysterious as all that, my dear Lorna. But it is a little early for putting theories into words. Briefly, it is quite possible that the so-called glazier not only stole the picture, but that he also shot your uncle. In any case we must try to find him, and the police may have difficulty in doing that. But that is only one possibility.

"Then, of course, there is the possibility that Cullen Forbes came back after his first call. But improbable, I think, because, being a business man, he rested on the appointment he made for today."

"Then why did he run away?" demanded Lorna almost fiercely.

"Ah, that is something that needs explaining. He is in close touch with city politics. Some friendly police official may have told him more than he should and decided him to slip out of possible garish publicity. His wife may have urged him—foolishly—to go away. Some friendly newspaper man may have tipped him off and thrown him into a panic. Don't forget, Lorna, that a big New York business man has more resources than an Eastern potentate, though not necessarily more sense. If he is not guilty, as I believe, he has done a thing bordering on the idiotic. The jockey—Cross—the maids and nurses—all possibilities, but highly improbable."

"Then who—who?" queried Lorna.

"Who but X—the Person Unknown? Does that sound foolish? You asked for a little—it's little enough. I am thinking aloud for you. I am seeking X—the Person Unknown."

"I see," sighed Lorna—"I mean, I see a good deal less than I did before, if that is possible."

"The difficulty is that the person may have come from either inside the house or outside. Once you think of the outside, you have a large section of the world to draw upon."

"Inside?" gasped Lorna. "You really think it's possible someone here—?"

"There's one serious obstacle against the outside theory," Ross explained—"that is the open door when I arrived."

"Oh, I see, I see! You mean a person coming from the outside and going out again would not leave the door ajar?"

"Well, consider, Lorna. Wouldn't every instinct urge such a person to shut the door as tightly and securely as possible upon his deed?"

"But aren't there exceptions, Professor Ross!"

"Oh, yes, of course. But other things being equal human nature works along certain well-established lines."

"How horrible!" Lorna impulsively put her hands to her face. "How perfectly horrible! Oh, I do think it must have been that wretched glazier. Who else could it be? He must have been insane to kill Uncle Jim for the sake of a miserable picture. He must be put out of the way before he can do any more harm."

Jimmie, returning, burst in with ill-suppressed excitement. "I have retained the Bennington agency," he announced with naive self-importance. "They believe they can check up on Erzeroff very quickly—possibly in twenty-four hours. So if you don't let me go sleuthing him, Professor Ross, there is no justice this side of Paradise."

"A Watson talking of justice!" cried Lorna. "When we ought to be saying, 'Marvelous, marvelous!' Did you ever hear of such a thing?"

"First let us eliminate the if's, my children," suggested Ross pacifically. "Then we shall hold a council of war, and like the Jesuits, we shall use the fitting instrument for the designed work, a.m. D. g."

15
Ross and His Acolytes

There is a convention that demands the narration of a crime to be bursting with bomb-like detonations every ten minutes. The newspapers, those actual transcripts of life, tell a different story.

Not that the newspapers, in the present instance, did not detonate as expected—for forty-eight hours. Goold had been a mighty citizen of Manhattan, and the press of the Seven Million, indeed, of all the one hundred and twenty million, desired long juicy columns of news.

Goold's death by shooting—already an immense sensation. Murdered! with a .32 calibre revolver—by some person unknown! Another sensation! Simultaneously with the murder vanished the famous Rembrandt, "The Tartar Chieftain!" Wells had finally parted with this piece of information also. The Rembrandt Murder—it made a convenient headline.

The police had many suspects. They were seeking with all their might for a glazier, a foreigner, who replaced a pane of glass about the time of the shooting.

New sensation! Police Commissioner Wells had sent out an alarm over the seas to turn back Cullen Forbes, a citizen almost as eminent as James Goold, who had happened to depart for an unknown destination the night of the murder! Were the two facts connected? No one ventured to suggest that. But the two men had long been friends and associates in many enterprises. Cullen Forbes probably had information the police desired.

The District Attorney, his whole office in a fever of investigation, had found nothing thus far among Goold's papers betraying the slightest clue to the murder. The investigation, however, was still in progress.

New sensation! Cullen Forbes was steaming back in his yacht toward Manhattan, more or less convoyed by a Coast Guard patrol which overhauled the yacht off the coast of Bermuda. Forbes said he was returning voluntarily—did not get the Police Commissioner's message owing to the fact that his wireless was out of order.

Goold's autopsy revealed nothing that hadn't been settled by the first glance of the Medical Examiner. A .32 bullet fired at close range had been lodged in the brain. The bullet was the same as those in a package found in Goold's desk drawer. The pistol, however, which must have been there, was still missing. Goold's body was placed in the family mausoleum at Woodlawn.

In short, as the *World* observed editorially, there was, "a great deal of publicity, a great deal of noise, a great deal of police activity, but actually no knowledge whatever!"

Jimmie Trumbull, in the meanwhile, had heard from the Bennington Agency that Prince Erzeroff had been staying at a hotel in Indian Springs, Southern California, that he had left there some time ago, that he had fallen ill in New York and had been a patient in the Post-Graduate Hospital, but that within the past week he had left the hospital and had disappeared, no one knew whither! If Mr. Trumbull desired, the Bennington Agency would endeavor to trace the man, though there was no telling how soon they could find him. Mr. Trumbull did desire, and the search went on.

The one thing that preoccupied Ross, perhaps more than the murder, was the return of Sheila and Cullen Forbes.

Her letters, so far as he knew, had not been found among Goold's papers. They were pretty certain to turn up sooner or later.

"And then," he reflected somberly, "we are in for it—they and I. A chance for all three of us to be arrested on a murder charge. Delightful!"

The reading of the will had been postponed owing to Mrs. Goold's condition. She lay in a half coma, a sort of daze of sorrow, moaning softly from time to time.

"Jim, Jim! Oh, why have you left me, dear?"

She was in a pitiable state and the doctors had grave difficulty in maintaining her reason.

At moments, when Lorna endeavored to comfort her, she would cling to Lorna's hand, passionately press it to her heart, then abruptly thrust it aside and repeat her constant plaint.

"Jim, Jim! Why have you left me?"

"Love seems to be a very terrible thing," murmured Lorna half to herself after recounting this to Ross. "Look at my poor aunt. Look at what you risked for Sheila Forbes, Professor Ross! Look at the condition it brought poor Uncle Jim to—and maybe it's responsible for his death! Uh—!"

"I hope you don't fancy I'm in love with Sheila?" protested Ross quietly. Lorna looked at him with the deep searching look of the young who are just discovering the secret world of the human heart.

"Well, what then?" smiled Lorna. "Just a knightly act to shield poor Sheila's reputation—these days?"

"Partly," nodded Ross.

"Partly," she repeated. "What's the other part?"

"An irresistible impulse to mess up in other people's affairs," he answered with a laugh and the little rising inflection peculiar to him. "I did hope to help get Sheila out of her mess," he added. "As I told you, I knew her as a kid with pig-tails. For the same reason I'm sorry to have you two youngsters mixed up in this—but there's no help for it now."

"You must think we are kids," muttered Jimmie almost shamefacedly.

"No, James—on the contrary. It's a sort of instinct. We elders like to think of our young as clean and unsullied."

Jimmie flushed and looked away. With Lorna, or any other contemporary, he might have discussed these things in the jargon of a Freudian lecturer. But before Ross, it was difficult.

"You see it works both ways," laughed Ross reading his thoughts. "You want to keep your elders clean, too."

"But," broke in Lorna, as from a troubled daydream, "I don't see how the Callahan type of mind has failed to arrest you by now."

"If you don't see it now," Ross grimly smiled, "Callahan will fail to see it utterly as soon as he has questioned the Forbeses. Sheila will, of course, be cleared. There she was in her apartment giving me tea. Her servants will doubt-less swear that she remained there. But for her husband and for me, things do not look nearly so bright. I've got to do my level best to find the real criminal and you two have got to help me. From now on, you're both promoted out of the role of Watsons to that of full-fledged and very necessary assistants."

"Only use us!" cried Lorna with genuine anxiety in her voice. Through Jimmie's mind as he sat watching Ross, there suddenly shot the pictures of Ross behind bars, Ross strapped in the electric chair—and his young vitality re-volted at the images. A pallor swept his cheeks.

"Gee!" was all he could gasp.

"Yes," smiled Ross with the look of shrewd kindly penetration peculiar to him. "The contrivance at Sing Sing is not a pleasant one to contemplate even for our guilty enemies, let alone our innocent friends!"

Loma's lips whitened and she glanced away.

"There can't be quite such miscarriages of justice as that," she answered with sudden vehemence.

"Can there not?" said Ross lightly. "I have seen many. One business of the good detective is not to permit any. That is what we must concentrate upon. The only thing we can do now," he turned to Jimmie, "as soon as you hear from the Bennington people, is to check up on Erzeroff. I have some other schemes in my head but it's too early to talk about these."

At that moment the telephone bell rang. It was Commissioner Wells, himself, the Imperial, and he desired to speak to Ross.

"Know where I am, Ross?" came the harsh somewhat breathy voice over the telephone.

"Not an idea," said Ross. "In your office, I suppose."

"No, I am at the District Attorney's office. And do you know to whom I've been talking?" Ross remained silent. This manner was doubtless Wells's way of being mysterious.

"Cullen Forbes," came the stage whisper over the wire. "He is still here. I want you to come down here. Callahan is here, too; and, of course, the District Attorney. Could you hot-foot it, rather—we're in a hurry."

"Very well. Traffic permitting, I can be there in about twenty minutes. Now it begins," he smiled to Lorna and Jimmie as he put down the receiver. "Cullen Forbes has been herded in. He is at the District Attorney's office, and much depends on whether he is a wise man or merely a good business man. The two do not always go together."

"Oh," gasped Lorna suddenly realizing the uncertainty, the precariousness of life. "I can't believe Cullen Forbes would do such a thing. Poor Sheila! I wish we could go with you!"

"Into the lion's den?" he smiled. "But let us hope for the spirit of Daniel. You have work to do here, in any case, Lorna."

"Work? What?"

"Keep a sharp eye and a clear open mind upon everything that you can observe in the house. There is a way of not listening to servants' talk, but of hearing it. That nurse, Miss Baker, interests me. Please converse with her whenever you can, but don't seem to be drawing her out. You don't need to with her kind. And the other nurse, Miss Kelly—she spoke of a certain mysterious dread that to her perception seemed to overhang the house. It may be moonshine and bad astrology, but I would give something to know just what it's based on, and what it simmers down to. A girl like you, Lorna, could learn much by simply keeping your antennae out for knowledge without seeming to do so."

"I'll do my best," said Lorna dubiously, "but I'm beginning to think that my congenital stupidity has been intensified by a college education."

"On that, too," smiled Ross, "I'd keep an open mind. You'll both hear from me as soon as I have anything to communicate. Meanwhile, let me know the Bennington news as soon as possible after you get it, James."

At the door, as Cross was about to open it for him, he murmured more confidentially than was his wont,

"That glazier, sir—I've been thinking it over. After the way you put it, I feel absolutely certain he was a Russian, sir. There was something in his eyes—a queer sort of light. You might call it—something fanatical—I mean to say, something not quite natural. 'Shouldn't wonder if you'd been up to something'—that's what I said to myself. Only I didn't think of it again until you suggested he might be Russian."

"Very good, Cross," Ross nodded carelessly. And as he ordered his taxi to drive him to the Fifty-ninth Street subway he saw out of the tail of his eye, a checkered taxi patiently following him.

16

Cullen Forbes in the Net

"Come in, come in, Professor," sang out Wells when the District Attorney's man showed Ross into the private office. "You know District Attorney Burton, don't you, and Callahan." The District Attorney rose long enough to shake hands and Callahan came round the long table, behind which he had been sitting like a grim inquisitor, expressly for the purpose. "Sit down," went on Wells. "Truth is, Ross, this thing is—getting my goat."

Burton resumed his seat, with one leg hanging over the arm of his swivel chair, to show that he was informal and no respecter of persons. Wells ran his hand over his hair and Callahan after a moment's unbending for social purposes, returned to his seat and his grimness.

"We've got Forbes in the next room," Wells began again without losing time. "He has a good alibi, but not quite good enough. He had been talking to Gillette, his lawyer, at the Varsity Club some fifteen minutes after he left Goold. Forbes is not a member of the club. Gillette is. Well, it appears that Forbes left the Club at exactly five-thirty on his way home. Gillette confirms that. But—mark this: He did not come home until six-thirty-five—on his own statement. Where was he all these sixty-five minutes? Get me? It doesn't take sixty-five minutes to go from Fifty-third to Ninety-second Street. Regardless of traffic conditions you and I could do it in fifteen minutes in a taxi, or even in a bus."

"Possibly he walked?" suggested Ross mildly.

"Yes, but here's the singular thing." Wells moved his right index finger impressively up and down. "He got out of a taxi. The doorman of his own apartment house has stated that positively. The Inspector here has checked up on that. Question is, where was Forbes during at least thirty-five of these sixty-five minutes?"

"And he won't say?" from Ross.

"Nothing more than that he was on his way home."

"Did he tell you the object of his visit to Goold earlier that afternoon?"

"Absolutely not, Ross. Forbes positively refuses to speak of his reason for his visit to, or his quarrel with, Goold." Ross smiled slowly.

"I suppose," he said, "the Inspector is thinking of checking up on the taxi drivers of New York to see if he can find the one who carried Forbes."

"Yes, I was, at that, Professor," returned Callahan with the grimmest of his looks, "and a sweet job it'll be—with about fifteen thousand of 'em. That's what I'm thinking. Forbes says he can't remember even the color of it. Doesn't want to very hard, I guess."

"He admits," went on Wells, "that he heard of the murder before eight o'clock in the evening. A newspaper man he won't give away, telephoned him to his apartment. Well, we can find out who the man was and take his police-card away. Much good that'll do us. We can arrest Forbes, of course. But suppose his alibi is good? Very serious thing to arrest a man of his prominence if he's innocent."

"Very," Ross emphatically agreed.

"We'll see he doesn't leave town again. But Burton and I feel his quarrel with Goold might throw an important light on the case, if only he weren't so pig-headed about telling us. That's one reason we sent for you, Ross."

"Me? What can I accomplish where you have failed?"

"We believe," Burton suddenly broke the momentary silence, switched round and set his feet squarely on the floor, "we believe that you could help us in this, Professor Ross, that you know, and that you are going to tell us."

Burton's heavy forensic manner with every word weighing a ton, which so overawed criminals in the dock, now came to the fore accompanied by a corrugation of the brow and a snapping of the jaws.

"I see," said Ross, slowly, thoughtfully shaking his head. "Is that information so really vital to you? I hardly think it is."

"We are the best judges of that, Professor." The District Attorney showed his two rows of very solid teeth. "You are working with us, aren't you? However, even as a mere citizen you would hardly wish to be in the position of withholding information from the police or the District Attorney."

"Not if it were vital—no," said Ross decisively. "But here is a question of betraying a woman's confidence—a confidence which probably has no bearing at all on the crime, or at most, an indirect and remote one. Nor do I believe Forbes guilty of the crime."

"Very well, Ross," Wells was suddenly suave, conciliatory, the embodiment of pure reason. "Granting all that you say, we are still instruments of the law—and we're having a hard time with this case—which means a good deal to this city and to us. We really feel you ought to tell us. Put yourself in our places, Ross. Wouldn't you feel as we do?"

"I see your point of view perfectly," agreed Ross, "but I must positively consult the lady before I can make any such decision."

"No need of that," the District Attorney's heavy jaws moved triumphantly. "Suppose I tell you the story, and you can check me whether I'm right or wrong? Fair enough? Well, we know—and by we I mean everybody in New York who knows anything of what's going on—that this Sheila Forbes, or Mrs. Brice, as she was then, was for more than two years Goold's mistress. We know they had a tiff and Goold went abroad on business, without Sheila occupying the bridal suite on the same steamer—as she had done once before."

Ross listened spellbound, for here was information he had not received.

"We also know," Burton continued in his categorical manner, "that Forbes, always something of a rival of Goold's, was madly in love with her. Goold chose his time to go rather suddenly—when he learned that Forbes was sailing on the *Sylvanic*. But that proved to be one time, anyway, when Forbes got the best of him. When he learned, and he has ways of his own of getting information,—when he learned that Goold was sailing, and alone, Forbes simply did not board the steamer. Do you follow me, Professor?"

"He cancelled his passage?"

"Not at all; on the contrary. He sent some luggage aboard. But he never sailed. Once Goold was gone, he laid siege to Mrs. Brice, or Sheila, and he can work fast when he has to—as many of his rival companies have learned. Before Goold could return he had seized the fortress. That's as much as we know. But we also know that Goold and Forbes had not been very good friends since. They sat on some of the same boards of directors, so we've been able to check up on that. But the question we want you to answer is, what did Forbes and his wife want from Goold? That butler spoke of letters. What letters? What about?"

"You know so much more than I, Mr. Burton," Ross smiled disarmingly, "you hardly need waste your time on my ignorance."

"Possibly," said the District Attorney, lighting a cigarette with deliberation, "but what kind of letters? Love letters? Perhaps love letters," he answered himself. "But, heck, what of it? Mean to say a man in Goold's position would have used love letters written to himself to blackmail a woman? Hell! Goold was no gigolo! Besides, where are those letters? We've failed to find them. What was there about that mess that may have led to the murder of Goold?"

"Then you've abandoned the theory of the Rembrandt thief as the murderer?"

"Abandoned nothing!" all but shouted Burton. "But we've got to know everything! What about those letters?"

"Yes, yes," chimed Wells. "That's what we have got to learn. And if you know, Professor, consultant or no consultant, it's your duty to tell us."

"There is always the chance," suggested Ross, "that the eavesdropping butler may have misheard."

"I've thought of that," put in Callahan who had sat by with singular forbearance, "or he may be screening somebody—maybe himself."

This spectacular diversion gave Ross a respite, but it was of short duration. Burton pressed a bell with energy, his somewhat pendulous cheeks flushing.

"Dempsey," he called to the man who appeared at an opening door, "ask Mr. Forbes to come in here." Burton was determined upon high-powered action.

"Mr. Forbes," said Wells with considerable deference, "you know Professor Ross, don't you."

The man who entered was tall, weighing about 170 pounds, yet with a sort of panther-like litheness in his

movements, a keen wiry specimen of the American business man. His blue eyes held something at once of the
gambler, the dreamer and the man of action; and there
was somewhat about him of the fiery Southerner. His
face, clear cut almost to the point of sharpness, had a set,
almost a dangerous expression.

"I have heard a great deal about Professor Ross," he
said easily, shaking hands. "I'm glad of the opportunity of
meeting him."

"Sit down, Mr. Forbes," began Burton briskly, "here's
the point. We'll put all our cards on the table before you.
Professor Ross knows the reason for your quarrel with
Goold. If it embarrasses you to tell us, will you, or Mrs.
Forbes, give him your permission so he can make it clear to
us and allow this investigation to take its proper course?"

"I don't give a damn what Professor Ross knows,"
Forbes answered with a visible effort to control his rising
anger. "You'll get nothing from me on that subject. And I
will certainly give no one permission to discuss my private
affairs. I won't have my wife's name dragged into this,
I tell you. I can only repeat what I've told you. I am as
innocent of Goold's death as you are. Don't try third
degree stuff on me, Mr. District Attorney. You're barking
up the wrong tree, and that's all there's to it."

"You were overheard asking Goold for some letters
the afternoon before he died," Burton pressed on with a
sudden blandness that was almost kindliness. "Now, Mr.
Forbes, why take this tack? Suppose they were private?
Give us an idea what it was all about, and if that elimi-
nates you from the case, why, don't you see that's so much
the better all round?"

"I tell you, you're wasting your breath. I can't tell you
and I won't. And if Professor Ross knows, though I don't
know how that's possible, and is the gentleman I take him
to be, neither will he."

"Very well, Mr. Forbes," Burton almost sullenly murmured. "You may come to regret your obstinacy. Such high-handed conduct in a case of this sort is inadvisable. You may go now. You will please not leave the city until I give you permission."

"Good day, gentlemen," Forbes rose with alacrity, and Callahan rose, too, obsequiously accompanying him to the door.

Forbes's exit seemed to delete a whole field of energy from the room. However the course of events might develop, it would move anything but smoothly where this high-spirited individual was concerned.

"You wouldn't think it possible," began Wells as soon as the door had closed behind Forbes, "that a twentieth century business man, who's made millions of dollars, should be so childish, would you!" He spoke as one making late in life some sad discoveries concerning human nature.

"They still breed that type in the South," growled Burton, "the chivalrous fire-eater, the man who'll go to hell for a woman, and so on. He'd better cool down, though, or he may find that even he can't stand the temperature of hell."

"It looks, Professor Ross," Burton suddenly resumed the bland manner of a few moments earlier, "as though it's all up to you just now. Tell us all you know, for God's sake, and let's get on with this case like men, not children."

"Yes, yes!" Wells joined in more vehemently. "Let's put an end to this, Ross. What do you know about those letters?"

"Forbes said," began Ross quietly, "that I am no gentleman if I tell you. However, it was you gentlemen who told *me*. Anyway, I am not disturbed by his judgment. But why are you so sure, assuming the letters did exist, that Goold would not have used them, if you can picture him mad with jealousy? Use them, not necessarily publicly, but as darts to make Forbes and his wife miserable?"

"But if Forbes already knew of these letters!—" broke in Burton, "then the letters would have been no news to him, don't you see?"

"Yes, I see. But, in the first place Sheila Forbes didn't know her husband knew. In the second, according to the butler's testimony, it was only the afternoon of the murder that Forbes spoke to Goold of the letters. Up to that time Goold may have believed that Forbes was completely ignorant of them."

"Yes, I see!" cried Burton, whose mind moved more quickly than Wells's. "But even granting all that, just where do you come in, Professor? I don't want to be rude, but that's what I can't understand."

"That is simple," said Ross, realizing that stubborn reticence now could do no one any good. "Sheila and I are old friends."

"What! you, too?" exclaimed Burton grinning ruefully.

"Not in the sense you mean, Mr. Burton. I knew Sheila as a little girl in California. We were neighboring families. And by the way hers was an excellent one. She came to see me at King's when she heard I had joined the faculty. The afternoon of Goold's death was the first time I called upon her."

"And on that first visit she told you all about her affair with Goold?" exploded Burton incredulously.

"Not only that, but asked me to intercede for her with Goold—she didn't want her happiness broken up—smashed as she put it."

"The devil!" cried Burton. "Women are certainly even queerer than I thought. Quite a pair, these Forbeses."

"You forget that they are wildly, tenderly in love with each other."

"I don't forget," grunted Burton. "I learn. You agreed to intercede and made your appointment then and there by telephone from the Forbes apartment—is that right?"

"Yes—and when I came the doors were ajar and Goold was dead."

"Yes," said Burton, "and that, if you ask me, makes it look even darker for Forbes. Either Goold was killed in process of a robbery, or those precious letters of Sheila's are responsible for his death. We have got to face both possibilities until we eliminate one of them."

"Exactly," chimed Wells. "We have got to find that glazier and we have got to watch Forbes like hawks. It looks to me, we have narrowed it down to workable dimensions at last."

"If I believed either one of these two to be Goold's murderer," Ross smiled pleasantly, "I should drop all interest in the matter here and now."

"What!" shouted Wells. "You have another idea—and you won't tell us?"

"I have several notions, Commissioner. But none of them are in tellable shape—for the reason that they are not ideas."

Burton, Wells and Callahan stared at him with expressions of incredulity, at once comic, angry, and pathetic.

"In heaven's name, why don't you tell us what you are doing?" almost begged Wells. "After all, we are the police. We could help you, you know."

"Oh, I may call for your help at any moment," Ross reassured him lightly. "But now, if you will excuse me, I must go."

"Is that a promise—about letting us know?" Burton grinned good-humoredly.

"Absolutely!" laughed Ross. "You may count upon it. You have the whip-hand. I cannot do without you."

"Then good luck to you," and Burton held out his hand. "That man," he said to himself, rather than to Wells and Callahan after the door had closed behind Ross, "is either a genius or a charlatan. And somehow, I don't think he is a charlatan."

17

The Man with a Mission

Behind him as he walked briskly away from Center Street toward the subway, Ross could see out of the tail of his eye his shadow following him at the usual distance.

"Enviable creatures, those geniuses," he reflected. "Sherlock and all the rest of 'em; somehow neither Scotland Yard nor any of their creators ever thought of shadowing them. Pastoral simplicity I call it."

He had no sooner entered his own apartment than the telephone rang. It was Jimmie Trumbull.

"I have rung you before, Professor Ross, I know now—"

"You have something to tell me, I take it, James?" Ross quietly interrupted him.

"Yes, sir, about that—"

"Quite so, Jimmie. I understand. You are perplexed about the reading assignment I gave you after the last lecture. In that case, why not drop in and see me?"

"Yes, sir," gulped Jimmie, now perceiving his mistake. "I thought—"

"Ah, yes. But it is quite difficult to discuss academic work over the telephone, don't you think?"

"Yes, sir."

"Then we agree. I shall wait for you, James."

Less than fifteen minutes later Ross was admitting Jimmie Trumbull.

"Am I a half-wit?" he asked as he came in, and he answered himself, "I am. Stupid of me trying to talk to you over the telephone."

"Not precisely stupid, James. The telephone is often used for conversation. But since Mr. Callahan and the District Attorney are displaying an unhallowed and, I fear, a damaging, interest in our humble efforts to aid them, they may possibly have suborned the young African below to listen in on us. Natural enough. Now what have you got, James?"

"Briefly, this. I know now where Erzeroff is."

"Not, I trust, in distant California?"

"No, sir. Luckily he's no farther away than Westchester County, a mere step."

"Excellent!" cried Ross. "And where do we arrive after we take the step?"

"At the Ali Baba," answered Jimmie triumphant.

"Sounds cryptic—and Arabian."

"Have you never heard of the Ali Baba?" Jimmie demanded in wonderment.

"Alas, no, James. Not being a New Yorker, I have much to learn."

"Well here's one thing I can tell you, Professor. The Ali Baba is the last thing in comfort and luxury in the way of a rest-cure. It's a hotel, a sanitarium, a spa and a retreat all combined. The rates are high, but the service is as nearly perfect as you can get."

"Aren't you mixing it up with the prevalent notion of Heaven?"

"Sounds that way, but that's what it is. I once had an uncle staying there. He drove up there one day with a friend for lunch. He had no luggage, nothing but the clothes on his back. But he liked the place so much he wanted to remain. The proprietor told him he needn't worry about luggage. They gave him everything; linen, underwear, dress clothes, brushes, razors—everything he could need—and the best food and wines in the country. Everybody there is the guest of the proprietor. It's like an English house-party—plus."

"Interesting," observed Ross. "How much I should like to see an itemized bill of the place!"

"No bill there is ever itemized. The butler simply places a bill on your table in your room before you leave and you settle with him. The proprietor being host, never talks money with his guests."

"And no disagreements arise?"

"No one has ever disputed a bill there," exulted Jimmie, as though the place were his own. "You get too much for your money."

"Ah, James," sighed Ross, "a laborious life has excluded me from much."

"Well, you'll see it now, Professor."

"I fear not," said Ross. "It is you, my dear Watson, who are destined to revel in that paradise."

"You really would send me, to the Prince?"

"Precisely that, Jimmie."

"But I don't speak Russian."

"That you may safely hold the last of your worries. Your careless and picturesque English will see you through."

"Sounds great—but just what do I do there besides eating high and sleeping soft?"

"Chiefly, you will observe, James—just simply observe —without seeming to do so. Your innocent manner should carry you far."

"Fair enough," grinned Jimmie. "It's all about as clear as mud to me."

"It will be clearer before you start. And that reminds me, James. I want you to accompany me tonight on a little jaunt, can you manage it?"

"If it's any nearer than Siberia, I can start now."

"Blessed youth! Our destination is no more remote than the East Side of Manhattan Island."

"Let's go," said Jimmie.

"You forget I am watched—I and my comings and my goings."

"And your ox and your ass," appended Jimmie in a high state of glee.

"No. Luckily it is the ass that does the watching. On this particular excursion, however, I do not desire to be watched, so I shall have to give my guardian the slip. Could you manage to meet me at eight o'clock this evening at the Brooklyn Bridge Terminal of the elevated?"

"Certainly could, Professor. But—"

"And could you wear passably old clothes, some time-worn articles? You understand, dark shirt, battered hat, that sort of thing—protective coloration for our proposed environment. I will do the same."

"Sure," said James. "But how will you get away from your sleuth?"

"Elementary, my dear Watson. In fact, rudimentary. If I can't lose my sleuth in the New York subway then I had best leave crime detection alone. Wait on the platform for a Brighton Beach train, but don't take the train. I may be a few moments late. But eventually I shall appear."

At five minutes past eight, Jimmie Trumbull, intent upon the variety of humanity which seemed mysteriously intent upon going to Brighton Beach, was startled by a touch upon his shoulder.

"Well, old scout," and Ross's genial smile was close to his own eyes, "I see you are going to Brighton Beach. But let us do nothing we might regret." Jimmie followed with a mystified grin.

"Just where are we going, Prof?"

"I have a fancy to be Prince Florizel of Bohemia to-night—to visit the haunts of our melting pot."

"Slumming?"

"Yes, in a way." At Duane Street they boarded a trolley. "I have a little theory I'd like to work out. It's a bit wild, but it may yield results."

At Grand Street they left the car and walked leisurely northward. Before various eating houses of that teeming district Ross paused, gazed into the windows, but being dissatisfied with the ethnic groups he observed therein, he marched on. Now and then when he saw the right lettering upon the windows or over the door, he would enter, Jimmie following blankly, for he was in a world wholly alien, and they would linger over tea, or coffee. The tongues of the places were various but strange, and generally Ross stayed no longer than the time necessary to smoke a single cigaret.

"Here is a queer dump," said Jimmie as they paused before a dingy place that bore upon its window in pre-Raphaelite lettering a legend in an unknown tongue.

"Yes!" murmured Ross. "I myself feel drawn to this dump. Its sign reads, 'Ivan Tcherabin: Billiards.' Let's go in, James."

Men were drinking tea out of glass tumblers or from thick saucers. Some were eating, some playing dominoes with sebaceous counters or strange card games with fabulously greasy decks. In one corner of the room sat a bearded man, a laborer seemingly, with a flat Slavic face and nose, and softly, dreamily he was playing an accordion.

The light in the center of the room was garish. Ross, with Jimmie following, took the only vacant table in a corner.

"*Tchai!*" ordered Ross. The waiter, who took their order for tea, was clad, not in the chromatic silken blouse of the expensive imitation Russian restaurants, so many of which have sprung up in New York since the Russian diaspora, but quite simply in the shirt-sleeves of a very black shirt protruding from armholes of a much-stained vest. His trousers were tucked into the tops of knee-high boots.

"They advertise this as a billiard-room," animadverted Jimmie, "where is the billiard table?"

"Slavic efficiency," said Ross in an undertone. "It probably started as a billiard room, and it was too much trouble to change the sign."

The waiter put before them two tumblers, thick and rather sticky, with a faint amber liquid, a tenuous half-slice of lemon floating in each. As an afterthought he then brought two saucers. When Ross gave him half a dollar, he received forty cents in change.

"Do we have to drink this?" murmured Jimmie dubiously.

"When in Rome—" said Ross, and taking a lump of sugar he bit off a fragment and began to sip the anomalous liquid with every sign of relish.

The man with the accordion was still softly moving his fingers over his little keyboard. Then, with a glance at Ross and Jimmie, he began a more definite tune.

Ross smiled appreciatively in his direction. "The song of the 'Blind Musician,'" he whispered to Jimmie—"quite sticky with sentiment—known to every peasant in Russia. The minstrel is playing it for our benefit."

Even in their American environment these Russian workmen could not resist it. The checker-players were moving their pieces more slowly. The hands of the card players grew languid and were still. Before long all the room was listening to the plaintive strains of a ballad that may have antedated Homer. When the musician finally ceased, a deep sigh escaped those alien breasts.

Ross moved over to the accordion player and laid a coin on the table before him. The man's eyes gleamed.

"Do you know the 'Razkamarensky?'" Ross asked softly in Russian. The man nodded but made no move to take the coin or to play the song. Ross returned to his place.

"I wish I knew what you were driving at, Prof," murmured Jimmie.

"You may think it odd, James, but I am aiming to get a little information. Patience is the detective's foremost virtue." Jimmie looked blank.

The card and checker players were just beginning to emerge from the solemn state induced by the "Blind Musician" when the man with the accordion suddenly struck up the "Razkamarensky."

That famous and somewhat ribald ballad of a mujik from Razkamarensk who felt merry and "let himself go" is quite irresistible to anyone, but notably to the Russian mujik himself. Heads began to nod, hands to beat the measure and feet to accentuate the rhythm. "Vanka! Vanka!" Some of them called thickly. Suddenly the booted waiter began to shove chairs and tables aside to clear a space. Then he began to dance. With arms akimbo, now squatting on his heels, now flying into the air, now creeping, now leaping to the ceiling like a highly trained gymnast, that boy was dancing the wild dance of the Razkamarensky. Faster and faster he whirled and flew, with a wild ecstasy, a savage abandon, until he fell exhausted to the floor.

The customers applauded loudly and dragged the boy to one side like a sack of meal. A faint smile parted the lips of the musician. Ross grinned appreciatively, in his direction; then, as the turmoil of shifting chairs and tables was still in progress, he nudged Jimmie and together they went over and sat down beside the sombre accordion player.

"I have heard only one man play the Razkamarensky as you have played it," Ross told him, "and that was in Siberia." The man scrutinized him narrowly from under heavy eyebrows and nodded.

"I am a Siberian," he muttered.

"He was a pilgrim, a religious," went on Ross wistfully as though adrift upon the gentle tide of his own memories, "and he belonged, I believe, to the sect of the Khlysts."

"*Da*—I also am a Khlyst," the man nodded.

"Marvelous!" exclaimed Ross. "I did not know there were any in this country."

"We are everywhere," muttered the peasant as though carried away by his own vainglory, "in Russia, in Siberia, in China, throughout the earth."

"Ah, you are men with missions, pilgrims," observed Ross, reverently, "moving over the world."

"Over the world," the man breathed heavily. "*Da*. The Head sends us and we go. He calls back and we return— if we can, if we can, brother," he concluded in a sudden burst of religious zeal. "There is no redemption except through sin."

"No, none," Ross chimed in quickly. "I know that is the creed of the Khlysts."

"Surely," the man retorted, solemnly argumentative, "only a man who has sinned can repent. What is there to repent if you have not sinned?"

"Are you to remain long in this city?" queried Ross. "For it is a joy to me to hear you play."

"I stay until I am called. Be it a day or be it years."

"I understand," nodded Ross. "Yours is but to obey. Well, brother, I must go," Ross slipped a bill into the man's hand. "I will come back to hear you and to speak with you. Farewell."

"With God," the man answered solemnly. "I am here today, but tomorrow who knows?"

"Exactly," smiled Ross. "I shall not forget."

When they left Ivan Tcherabin's eating house, Jimmie inhaled a deep breath and uttered the single expressive sound, "Gee!"

"Precisely so, James," murmured Ross. "It is indicated that tomorrow you start for that oriental paradise you described—The Ali Baba."

"I wish I understood Sanskrit," sighed Jimmie. "Perhaps I might follow you, then."

"Hardly necessary, Jimmie. For oddly enough I don't know much Sanskrit myself, except to read a few sutras. Besides, you will no doubt find Erzeroff a cosmopolite speaking every modern tongue. Make friends with him. Learn all you can about him. Your best character is that of a well-to-do young man compelled to rusticate for a while."

"But suppose the police are already watching him?" suggested Jimmie dubiously.

"So much the worse, as the French say. But I scarcely think so. You see, my peculiar theory regarding Erzeroff would be too far-fetched for Callahan."

"But what am I supposed to find out?"

"Well, supposing Erzeroff were to have the Rembrandt painting, The Tartar Chieftain, in his possession—that, as reporters say, would be news. But everything else about him would be news, James. Your role is much that of an observant child. Is that clear?"

"Clear as mud," said Jimmie heavily, "but I'll do the best I can."

"You must, Jimmie. For, mark you, there are two problems before us. One is to find the murderer of James Goold. The other is to save the wrong person from the electric chair. And if I know anything of Messrs. Callahan, Wells and Burton, they are determined that someone must be executed or at least sentenced—even if it be one of ourselves."

18

Ross Receives Visitors

As Ross approached the corner of his apartment house he saw a very anxious man intently peering in his direction and then suddenly relaxing as he recognized him under the street lights. It was his shadow.

"Good evening," Ross greeted him politely. "We might as well be sociable, don't you think so?"

For an instant the man simulated surprise. "You speakin' to me?" he queried.

"Yes, I am. I have reason to believe you are my bodyguard. I am very proud of the distinction, but it must be rather a bore for you."

The man grinned uncertainly. "Say, Professor," he admitted, "I'll have to hand it you. You certainly did give me a chase down there in the subway."

"I am sorry," smiled Ross. "I'll try to make it easier for you."

"Say, I'll say you're a white man," the plainclothes man responded enthusiastically. "It ain't no fun. You've said it. But I've got my wife and four kids and a living to make. See?"

"I see, of course," nodded Ross. "Come up some time, when you're bored and cold. Tell you what I'll do. When I think conditions are auspicious, I'll flash you a signal by putting a lamp in the window. You know my apartment, don't you? Good. The lamp will mean, 'Come up and have a smoke.'"

"Oke," said the detective, impressed. "It'll be a pleasure."

"Excellent!" cried Ross with a joyous squeak. "Life is in reality so very simple, isn't it? In the meanwhile, good night." The man responded with heartiness.

When Ross entered the doorway he found a lady, a fur hiding the lower part of her face, shrinking into a corner of the visitor's bench in the hall. He endeavored to conceal his astonishment when she rose at his approach and he beheld before him Sheila Forbes.

"Come up, won't you," Ross shook hands with her pleasantly, as though her presence were the most casual and meaningless occurrence in the world. "I hope you haven't been waiting long."

"I had to see you," breathed Sheila as the African boy slammed the door of the elevator. Ross nodded and by a sign conveyed to her that silence here was even more imperative than her need for speech.

"Now, Sheila," he began as soon as the door of his apartment had closed behind them, "I need not tell you that your coming here is unwise, even dangerous?"

"I know, I know," she cried. "But I had to see you, Roland. I am so utterly miserable!"

"Sit down, Sheila. Five minutes is the longest time you can afford to remain here. Now what is it, child?"

"Oh, I am so terrified. All this publicity! My letters will come out—and it will be so horrible!"

"Is that all?" Ross smiled whimsically. "They say every woman is an egotist. Well, we are all that. However, let me tell you, Sheila. Your husband knows they exist, though so far they have not been found."

"He knows!" she gasped, and then she moaned against her furry sleeve. "Oh, then everything is smashed—and they will blame him for the murder!"

"He has a pretty fair alibi—though he won't say why it took him over an hour to get home from the Varsity Club the afternoon Goold was murdered."

"And do you think they'll blame him—for that?"

"It depends how desperate they are for a victim."

"Roland, I can't bear it. I'd rather die than have him suffer. You don't know, oh, nobody knows how chivalrous and how—stubborn he is! I love him! I won't have him suffer!"

Ross was not a little amazed at the depths of passion in this otherwise somewhat shallow young woman.

"Sheila, my dear," he took her hand gently, "I've promised you to try to find the letters. I'll do my best. I make you another promise. I'll do my best to prevent any harm coming to your husband. What more can I say?"

"Oh, Role, dear," she pressed his hand to her cheek, "you're a perfect angel to me! It's only you now, my only friend. If you don't help me, nobody will. And I tell you, I'd rather die than let a hair of Cullen's head suffer!"

"Now, don't let's be melodramatic. It's a bad situation. Personally, I feel sure that your husband did not kill Goold. But to find the person who did—that is another matter. However, I have hopes of doing that sooner or later."

"You darling!" sighed Sheila. Then with a sudden child-like transition she added, "I suppose now I look a fright, crying and all?"

Ross laughed outright. "You're a peach, Sheila. But now you must go. Do you know I am watched?"

"Oh, dear. Then they will know I've been here?"

"Possibly. You're a very headlong child to come without an invitation." Her face conveyed a wide-eyed hurt. "Sounds very ungracious, I know," he went on. "We must get you out of here with the least possible publicity."

"Now I'm afraid!" she shuddered. "Is there no back way?"

"None. But we'll have to make the front way safe for
Sheila."

Ross lifted a standing lamp from his study table, raised
the shade some eighteen inches and placed the lamp on
the window sill. Sheila watched him as though he were
performing a magic rite.

The man on the pavement opposite, seeing the lamp
and Ross's face in the window, gazed dubiously for a moment, looked about and began to move slowly across the
street.

"Good. There comes my guardian angel," Ross spoke
rapidly as he planned the moves.

"Now, Sheila, come with me to the elevator. As soon as
we hear the door slam below, our Hawkshaw will be in the
cage mounting upward. Then you, child, without undue
haste, like a little lady, will walk down the six flights and
walk out through the front door. Hail the first taxi you
see."

"But suppose the elevator boy should get down before
me?"

"He has already seen you. Besides, I shall try to detain
him while I fumble in my absent-minded way for largesse."

"Oh, dear, you are just splendid, Role!" Sheila in an
ecstasy of gratitude kissed him warmly upon the lips.

"Look what I work for!" he murmured whimsically, and
Sheila laughed. He conducted her quickly to the elevator
shaft. "No use denying, Sheila," he added, as the hall light
fell upon her face, "you are terribly, dangerously beautiful. No wonder your husband—"

At that instant the grating of the door and its slam
resounded below and swiftly, with gestured directions,
Ross steered Sheila to the stairs which wound in and out
behind the shaft. By the time the cage reached the seventh
floor, Ross, his smile of hospitality already prepared was
waiting to greet his bodyguard.

"Ah, here we are, Mr.—Mr.—and William," he turned abruptly to the colored boy, "it's so long since I gave you a cigar, I can hardly recall the occasion. Can you?"

"No sir—not jes' this minute, sir, I cain't."

"Ah, I feared so. That is a parlous state—must be remedied at once, eh?" In pocket after pocket Ross fumbled with a sort of vague professional intentness. "Let me see, let me see," he murmured. "Ah, here it is, at last." His fingers returned to the earliest pocket investigated and produced a long dark cigar.

"Thank you, sir—thank you, professah," all the thirty-two white African teeth gleamed in a gala of gratitude.

Far below, Ross felt sure, he heard the front door closing.

"Come in," he said genially to the attending plain-clothes man. "I feel I owe you, too, a cigar."

The man thought of his own crowded flat in the Bronx, smelling of kitchen, and gazed about him at this haunt of scholarly peace. Being a poor conversationalist, his talk was not enlivening to Ross. The visit, however, had served its purpose even before it had begun. It was eleven o'clock and Ross was just devising a tactful way of getting rid of his visitor when the telephone rang.

"Now to put a nice red cap on this climax," reflected Ross, "Cullen Forbes himself ought to crave an audience." The visitor announced by the hallboy, however, was Jimmie Trumbull.

"James!" exclaimed Ross opening the door and casting a glance over his shoulder at the district visitor within, "how delightful! What could possibly bring you at this hour? But come in, and welcome. The more, the merrier."

By now, however, Jimmie was an experienced sleuth.

"It's these papers, Professor. I thought I studied the stuff pretty hard and I can't see why I flunked the exam."

"One of my students," explained Ross blandly to his prior guest with an urbane wave of the hand in place of an introduction. "A teacher's time," he added plaintively, "is never his own."

"I am awfully sorry, sir," apologized Jimmie with realism, "but I happened to be passing and saw your light, so thought I'd drop in."

"Sit down, sit down," urged Ross. "You know every teacher at bottom feels honored by a visit from one of his students."

"Guess I'll have to be going," muttered the plainclothes man awkwardly. "Great smoke that was. Thank you very much, sir."

"Well, if you must," Ross held out his hand. "You and I are servants of the public. There will be more little smokes here I trust. Good night to you."

"Good night, sir. Much obliged."

"James," began Ross as soon as he heard the elevator close in the hall. "I will take you to my heart of hearts. You're a splendid conspirator! As you gather I was making friends with my shadow. Your style was, I may say, classic. Now, you must have something, or you wouldn't have come."

"Yes, sir. When I left you I thought I'd give Lorna a ring, on the chance she might want something, or just to say hello. And she wanted me to hot-foot it up there to her place. Well, she had the photostats of Erzeroff versus Goold, and she's all excited about the stuff. You see, the lawyers for Erzeroff were Cullen Forbes's lawyers, Gillette, Ward and Ward."

"And she thought that might have a meaning," speculated Ross. "Well it may have. Clever girl, Lorna. I fancy the love lost between those two gentleman was not prodigal. Still what else did Lorna hear?"

"Oh, she is jealous about my going out on Erzeroff's trail," laughed Jimmie. "Wished she were going, too, and all that."

"Hardly possible," murmured Ross. "Besides, I have other uses for Lorna."

"Did you really get anything from that queer isskyvodsky place we went to tonight, Prof?"

"Strange as it may seem I believe I did, James. I believe that old devil Rasputin's friends, the Khlysts, are somehow connected with the case we have in hand. Great old melting pot ours! Rasputin and Cotton Mather, Jonathan Edwards and Erzeroff and Dr. Nicholas Murray Butler— all meet in our strange brew of a nation."

"Of course, that's all Greek to me," protested Jimmie.

"Never mind, James. You start tomorrow on your rollicking career to become the friend of a prince. But put not your trust in princes. Watch your step. If you see anything out of the ordinary, or if you have reason to think Erzeroff is being watched, or engaged in any secret business, you are to pluck the heart of his mystery. At least you are to let me know. For purposes of communication, whether by letter, wire or telephone, we'll call him Mr. X. The one instruction is, keep your eyes and ears open."

"All jake, Prof. The next time you hear from me it will be from somewhere out Westchester way. Wish me luck."

"All the luck in the Universe, James."

"And that's plenty," Jimmie put out his hand. "Good night, sir."

"Good night, my lad. And by the way, make it a point to see whether you yourself are watched. I hardly think you will be, but it's always better to be aware than unaware." With a nod Jimmie vanished.

"Ah!" sighed Ross whimsically, "the cloistered ease of the scholar is neither so cloistered nor so easy as commonly reputed. But then," he lit a final cigarette before going to bed, "I am not a scholar and have never lived cloistered, nor yet easily."

He took off his coat and was just slipping off his shoes when the door-bell rang.

"Now what on earth—" he murmured to himself.

"Surely not another visitor, or—he would have been announced." He opened the door.

It was Callahan.

"Angels and ministers of grace defend us!" began Ross genuinely astonished. "You, Inspector, and at this hour?"

"You sure will have to excuse me, Professor," grinned the Chief. "I couldn't resist. I knew you were in and—to make a long story short, you'll spare me five minutes, won't you?"

"I'll spare you ten, Inspector. I was just going to bed, but there are no fixed hours for a distinguished visitor."

"Yes, I know," nodded Callahan removing his hat, "you'll give me anything except information."

"On the contrary, Inspector. Only sit down and my house, and everything in it, as the Spaniards say, is yours."

"You mean that?" Callahan sank his tall frame into the best chair without removing his overcoat.

"But of course. Why not, Inspector?"

"Why not? That's what I don't get."

"Cryptic, yet I do believe you mean something, Inspector. Don't keep me in suspense."

"You mean cards on the table?" challenged Callahan with a great show of geniality.

"The entire deck," laughed Ross.

"Good, then here goes. One of my men saw you on the East Side down in the Hunky quarter tonight. It was none of his business, so the damn fool didn't follow you. Besides, he thought—he knew—" and Callahan paused, confused.

"Knew, you mean, that I was already provided with a shadow?"

"Well, yes, put it that way if you like. Anyway, I came up myself to talk to the bird outside here from the District Attorney's office and he admitted you'd given him the slip for about two hours or so tonight. Now, what I mean is, you didn't just go slumming down there, did you Professor? Heck! What's the big idea? Why not give a feller a show?"

Ross smiled. "If only I had the big idea I should share with you with all my heart."

"Yeh?"

"Yes. It was no idea at all. It was just a notion. I have hundreds of them a day. Whereas, ideas, as we both know, are scarce."

"Razzing me again, ain't you, Professor?" Callahan's geniality was positively oleaginous. "I don't want much, only just results."

"Ah, precisely, Inspector. Your moderation moves me to tears. But I ask you, have you known results to come in a moment?"

"Yes, I know. But this ain't a moment. The man who was killed was Goold. Do you read the newspapers any? Do you see what they say about the police—about my bureau? Time goes on and we haven't got a thing to show, not a damn thing! See our fix?"

"Do I not!"

"Honestly, Professor, I am stuck in this case. It's a big case, one of the biggest, and I don't know where to turn. Now what I say, if you got any ideas, why not give us a hint or two, so I could say to the newspapers, 'rapid progress is being made'—see my point? That would make life a little easier for yours truly."

"I am touched, Inspector, profoundly touched."

"And if you did that," Callahan continued eagerly, "I might suggest to the D. A. to take that fly cop off your trail, got me? He's not much good anyway if you can lose him any time you've a mind to. Why, I could give you twenty men to work for you, instead of on you, like that mutt down below. Get me?"

"Indeed I get you, Inspector," laughed Ross. "It would be very pleasant. But how can I give you what I haven't got? I am in process of trying to construct a theory—to gather the materials for one—and here you want me to deliver, on the spot, the finished product, like one of those mail-order readymade houses."

"Hell! You drive me crazy, Professor!" exploded Callahan with a sudden release from his inhibitions. "There's times when I think you know more than I do, and then there's times when I don't think you know a damn thing!"

"Personally I favor the latter view," all but drawled Ross with marked detachment in face of the other's emotion, "especially for what is sometimes called the nonce."

"There you go!" cried Callahan grinning in spite of himself. "Do you think any detective ever talked like that outside of a book?"

"Ah, my many shortcomings! But believe me, the minute I have something tangible, it is yours without even the asking. It must be yours, Inspector, for you are the Power!"

"All right, all right, go ahead. But sometimes I think if you do anything on this case, I'll eat my hat."

"I trust not," smiled Ross. "It might disagree with you."

"Better than that, I'll buy you a new one."

"Excellent! Hats are, I admit, one of my economies. Yet I was planning to buy one next week. Your gift will be much appreciated."

"Next week!" flung out Callahan, rising from the embracing chair, "I'll buy you two of the best if you earn 'em in that time."

"That were rank extravagance," laughed Ross. "You know my name is Scotch."

"You're like a woman, Professor. Can't get along with you, and can't get along without you."

"That," said Ross, "is a high compliment I shall do my best to deserve."

"At that," muttered Callahan, "I'd like to see you Police Commissioner of New York some day."

"Heaven forbid!" Ross threw up a protective hand. "That sphere is designed for more exalted intellects."

For some reason Callahan roared with laughter.

"Well, I didn't get much out of you, did I, Professor?" he murmured sadly.

"What can I give of my poverty, Inspector, but my good will?" Callahan's face gradually hardened. He took his hat and moved to the door.

"Well," he observed in a calm voice which the hard look in his eye belied, "if that man Forbes don't come across with a better alibi soon, I guess we'll have to lock him up for safety. At that, we haven't such a bad case against him right now. He's a big man, but we're dealing with a big murder. Get me?"

19

Lorna of the High Heart

Friday being a day when Ross had no afternoon lecture he had cordially invited himself to lunch with Lorna, and let it be said quite frankly, he enjoyed being alone with her, without even the pleasant company of Jimmie.

It was one of those brilliant October days with a tang in the air that brings energy and ambition even to the ailing and aged. To the young and hale it brings a wistfulness and at the same time a renewal of the eternal zest for life.

Ross was far from being a poet, but somehow Lorna in her exquisite young perfection made him think of Rose Aylmer. Phrases were running in his head, "The sceptered race," "The form divine"—

—"every virtue, every grace!
Rose Aylmer, all were thine."

"Absit omen!" he reflected. Those lines were in the past tense. Thank Heaven! Lorna was very much of the present.

"Every time I think of it," he began rather abruptly for him, "I don't quite like the idea of your being so alone in this house, Lorna."

Her clear eyes searched his face, but her heart was beating a trifle faster. She was always happy in his presence.

"Why," she smiled, "you don't think anybody will try to murder me, do you Professor Ross?"

"No, no—I don't mean that. But the atmosphere is for the moment somewhat oppressive, not to say lugubrious."

"There is a whole house-full of servants and nurses," she reminded him. "And I am not easily frightened."

"Don't I know that? You are Lorna of the high heart. Thank God for the younger generation. It has such oceans of common sense."

"I am beginning to doubt that," she smiled brightly into his eyes. "You want me to watch, to study the people in the house, and I can't seem to see a thing."

"Lorna, have you ever heard of Ivan Lermolieff?" he enquired irrelevantly.

"No, never, Professor Ross. Was he a detective?"

"A detective in a way. He was, as a matter of fact, an art critic. He revolutionized art criticism and art appraisal by using Sherlock Holmes methods before Sherlock was invented. He showed the necessity of observing small details in determining the genuineness of a painting. Small details—they are innumerable—that the old masters themselves didn't know as characteristic of them. These are the marks of genuineness. I shall take that up in class one day."

"Is there anything you don't know?" smiled Lorna.

"Tons—but have you begun to use the Lermolieff method on the people about you?"

"On whom, for instance—on Cross?"

"Cross offers a rich field. But he's not alone. There are the nurses, for instance."

"If I had your eyes and your brain," said Lorna, "I suppose I should have seen whole histories in those rather ordinary women."

"Tut, tut, Lorna. You do yourself injustice. The greatest revelation in my life is the way you and Jimmie have taken hold. When you have lived as long as I have, you'll be—whirlwinds."

"Good old Jimmie—possibly he will be a whirlwind some day. But I—I feel like stagnant water."

"Water reflects, Lorna. That is your function. You spoke of the nurses as ordinary women. They may be, probably are. But two things in their testimony have been haunting me ever since. It was Miss Baker, the day nurse, I recall who went to Cross's pantry for the eggnog. She had answered all questions stupidly, but frankly enough. When, however, Wells asked her whether she went directly back to your aunt's room, for some reason she turned pale."

"You are sure of that?"

"Positive. The meaning may not be important, but there is a meaning to that pallor, I feel sure."

"And you want me to find it out?"

"It would be so helpful to you in whiling away time," smiled Ross.

Lorna gazed at him gravely, inquiringly for a moment.

"Of all people," she declared, "I should think Miss Baker would be less likely to commit a murder than almost anybody on earth."

"Ah, but who said she did, my dear Watson? I am speaking of getting a piece of knowledge, and you talk of her doing murder. Besides, Lorna, every human being on earth is capable of the worst crime on earth. That is our grim inheritance from a savage ancestry. And we are all members one of another—of the human race."

"Then how about the simpering Miss Kelly, the night nurse,—do you suspect her, too?"

"I suspect nobody and everybody, Lorna. That is not the point. But Miss Kelly, as it happens, interests me even more than Miss Baker. Expression in words is not her forte. But she spoke—"

"I know," broke in Lorna. "Of something uncanny going on in the house, something queer that she couldn't explain. She's told me. And now all the maids are peering like Sybils and gliding about the house like shadows. I'm beginning to feel creepy myself."

"Are you? Good. That's a beginning. Miss Kelly also spoke of an atmosphere of hostility—hatred, I believe, was the word she used. Did she tell you that also?"

"No, she hasn't, Professor Ross. But I'm sure she will if I listen to her. She can rattle on like a model T Ford, and will, whenever I give her the opportunity."

"Precisely what I would entreat you to do. Give both of those nurses every opportunity. By way of distribution of effort, I would talk more with Miss Kelly, but I would watch Miss Baker as closely as possible short of leading her to suspect she was watched."

"I am staggered, Professor Ross. I'll do it, of course—but, Miss Baker—I might as well watch the cook—a far more interesting personality."

"Remember Lermolieff, Lorna—his doctrine of little things. And by the way, have you ever noticed a penchant on the part of the Baker for any male in the house—Cross, for instance?"

Lorna laughed softly. "I'd hardly call it a penchant. I think she dislikes him more than she dislikes most men. She hardly has a good word to say for him."

"Splendid! Did she ever say any word, good or bad?"

Lorna was uncertain for a moment.

"Yes, I believe I once overheard her saying to someone, perhaps it was to Miss Kelly, that she believed that French girl, Amalie, was 'running after' Cross—that was the phrase, I think."

"Ah, a touch of jealousy! Now see, Lorna, how much you really know," Ross pointed out. "How many little things! If I assure you they are of the value to me, may I count on you to gather more?"

"Of course. Though I confess my idea of helping you wasn't—didn't—"

"Didn't run to servants' gossip? Never mind, my poor Lorna. As a faithful Watson you will nevertheless carry on, won't you?"

"Certainly. Mine not to reason why. Mine but to snoop or die."

"Far from it," protested Ross with a delighted squeak. "Presently you shall know all there is to know. This is laboratory work in Criminology, you remember. In a laboratory we gather facts to prove or sustain a theory. Did you notice, by the way, that in the Erzeroff Case, Cross was the only witness to the gentlemen's agreement between your uncle and Erzeroff relating to the missing Rembrandt?"

"Oh, yes, it all came back to me when I read the stuff. Cross was at that time a temporary valet whom Uncle Jim engaged in England. The transaction occurred in a hotel in Paris. Cross testified that he heard Erzeroff definitely say he was selling the picture not—not—"

"Not hypothecating it?" supplied Ross.

"Yes, that was the ugly word."

"Cross then was a good deal more involved in it than we at first knew. It was after that your uncle employed him as butler?"

"Yes, Uncle Jim liked him and brought him back."

Ross fell into a silence which Lorna did not disturb. She was suddenly realizing the vast number of implications, of ordinary human inter-relations that begin to emerge with a sinister meaning in the event of an unsolved crime mystery.

"If Callahan knew that," began Ross speculatively, "I can just see how his mind would leap into contortions.

He could easily evolve a theory that this was Cross's hold upon your uncle—partners in crime—that they quarreled. Possibly your uncle wanted to discharge the man. That then Cross shot him."

Lorna all but leaped from her chair.

"But how crazy that would be! Why Uncle Jim swore by Cross!"

"Yes, but I am only showing you how a mind of the type of Callahan's might work. And I know Callahan's mind."

"Then why wouldn't he think Cullen Forbes did it because the Prince and Forbes had the same lawyers in the law-suit?"

"As a matter of fact, Lorna, Callahan already thinks so—even without that piece of knowledge. That shows you our need of gathering accurate facts."

"So that is what's running in your head, Professor Ross," Lorna smiled a gentle accusation. "You are always thinking of Sheila, of protecting her. It certainly speaks well for her that she can inspire such a loyal friendship—unless," added Lorna and paused, a faint flush on her cheeks making her the more exquisite.

"You mean," said Ross, "unless I am after all in love with her." Lorna's confused laugh was a confession. "I can assure you, Lorna, that I am not. I can be very fond of a child, but I cannot fall in love with it. To me Sheila is a pretty child. You are much, much older than she—" Then suddenly Ross paused, and they both laughed in a delicious unison.

"What a queer race we are!" he exclaimed and Lorna suddenly had an impulse to activity, to move about the sitting room to look out of the window.

"A gorgeous day for Jimmie to begin his sleuthing!" she exclaimed, a new zest and energy in her voice. "I wish I could see what he is doing!"

"Ah, Jimmie preoccupies you a good deal?" murmured Ross. "I don't wonder. He's one of the best."

"He's a very nice child," she murmured almost demurely, with a glint of mischief in her eyes. "And who doesn't like to play with children?"

"How almost fantastically beautiful she is," Ross silently reflected—Then: "Good God! Am I, in my old age, turning into a sophomore with a crush?"

For the first time in many years Ross felt his cheeks grow warm. But for some reason he felt absurdly light-hearted. The telephone bell sounded.

"Ah," he said, "that may be Jimmie reporting his arrival at the Ali Baba?" Lorna picked up the instrument.

"Yes," she said, her face clouding. "Professor Ross is here. Do you wish to speak to him? Callahan!" she added covering the mouthpiece.

"Speaking of angels," murmured Ross taking the receiver. "How are you, Inspector," he went on, "am I to gather you wish to speak to me?"

Callahan's speech lasted for some time, punctuated only by monosyllables from Ross. Finally, with the phrase, "I think we can manage it," he put down the instrument.

"Callahan! Callahan!" he murmured, "wherefore art thou Callahan? Briefly, Lorna, Callahan wants us, you and Cross and myself, to come down at once to the District Attorney's office. The Grand Mogul has some new information and he desires politely to ask us a few questions. In his politeness, therefore, he has commissioned Callahan to summon us to The Presence."

"And we must go, I suppose?"

"I fear we must. I could almost wager some happy sleuth has come upon the traces of the Erzeroff law-suit and Burton feels vastly important with his discovery. We will go in a taxi, Lorna, and we will bear with us our Cross, to chaperone us."

As events proved Ross was only partly right. For the Grand Mogul had indeed come into possession of a fact—a fact that had not entered Ross's immediate conjectures.

20
Burton Springs a Surprise

Upon the very threshold of the Criminal Courts Building, Lorna and Ross were joined by a brisk and preoccupied Police Commissioner who greeted them with an effort to smile.

"Ah, Miss Storey, I am very glad to see you," he shook hands nervously. "Shows me you have to some extent got the better of your very natural shock. Great thing, youth. Helps us over many a rocky place." Having delivered this piece of oracular wisdom he turned a less smiling face to Ross.

"Professor," he nodded brusquely as they arrived at the ancient elevator, "you are in my bad graces. You haven't communicated with me in ages."

"True, alas, Commissioner, but with regrettably good reason. A famous oracular Spaniard, Baltasar Gracian, once said, 'He who speaks lightly soon falls or fails'. He also said, 'Do not be the slave of first impressions.'"

The ghost of a smile flickered upon the face of Cross who held himself respectfully aloof from his titular betters.

"All very well," grumbled Wells. "But that Spaniard of yours didn't have a business like this on his hands."

"He was a man of profound experience, Commissioner."

By this time they were treading the corridors pervaded by the peculiar sordidness which aging public buildings assume and, Wells leading, they entered the outer room of the District Attorney's office. Two or three men were waiting, all depressed and seemingly dejected by their surroundings. Callahan was just emerging from an inner room and his face lighted up with a good imitation of enthusiasm at sight of his chief. Brusquely he brushed by the attendant, whose broad Irish face was already prepared with that Hibernian suavity which pervades all American municipal institutions.

"Thank you for coming, Miss Storey," he began gallantly, seizing her small gloved hand in his large one. "We don't have visitors like you here very often. Commissioner," he added deferentially, "the D.A. is waiting for you and Professor Ross—for all of us, right in there now." And like a somewhat clumsy destroyer he officiously convoyed them to the inner sanctum.

Lorna in her dark clothes, touched at the throat with the white of lace, with her flower-like face beneath the small black hat, did indeed present a picture rare in those tessellated halls. Even the District Attorney, as they entered, instantly responded to her appeal. Somewhat heavily he rose from his swivel chair and moved quickly forward to greet her.

"Miss Storey," he said, "I am greatly obliged to you. I'm sorry I had to ask you down here, but I am under great pressure of work, and for other reasons it seemed best that we all meet in this office. Hello, Commissioner," he added more negligently. "How do, Professor Ross."

Chairs were quickly found and only Cross remained standing aloof and respectful in the background.

"You are—" he gazed with a momentary bewilderment at the tall figure in the rear.

"Cross, sir."

"The butler, you know," chimed in Wells.

"Oh—oh, yes. I won't keep you long. Cross, you were a witness in the suit that Russian, what's his name—

Erzeroff, brought against Mr. Goold for the recovery of the Rembrandt—according to the record." Ross and Lorna exchanged glances. That was evidently Burton's great bomb-shell.

"Yes, sir. I was," Cross answered quietly.

"Your testimony I know," went on Burton with a furrowed brow. "But after it was all over, at any time, did Mr. Goold speak to you of the case?"

"No, sir. I cannot remember that he did. Mr. Goold was not a talkative man, leastways not with the servants, sir."

"He never mentioned Erzeroff again?"

"No, sir."

"Did you ever hear of Erzeroff threatening or complaining, or at least communicating with Mr. Goold apropos of the result?"

"No, sir. Prince Erzeroff was in his way, if I may say so, quite a sportsman, sir."

"H'm—yes—yes," Burton appeared abstracted, as though thinking of something else. "Did you, by the way," he went on as with the merest of afterthought, "ever happen to hear Mr. Cullen Forbes discussing the picture or the law-suit with Mr. Goold?"

"You mean before the trial or after, sir?"

"Any time." Burton suddenly appeared more alert.

"Well, before the trial, I remember Mr. Forbes saying to Mr. Goold, partly in fun, I believe, 'Jim, any time you don't want that picture, I'll take it off your hands.'"

"What was Mr. Goold's reply?"

"I don't know, sir. I left the room at that point."

Burton looked displeased. "You never heard the matter mentioned again?"

"No, sir, not by anyone."

Burton nodded perfunctorily. "That's all about that," he said. "Now about another matter. You know the nurses in the house pretty well, don't you, Cross?"

"Fairly well, sir."

"That day nurse, Miss—er—Miss Baker, should you say she was an exceptionally emotional person?"

"Emotional?" repeated Cross perplexed. "I am not sure I know what you mean, sir."

"Well, is she particularly gloomy, over-religious, fanatical on any subject—religion, morals, anything?"

Cross hesitated a moment before replying. It appeared as though the mastery of his features offered him a momentarily acute problem. He was however long accustomed to control.

"No, sir, I never noticed," he answered evenly. "If anything, I should have said she was rather inclined to be jolly—out of the sick-room."

"Jolly, eh? How do you mean that?"

"Oh, she always liked a bit of a chat whenever she came to the pantry, and she'd always smoke a cigaret. You see, sir, she was safe from prying eyes in the pantry—her being middle-aged, and all that." Lorna and Ross exchanged glances.

"Did she do that on the afternoon of the—tragedy?"

"Yes, sir. She generally stayed fifteen, twenty minutes."

"I thought," Callahan fairly jumped at him, "you said it took you ten minutes to make that eggnog?"

"I did, sir. That was correct. You did not ask me how long Miss Baker stayed. As a matter of fact I left her there when I returned to the basement."

Burton glanced at Callahan, then at Ross and Lorna.

Ross's eyes alone betrayed no amusement. Miss Baker's pallor was at least partly explained. Burton turned again toward Cross.

"Now, one more question, Cross. Did you ever quarrel with Mr. Goold, or have any words or disagreement at any time since you have been in his service?" This time a wave of very genuine astonishment swept the butler's features. For a moment he stared in amazement at the District Attorney.

"I, sir? Quarrel with Mr. Goold?" he all but gasped. "Such a thing could not happen. I know my place. Besides, Mr. Goold was the most considerate employer I have ever known, sir."

"I guess that is all, Cross," said Burton somewhat dully. "You may go."

"Thank you, sir," replied the butler and with grave dignity walked out of the room. Callahan looked down with exaggerated fixity at the table before him. If he had inspired the question, he was not enjoying the results.

"That is one reason I asked you down here, Miss Storey," Burton turned with a more lively air toward Lorna. "You don't happen to know of any trouble between your uncle and this butler during the time he's been in the house, do you?"

"No, Mr. Burton, I don't. I should have said that Cross has always been happy in his place and my uncle placed great reliance on him."

"Nothing at all," interposed Callahan suddenly with the bravado of the defeated, "that might make you think that butler had any sort of a hold over your uncle?"

"No, nothing," Lorna shook her head almost absently and Ross could not resist a faint enigmatic smile.

"You, Professor Ross," boomed Burton with a rueful grin, "seem to think it's funny. But we have to follow up all lines. Now, see if you think what's coming is funny. Miss Storey, about Cullen Forbes: your uncle used to see a good deal of Forbes, didn't he?"

"Oh, yes—until recently, quite a good deal. Mr. Forbes used to come up from downtown with Uncle Jim quite often, and sometime he'd simply drop in—yes, they were quite chummy."

"And that ended with Cullen Forbes's marriage, didn't it?"

Lorna flushed perceptibly, but in an instant she answered with her usual poise and naturalness.

"Yes, roughly, perhaps. Anyway, they stopped seeing so much of each other, at least uptown, a few months ago." Burton nodded pleasantly.

"Was Cullen Forbes ever a neighbor of yours?" he asked with a negligence of tone that seemed almost perfunctory.

"A neighbor?" she repeated. "No. Not that I ever knew."

"Did you know that he owns the house directly opposite the gallery entrance on Sixty-second Street?"

"No!" she answered in a tone of unfeigned surprise. "Does he? I never heard of it before."

"Do you suppose your uncle knew it?"

"How can I say? He certainly never mentioned it to me." Burton, out of the tail of his eye, was glancing covertly at Ross. Ross's impassivity, however, was no criterion to the shock of amazement he was experiencing. Inwardly, he was saying to himself, "if that young woman, Sheila, and her husband want my help, they'd better take me a little farther into their confidence."

"H'm, yes," proceeded Burton easily. "Forbes has owned that house for some time—some years."

"Did you know it, Professor Ross?" Burton could not resist this easy victory.

"Absolutely not," responded Ross in a tone of detachment.

"Now just one more question, Miss Storey," Burton became more business-like. "Have any other nurses been employed at your house besides the present ones, Miss Baker and—let me see—Miss Kelly?"

"Not for a long time, Mr. Burton. In the first weeks of my aunt's illness there were some rapid changes. But after these two came, they have suited her pretty well and they have remained."

"Then, that will be all for the present, Miss Storey. Thank you very much. If you are waiting for Professor Ross to escort you home, would you oblige me by waiting in the next room? Just a few minutes. I shan't keep him long." He smiled with an urbanity unusual for him and opened a door into a room that was evidently the office library. It was lined with calf-bound volumes in serried rows, the record of a world in disharmony. Lorna nodded smiling to the men and withdrew.

"Now, Professor," he lit a cigar and addressed Ross briskly, "I can tell you that Forbes's alibi doesn't look nearly so good as it did some twenty-four hours ago." And he paused.

"I am listening, Mr. Burton."

"You heard me say that he owns the house opposite the gallery door? Now, you, Inspector, tell the professor what you learned." Ross shifted his gaze to Callahan.

"May surprise you, Professor, but we've found the taxi that carried Forbes to his home that afternoon, after he left the Varsity Club."

"You're a genius, Inspector. There are said to be over twenty thousand cabs in New York."

"Oh, that was just luck," grinned Callahan modestly.

"But where do you suppose it picked Forbes up?" put in Wells unable to contain himself. Ross looked blank. "At Sixty-second Street and Madison Avenue!" Wells exclaimed excitedly.

"Yeh," nodded Callahan emphatically, and Burton broke in:

"And mind you, he owns the house opposite, and here's this fact as a rider—the house is vacant, unoccupied!"

"Pelion upon Ossa!" murmured Ross nodding with a slow smile. "And what do you conclude from all that, gentlemen?"

"Oh, come, Professor," Wells spoke up, checking Burton with a gesture. "You are supposed to be working with

us—not against us. Don't you think all that is very signif-
icant?"

"I fail to see that it has altered matters to any great
degree," firmly answered Ross—"though I admit the facts
are interesting. At what time," he added, "did the taxi pick
Forbes up, have you learned?"

"Exactly!" shouted Wells. "About twelve or fifteen minutes before it landed him at his apartment. Get that Ross?
How did he spend the forty minutes from the time he left
the Varsity Club until the taxi picked him up, eh?"

"I'll tell you, how—and this in confidence, Professor Ross," Burton spoke with an emphatic incisiveness he
ordinarily kept for juries. "He walked from the Varsity
Club to his empty house and looked across the street at
the Goold gallery windows. When he saw his opportunity—I don't pretend to say we've got every detail—he stole
across, either let himself in or was let in by some one, shot
Goold and walked out leaving the doors ajar. What could
be simpler? He walked east in a matter-of-fact manner
and at the corner of Madison took the first taxi that came
along. Home, James—easy as that. Up in his apartment he
probably kissed his pretty wife with great satisfaction and
considered his day well-spent."

Appalling as were these movements conjured up by the
District Attorney, the men could not help smiling, albeit
somewhat glumly.

"If you are as sure of your steps as all that," said Ross,
who saw that a reply was expected of him, "I don't see why
you don't arrest Forbes and go to the Grand Jury without
further ado."

"You forget that our case must be iron-clad," expos-
tulated Wells, "especially where a man as prominent as
Forbes is concerned."

"And that is where you come in, Professor Ross," Burton blandly took up the line. "We've got to establish the

matter of motive on a solid foundation. Quite frankly, we
want you to tell us everything you know about those letters—all that Sheila Forbes has told you. You must admit
the time for hesitation on your part is past. It's come to a
crisis too grave for any such childish trifling as that."

"Yes, exactly," snapped Wells. "We're in the fortunate
position of having one of us, yourself, that is, in on the
ground floor from the start. Lucky day," he forced an un-
convincing smile, "when I appointed you a consultant to
the Department, wasn't it."

"Sure was," responded Callahan with a broad answering
grin. The District Attorney looked matter-of-fact and expec-
tant, and being a better actor, he was the more convincing.

"I repeat," said Ross amiably, "I am surprised you
haven't arrested Forbes."

"Oh, he won't get away," growled Callahan and Burton
broke in:

"But you agree, don't you Professor, that it's a pretty good
case—and that it now hangs upon your testimony, eh?"

"Far from it," smiled Ross, and Wells and Callahan all
but shuddered at his blasphemy. For a moment there was a
tense silence in the room.

"You don't really mean, Professor Ross," began Burton
with impressively slow and distinct utterance, "You are
still determined to hold out on us, like a stubborn child,
or a pig-headed juror, do you? Why a priest who got the
stuff in the confessional would by this time have come
across."

"I question that," said Ross, "though that is not the
question. A confidence is a confidence. But—"

"But it's essential to the process of justice in this case!"
almost shouted Burton.

"But it is not essential," went on Ross with the same
evenness of tone. "Especially since I don't believe in your
theory."

"Have you got a better one?" demanded Wells. Burton said nothing. He pretended to be too outraged for speech.

"I was coming to that," Ross pursued amiably. "I have the rudiments of better ones. And in a few days I hope to do even better by you than mere theories. I hope to deliver to you the murderer of James Goold."

"Yes, so you say," grunted Burton rudely. Ross, however seemed not to have heard him.

"I cannot say enough for the cleverness of Inspector Callahan and his men in discovering the taxi driver who carried Forbes—the empty house, and so on."

"It was my men who found out about the house," cut in Burton.

"I am immensely impressed," and for all his quietness of demeanor Ross seemed to be dominating the conference, handing out badges, as it were, for good conduct. "But," he went on, "it will all prove to be irrelevant. The murderer of Goold will prove to be not Forbes, but someone so entirely different you will be amazed."

Burton attempted a laugh. But the others were too impressed to do anything except sit and gaze at him.

"In a few days, I think you said?" blurted out Wells.

"That was what I said."

"In about how many days would you say, Professor?" demanded Callahan with an effort at jocularity. "Be a sport and give us a line."

"I am no prophet, Inspector. But the middle of next week should see the end of this business."

"God! Professor!" cried Callahan leaping from his chair. "I could lick you, and then again I could kiss you. Want any men, any help? Only say the word. The sky is the limit."

"Thank you, Inspector. I may call on you at any moment."

Both Callahan and Wells were now smiling broadly. To tell the truth all three, even the District Attorney, were relieved that it did not appear immediately necessary to arrest Forbes.

"Just what are you doing about it?" enquired Burton almost casually.

"I am taking the best possible measures, Mr. Burton. I might conceivably be able to take better if your detectives did not follow me about so doggedly. I assure you it's a waste of the taxpayers' money."

"I am the judge of that!" snapped Burton. "However," he added more temperately, "since it seems to annoy you so much, you will be relieved of that burden."

"Thank you."

"Now we'll see the magic. I have your word and I take it, that nothing that's been said here is to be communicated in any shape or form to anyone?" Ross merely smiled. At that moment he concluded that Callahan was by far the finest of the three.

"And that you will not delay a minute more than is necessary in letting us know?" pressed on Burton.

"Minutes are long periods in a world of time," murmured Ross. "They have often proved fatal."

"Good!" cried Burton. "Then if the police are satisfied, I am."

Ross rose from his chair. "I fear, gentlemen," he said, "we have kept Miss Storey waiting an unconscionable time." Almost he added, "for wholly worthless reasons."

Once outside the building Ross handed Lorna into a taxicab to shut out as quickly as possible the depressing atmosphere of Center Street and the Criminal Courts Building.

"I expected to be called back and handcuffed to you any minute," smiled Lorna as she leaned back against the cushions.

"It was almost as serious as that," answered Ross, "but not quite. Burton had a bigger surprise than the Erzeroff case and Forbes's real estate ownership. But I punctured it somewhat, I think, by sheer bravado. In fact," he glanced backward and perceived no taxi following, "they have momentarily removed my bodyguard as reward for a good deed."

"So you're a little better off than when we came here?"

"A little. But I promised them the murderer by next week some time."

"Next week! I feel like the poor negro, who was to be hanged on Friday, writing to the Governor, 'And here it is Wednesday!'" Lorna's hand went to her heart. "Can you do it?" She scanned his face anxiously. "Oh, I hope so!"

"Yes, I think so, Lorna. With your help—and Jimmie's—" he added as an afterthought. "I can hardly conceive the things I could not do." And his whimsical smile played over his features, exactly as though they were jesting in her sitting room remote from thoughts of crime or criminals. She uttered a laugh, spontaneous and yet nervous, with a catch at her throat. Because what she actually wanted to do was to cry.

21
A Piece of Concrete Evidence

Jimmie, as good as his word, telephoned the next morning a message highly cryptic in which he evidently delighted.

"What have you been able to accomplish?" Ross asked him.

"Oh, just carrying on," came the lazy tone over the wire.

"Have you met Mr. X?"

"Him? Oh, yeah—a great boy—a regular pal." It was obvious that Jimmie did not consider the telephone sufficiently private and that the questions must come from the other end. His chief objective of making friends with Erzeroff was evidently in process of realization.

"Can you tell, are you, or is anybody else being bothered by curious eyes?"

"Not in the way you mean," was the ambiguous answer. Ross interpreted this to signify that so far as Jimmie could tell no detective from the outside was shadowing either Erzeroff or himself. It was possible, however, that within the Ali Baba itself there may have been some prying eyes.

"Is that all you can tell me, James?" queried Ross.

"That's all for the good old nonce," came the seemingly jovial answer. "But I'll call you again tomorrow, or maybe not before Monday. Hope I can convince you, you ought to take a vacation and come up here."

"No telling but you may succeed," laughed Ross. "I feel the need of dolce far niente. Meanwhile be a good lad—and carry on."

"My best to you all," said Jimmie with just the right pitch of suppressed hilarity in his voice that he meant to be characteristic of American Youth.

"I'll pass it on to her," said Ross, and Jimmie laughed.

"So long," he murmured and hung up the receiver. That Jimmie was upon the track of something, Ross was certain. It was a question in his mind how soon he ought himself to go up to the Ali Baba. It might, he thought, prove necessary sooner rather than later. After all, Jimmie was young, inexperienced, and his end of the case important.

That Saturday morning was cloudy and the fatigue of the week prompted Ross to linger in bed later than normal. It was nearly ten when Jimmie had called and Ross was not yet dressed. "Scandalous!" he murmured to himself and proceeded to make his breakfast coffee. He was humming a vague tune as he puttered in his diminutive kitchenette, but his mind, had some super-human photographer been able to take a flashlight picture of it, would have presented the appearance not unlike the wiring of a great modern telephone exchange.

Jimmie and Erzeroff—the Khlyst in the Slavic eating house—Callahan, Burton, Forbes, and oh, yes, Wells—Forbes and Sheila—poor Sheila—Helen of Troy caused a ten years' war—so mad was the world for beauty. Sheila—undoubtedly the cause of this Goold murder—horrible thought—

"Oh, come," he said to himself—"this won't do!" and by an effort of will he checked the entire confused stream of his consciousness, shut off the current from all the tangle of his mental wires and made his mind a blank.

It was a practice he often resorted to when he desired to clear his brain completely of debris and to make room for fresh vigorous thought. He sometimes wondered why we, accidentally immersed in the mounting complexity of our civilization, do not make more of this oriental practice. Once or twice he had spoken to his classes about it. But the nearer to blanks were the normal minds of his students, the more absurd and humorous were their reactions to the idea of deliberately making the mind a blank. For himself, however, he often had recourse to it in times of peculiar stress and always with beneficent results. It was very simple; he reared a mental wall which impregnably beat back all the confused crowding images that come swarming about it, until finally he was pervaded by interior stillness.

Suddenly he was awakened from his state of intense passivity by the sizzling of the coffee which was boiling over on the gas stove. He felt refreshed and free as he sipped the first draughts of the hot liquid, and then quite sharply, distinct as a sound, came the clear-cut thought, "I must go over that empty house of Forbes's facing the Goold gallery."

Whether that house was empty by force of necessity or design, it was not improbable that Forbes had used it as a point of vantage from which to observe—what? The obvious motive was jealousy. He may have wished to make sure that his wife was not visiting Goold.

Spying upon Goold!—It was grotesque, incredible, and yet possible. Human nature was a tangled skein. Big business man though Forbes undoubtedly was, Ross knew only too well how often the elements of childishness are apt to be fellow tenants with the ideas that make for large financial success in the cranium of the business man. Fortune-tellers are said to thrive upon the patronage of certain business men.

But, if Forbes had used that empty house for purposes of observation, then traces of him should be found there. Without hesitation he rang up Callahan.

"Well, this is a surprise," Callahan greeted his name over the telephone. "Glad to hear from you, Professor."

"I have a request to make," said Ross.

"Oh, I thought it was something you wanted to hand me. But anyway," went on Callahan suavely, "it's the first time you've ever called me, I'd rather give you something than not be called at all."

"I hope to call you many times in the near future," Ross assured him heartily.

"Oh, yeh?" said Callahan. "That's great! Now what can I do for you, Professor?"

"Briefly, I should like to visit that empty house, Inspector—the house in Sixty-second Street."

"Now, do you know I expected you to ask me that, Professor?"

"Really?"

"Yeh. I'm getting to be quite psychic myself, like that dumb cluck of a nurse. Only this morning, walking down to the office I said to myself, 'If the professor don't try to take a squint at that house, my name's Dennis.' And it hit me, I'd like to look over it myself."

"You mean you haven't seen it?"

"No, I haven't. One of my men saw it, though. He's a friend of the Holmes watchman on the beat, and the man let him in. I can tell you this: it's absolutely vacant—not a stick or stone in it."

"Yet, you wish to see it, don't you?"

"Yeh, I do. But here's the point. I was just turning it over. The place is now in the hands of a real estate agent. I don't want to attract attention, nor I don't want to go there with a search warrant. Those things get out. See what I mean? I was figuring the best way."

"Simplicity itself, Inspector. If you will tell me the name of the agent, I shall figure as a prospective tenant.

They'll send someone over with a key. If you will meet me there in one hour, we can both look together."

"I wish I had you on my staff, Professor," chuckled Callahan. "We could do a lot together."

"You have got me, Inspector. I am but one of your many minions."

Callahan sighed dramatically into the mouthpiece.

"Oh, yeh?" he said. "Well, the agents are Pierce and Ellebore. Now, let's see—it's ten twenty. S'pose we say eleven thirty—there at the house—that suit you? Good!"

And so it was arranged. The agents, when Ross telephoned them, assured him they would have a man there with the keys at eleven twenty, and they hoped very much he would like the house. It was a very fine house indeed, sir, one of the best on their rather exceptional list of exclusive house property.

At eleven twenty-five when Ross approached the house he saw a stocky young man, a future high-powered realtor, standing on the old-fashioned stoop of one of the few brownstone houses remaining in that region.

"Good morning, sir," said the young man. "A bright morning. Shall we go in?"

"I am expecting a friend to join me any minute, but—"

The youth opened the door and to tell the truth Ross was not sorry to have five minutes alone in the house without the cheering company of Callahan.

"I'll look out for your friend," the young man assured him. But he appeared somewhat surprised that the only rooms that interested Ross were the north rooms instead of the south exposure on which he lectured glibly. The second floor north, a large sitting room, directly overlooked the windows of the Goold gallery.

"See that house opposite? That's where James H. Goold lived," babbitted the young realtor. He paused abruptly, remembering that the murder might be bad for business.

The rooms were precisely as Callahan had said—absolutely empty. They were dusty, too. But still the dignity of the old New York house clung, the high ceilings, the walnut wainscoting running, at times with scroll work, all the way round. But the bath rooms were new and tiled in the finest modern manner. Very exclusive house property indeed, as the agent suavely insisted.

"I guess I see your friend," announced the young man from his post at a window and dashed down the stairs. It was then that Ross proceeded to open every door that normally probably nobody thought of opening—one of these was an electric switchboard box in the wall and the other a medicine cabinet with a mirrored door which was flush with the bathroom wall.

In the shelves of the medicine cabinet there was only one object. But it gave Ross a thrill as he swiftly transferred it from the shelf to the slanting pocket of his topcoat.

It was a powerful field-glass of foreign make.

For an instant it was a question in Ross's mind whether or not to inform Callahan of his find. Circumstances, he decided, must dictate.

"Why, hello!" said Callahan somewhat sourly. "Got ahead of me, did you?"

"Just a few moments," the young man spoke up cheerily. "No use waiting on the stoop like a bill-collector or plainclothesman. But I kept an eye out for you, sir."

"Oh, yeh?" said Callahan, and the young man wondered whether this man was as exclusive as he ought to be for this exclusive property. Their client, Forbes, he knew, would demand the strictest references.

"Well, what d'you think of it?" Callahan turned to Ross.

"Very well indeed. This is the upstairs living room. This is the north bath-room. Take a look at the bedrooms."

"Yeh, sure," said Callahan, and the young realtor wondered more than ever. These men did not address each
other by name; one appeared a man of culture and the
other, well—could they be expecting to make a gambling
house of this? This man who said, "Oh, yeh" had something of that air about him. Nothing doing if that was the
case. This was Cullen Forbes's property.

"I wish," said Ross, "you would show my friend the
downstairs rooms. Noble rooms, not to say palatial," he
added to Callahan. The young realtor was more than ever
convinced of the sinister possibilities in these potential
lessees. Callahan accompanied the youth somewhat reluctantly down the stairway. Ross, was no sooner alone than
he whipped out the field-glass with his gloved hand and
trained it upon the gallery windows across the street.

The shade was half way down over the window that was
his objective, but with the powerful lenses he could see
even in the obscure light Goold's desk, chair and all that
portion of the room. The glass in the gallery windows was
unusually good and offered no distortion.

"So this was Mr. Forbes's post of observation," reflected
Ross. "Childish and somewhat despicable, but still a long
way from murder."

He returned the glasses to his pocket and met Callahan
returning briskly up the stairs.

"Looks good to me," said Callahan. And then the realtor felt called upon to clear the air. He was going to have
no misunderstandings.

"Make a very fine home for somebody," he said, and
redundantly added, "for strictly residential purposes."

"Oh, yeh?" said Callahan. "Well, let's go and think
it over," he suggested to Ross, "unless you want to see
any more." Ross was satisfied with what he had seen and
as usual, when Ross spoke, the realtor's hopes rose once

more. They left him at the door and walked westward. The realtor turned toward Madison Avenue.

"Make anything of it?" demanded Callahan impatiently.

"I made this," Ross drew forth the glasses and held them up for inspection. "Very powerful field-glass with the best German lenses."

"What d'you know about that!" exulted Callahan. Then his face darkened. "Might have given me a chance to look across with them, up there in the house," he muttered.

"I thought of that. But it couldn't have been done without admitting that young man into our confidence. So I did the looking when you were inspecting the palatial rooms below."

"You were right at that," acceded Callahan. "What did you see?"

"Goold's desk and chair and that end of the room with a fair degree of clearness. Almost I believe I could have recognized a face there."

Callahan threw him a slanting glance. Surely, this was no defense of Forbes. There was no guile apparent in the face of Ross. He wished he could get the low-down on this professor bird.

"Certainly had a mighty strong interest in Goold's doings, did our friend Forbes, wouldn't you say so?" He was still watching Ross's features.

"Speaks for itself," nodded Ross. "And shows us, Inspector, doesn't it, that not all the foolishness of life is confined to the more humble individuals like ourselves."

"Humble, hell," said Callahan. "I wouldn't care to be in that baby's shoes right now for quite a bunch of his jack."

"Neither should I," agreed Ross pleasantly. "He is in for some unpleasant moments."

"I'll say so," said Callahan with emphasis. "Best piece of evidence in the case so far. Have to be a mighty sure substitute that would save him from being tried for the murder."

"I cannot go with you quite so far as that," Ross answered almost dreamily.

"What!" cried Callahan. "Mean to tell me a baby wouldn't see that?"

"Far from it, Inspector. A baby would undoubtedly see it that way. But not hardened sinners like you and I."

"You'll have to show me," Callahan laughed mirthlessly, but with great security in his tones.

"I'll do it easily, Inspector. We'll begin at the beginning. Incidentally, let's go into the Park and borrow a bench. Or those people here at Fifty-ninth and Fifth Avenue will think we are quarrelling." They crossed the street and struck into a pathway. Soon they found an empty bench.

"Consider, first of all," began Ross, "the fact that we found the glasses. Foolish as that little enterprise of Forbes's was, it bespeaks a carelessness that even the stupid criminal and the commonplace could hardly be guilty of. In fact, it argues a sense of security that is pastorally unimaginative, if you will, but certainly based on innocence, don't you agree?"

"I don't know whether I do or not," mumbled Callahan under his bristling mustache. "But let's hear the rest—if any."

"Consider further—what did Forbes want from Goold?"

"His wife's love letters to Goold—that's what he wanted!" cried Callahan triumphantly.

"Precisely—his wife's letters. He knew of their existence in Goold's possession and he wanted to get them and to delete them from the world. He had offered, you remember, to burn them unread in Goold's presence. His motive, I grant you, was a burning jealousy of the schoolboy type.

But above all, he wanted to speed them out of existence, so they would never again trouble the wife whom he loved, or break through into possible publicity and scandalize all concerned. Do you agree, Inspector?"

"Yes. I agree," Callahan enunciated slowly weighing his words, and watching Ross narrowly.

"Good! Then we are at one. Need I go further?"

"You bet you do!" grinned Callahan. "See, that only shows how crazy Forbes was to get those letters away from Goold. Nothing would stop him!"

"Yes, something would stop him! If he killed Goold those letters would eventually be discovered and almost certainly be made public! Don't you see, however much he wanted these letters he would do anything rather than kill Goold, unless he was absolutely certain of getting the letters by doing so. Otherwise, his interest would be rather in protecting Goold than in destroying him. For as you, or someone, said earlier in this case, Goold was Goold, and no blackmailer in any possible public sense, or a man who would carelessly risk his reputation."

Callahan's face clouded. For an instant he gnawed at his lower lip and gazed off into space.

"All the same," he said doggedly, "the District Attorney can make a pretty good case against that bird Forbes on just about what we got."

"Possibly," murmured Ross as though he had already dismissed the matter. "And Forbes's lawyers would shoot the case to pieces in about fifteen minutes of elementary argument and direct examination."

"Hell, Professor!" cried Callahan. "You make me miserable!"

Ross laughed. "It hurts me more than it does you, Inspector. But I should be a poor friend if I encouraged you in the ways of folly, in the ways good detectives should not go."

"All the same I want those glasses," declared Callahan.

"No one has a better right to them," Ross handed them over.

"I don't know, I don't know," Callahan murmured as if to himself. "I'll have to put it all up to the Commissioner and the D.A. They got to decide. That Forbes guy was too close to the murder, even if he didn't do it himself, for my comfort. I for one, would feel a lot better if I had him under lock and key."

"And you would regret it to your dying day," said Ross.

"Have to think it over," said Callahan rising from the bench.

"I would," said Ross.

"You're not going away anywhere, Professor—be in town, won't you?"

"I expect to be, Inspector. Command me."

"At that, that bird of mine was stupid not to have found those glasses," muttered Callahan as though regretting that Ross had had a hand in the business at all. "Anyway," he added, "I owe you one for that, Professor. Let me know anything I can do."

"I mean to, Inspector—very soon."

The two men separated amicably and went their various ways—Callahan downtown to his office and Ross to his favorite Russian restaurant in Fifty-seventh Street and then to his apartment. Both found messages awaiting them.

Callahan had upon his desk a sealed memorandum from Sergeant Burke to the effect that the man watching Forbes reported him as having taken a taxi at Forty-second Street and Lexington Avenue, upon emerging from the subway and driven to the empty house opposite the Goold gallery. After entering the house Forbes had reappeared a few minutes later with an expression described as "glum and strained." He then drove uptown to his apartment.

"Strained!" thought Callahan with a faint grin. "I'll bet he is strained. He'll be more strained before I am through with him." And he gave orders for redoubled watchfulness as to the movements of Forbes.

Ross found a message simply giving a telephone number and asking him to call. He knew the number to be Lorna's and he called her at once. It was then a few minutes past two.

Cross, who answered, said that Miss Storey had just left the house; that she would return soon, but in any case, could Professor Ross spare the time to have dinner with Miss Storey that evening at seven. Professor Ross could and Cross imperturbably as usual answered, "Thank you, sir."

22
Cullen Forbes, Gent

"If Jimmie doesn't communicate something of importance very soon," reflected Ross, "my offhand promise to show something by the coming week may prove abortive."

There was, however, in his consciousness that deep intuitive sense of security that he counted more important than facts. Callahan, Wells, Burton—they were already choked with facts, but the more facts they had the more at sea they appeared to be. Callahan, and for that matter the others, found it now all but irresistible to pin their hopes on Forbes.

Would the additional fact of the field-glass finally decide Burton to order the arrest of Cullen Forbes, wondered Ross? Lucky that Forbes was an exceptionally prominent citizen.

It was characteristic of Ross that, finding himself for the first time in days with a bit of leisure before him, he dismissed the entire case from his mind and opened William Alexander Percy's book "Sappho in Levkas." The love of Sappho for the shepherd lad Phaon in the masterly verse of this modern poet, full of restrained beauty, enchanted him like some new strange atmosphere blown from an unknown shore:

"To me, my kinship with immortal things
    Hath been too clear revealed that I should watch
    With willingness my retrogression to the clay
    And baseness mortals own as parent. . . .
    With all my spirits I have ever fought
    Life's battles; nor testing conflict shunned
    When righteousness made part."

"How beautifully that expressed the vocation of the detective!" reflected Ross with the amusement of one who knew its real meaning.

He was interrupted by the modern herald, with a tinkle instead of a horn, the telephone. His face, as he listened assumed an expression of grave surprise.

The speaker at the other end was Cullen Forbes.

"It happens that I am free, Mr. Forbes," he finally said, "and it would be a pleasure to come to you. But just now I should think that a most indiscreet proceeding."

Forbes responded with his usual energy that he "didn't care a damn about those people down there," that he knew he was being spied upon, that it made no difference to him, and that if Professor Ross would remain in his rooms for the next half hour, he would like very much to come to see him.

Ross reflected for a moment and then, with something of resignation in his tone, replied that he would be here if Mr. Forbes desired to come.

Reading poetry became more difficult then. But, as a matter of fact, Forbes appeared in considerably less than half an hour.

His greetings were brisk, genial, but with no attempt to be humorous.

"You'll have to excuse me for breaking in on you like this, Professor Ross," he went on, "but I'm fed up with the stupidity of those people. Five minutes' talk with a sensible man would be worth a lot to me."

Ross invited him to take a chair. Forbes mechanically held out a cigar case, nodded absently when Ross declined and proceeded to clip the end of his own cigar with fingers that belied somewhat the carelessness he assumed. Without a doubt Forbes was in the grip of a nervous agitation.

"First of all," he began with a long puff at his slender cigar, "do you know about that field-glass?"

"I do," nodded Ross and he admired the man the more for his brisk shearing away of ancient history and unnecessary detail.

"Good!" said Forbes. "That makes it unnecessary for me to go back to the year one. I know they think I am a damn fool and that the glass gives them a case. Well, I am a damn fool for leaving the glass there—but they're a long way from a case. Who found the glass by the way, did they tell you—and are you at liberty to tell me?"

"As a matter of fact I found it myself," smiled Ross.

"You did!" exclaimed Forbes, and his hearty laugh at least partly explained to Ross why Sheila was so evidently bound up in him. "Well, that beats the devil. And here I walk into the lion's den! I know you're a man of sense, but I wouldn't have come even to you if Sheila hadn't been at me for days. She thinks you're our best friend. I hope she's right. But it's that glass I was fool enough to forget that finally made me listen to her."

"Sheila is quite right, Mr. Forbes," began Ross gently. "I am your friend. But precisely what do you wish me to do now?"

"That's the deuce of it, Professor Ross. I don't know. I reckon they'll think that glass is damning evidence against me. Thing I want to know is, do you think so?"

"Not damning, Mr. Forbes, since you ask me. But it is evidence of sorts. It is at least unfortunate, you will admit."

"Admit! I'll proclaim it! Unfortunate—not to say stupid. But that doesn't say I killed Jim Goold, by a long shot—by any shot!" And he added a mirthless laugh. "Though mind, I don't know but at times I think he deserved it."

Ross remained silent, almost unconsciously appraising the character of the man before him.

"But you don't think I killed him, do you?" pressed Forbes.

"Not only do I not think so, but I have tried by what I believe to be unimpeachable logic to prove to the police that the very fact of the finding of the glass is against any theory of your guilt." The rising inflection on the word "any" reverberated gratefully in the troubled heart of the other.

That Forbes's somewhat dubious coolness was assumed was proved by his passing his handkerchief swiftly over his forehead and immediately pocketing it again as though he had been caught in some form of self-betrayal.

"Then that's that," he said. "I guess Sheila is right about you after all."

"But you are aware, Mr. Forbes, are you not, that I am not the police—not any of the authorities?"

"No? I thought you were!"

"I am merely an outside consultant. And just at the moment somewhat in bad odor with those authorities."

"Oh," and Forbes frowned unconsciously, "in bad odor, eh? Not on our account, I hope?"

"Partly, perhaps. But that doesn't matter. I shall live it down when I find the murderer—or the murderess."

"What!" cried Forbes jumping from his chair, and for an instant all the color was swept out of his face. "You think it might have been a woman?"

"Just as likely as a man. Our sex, Mr. Forbes, has no monopoly of crime."

"Oh," Forbes almost sighed, and by contrast his normally pallid cheeks now seemed almost flushed.

"You mean that generally? I thought—I thought you had someone specifically in mind." Ross was watching him closely losing not a trace of the play of emotion in this highly sensitive face that with some gallantry sported the mask of imperturbability.

"Mr. Forbes," began Ross with a quiet persuasiveness, as he lit a cigarette, "since you have taken the trouble to come and talk with me, why not let us celebrate the occasion by your actually telling me something?"

"Telling you what?" demanded Forbes with a sort of startled caution.

"Telling me something that you know and I do not."

"What do you mean, sir?"

"I mean, what you saw with those field-glasses at the various times when you trained them on Goold's desk through the window—everything!—and especially on the afternoon when Goold met his death. Don't you see, Mr. Forbes, how helpful that would be?"

A volley of colorful and diversified oaths broke from Forbes as he leaped, like a suddenly liberated mechanism, from his chair and groped for his hat, which, however, was at some distance from him in the little vestibule. His face was now all but purple.

"Hell!" he added like the final rumble of loud thunder. "I thought I was speaking to a friend and a gentleman. I admit I behaved like a fool and a cad. I had strong provocation. I am sorry, and I want to forget it. But to chew it all over again, like a dog returning to his vomit, me a Peeping Tom—bad enough, I admit! But I'm damned if I'll say anything about it. That's all of that, I guess, Professor Ross. Let 'em pin the murder on me if they want to. They'll have a tough job. If they had the brains of a rabbit, they would have found out long ago."

"Whether they will or not," Ross spoke quietly, "I don't know, Mr. Forbes. But I assure you I mean to find out. For Sheila's sake, if for no other—but for me there are other considerations. But then you see I am not a Southern—I am a mongrel, rather," he checked himself against offense. "We are actuated by different conceptions of duty. One of my duties in life is to help eradicate crime."

"Go to it, Professor," returned Forbes almost jauntily, "and I wish you luck. I will say, I think Sheila is right. You are a friend—and a very square shooter. I—I apologize for my stupid show of temper." And he held out his hand. Ross took and held it for a moment wondering more than ever how this adolescent-minded adult had managed to accumulate so large a fortune.

"Nothing to apologize for," smiled Ross. "Perhaps this meeting was necessary to both of us."

"I wish—I wish—" began Forbes almost gently for him. Then abruptly he gave a jerk to his head, indicating that he could not go on.

"Oh, don't worry," laughed Ross. "You have told me a great deal—and I am sincerely grateful."

Forbes looked startled for an instant, then abruptly he moved toward the door. His expression, more plainly than any words, said:

"I had better leave before I lose my self-respect."

In the queer boyish pride of the man lay all the key to his conduct; and his pride, reflected Ross, must have been a sorely wounded thing after he married Sheila simply because his passion for her had driven him past all resistance.

From his window Ross could see Forbes's taxi driving off; he could also see another taxi rolling along fifty yards behind with a certain discreet carelessness that was unmistakable. Forbes was being watched very carefully, and no one could blame Callahan for so watching him. For the knowledge this former rival of Goold's held concerning the murder was unique, whether or not he himself was the guilty person.

"And that knowledge," Ross reflected sadly, "must somehow be established without his assistance."

To Ross it appeared a positive and regrettable waste that genuine first-rate knowledge of a crime should thus lie fallow and unused. "Murder will out!"—ridiculous. It has to be dug for like radium.

The tranquil afternoon he had anticipated was turning out not so tranquil after all. Nevertheless he was determined to salvage at least a portion of it. And one of the ways of orienting his thoughts was to sit before his bookshelves, draw book after book from its space and turn the pages almost absently, so that titles, chapter-heads, page headings, opening lines, phrases, spoke to his subconscious mind, setting up currents of reflection. It amounted to a sort of assisted day-dreaming. Stekel on Cleptomania, some of the cases set forth in the stately prose of Roughead, even the elementary texts of Hans Gross—he was reminded of Emerson's dictum: If the authors knew how he read them, they would detest him. He used them as valves to open the currents of his own thoughts, then threw them aside.

Emerging as from a dream he walked over to the tinkling telephone with an intuitive certainty as to the appellant at the other end.

"Yes, Inspector," he said. "I knew you would call me. You are interested in my visitor of this afternoon. How did I guess it? . . . By virtue of irrepressible genius. Considering that you have men watching his every movement, it would be something of a reflection on you if you didn't know he had been here . . . No, I am sorry to say he didn't, Inspector . . . Ask him? I literally begged him for anything, anything at all. Like a headstrong boy. . . . No there I can't agree with you. . . . We shall get what we need without him. . . . Glad to cheer you, Inspector . . . Oh, yes, yes. He knew we had the glass. He is no expert in crime. . . . Quite. . . . Nothing has happened to change my belief. By the middle of the week we ought to see daylight . . . The same to you Inspector. Goodbye."

"I don't wonder," thought Ross with sombre amusement after he had hung up the receiver, "I don't wonder they call Callahan's most important department the Homicide Bureau. Their business is to slay their victims, of whom I am one, with endless unnecessary questions."

23
Jimmie Sends a Hurry Call

"With a bit of luck," reflected Ross as he sauntered through the Park swinging his stick, "this evening ought to yield something."

He was on his way to Sixty-second Street. And though the wind was easterly with a chill promise of rain in the air, the mere thought of seeing Lorna put him in good spirits. He was not in evening dress, but as a concession to ceremony he wore a dark blue suit under his gray topcoat which was exceedingly becoming to him. Notwithstanding his day's activities, he felt all the cheerful zest of twenty-five and decided that he must not show it. He was going to what was after all a house of mourning.

Lorna was of the sort, however, that does not parade grief for its effect upon others, unless those others would be scandalized by its absence. She was in a charming evening frock of jade-green silk, and the radiance of her expression when she greeted him conveyed nothing of hushed solemnity. Impossible for her not to be always herself and always natural. Yet she had that day been through an unpleasant experience.

"Very kind of you, Lorna," Ross murmured upon entering, "to ask a lonely bachelor to share your crust."

"So lonely," said Lorna, "that half New York, including the police department, is camping on his doorstep."

"I have no doorstep, Lorna. It's my only good chair they choose for their camping ground. But company is only company when you seek it."

"Well, I've sought you shamelessly," she said, "and since you won't let me sit in your chair, you must sit in mine."

By this time they were in Lorna's delightful sitting room and Ross settled in the deep chair indicated with the luxurious sigh of the hind let loose. Lorna was telling him of the visit that day insisted upon by Mr. Laimbeer, of Laimbeer, Strong and Laimbeer, Goold's attorneys. The old lawyer had decided that the will must be read to the family and procured the necessary permission from Dr. Humphreys to read it in Mrs. Goold's bedroom at eleven-thirty, when the invalid was at her best and brightest. "Just about the time," reflected Ross, "when I was finding Forbes's field-glass in the empty house opposite."

"But Aunt Julia is not at her best and brightest now, poor darling," concluded Lorna.

"Was it so very shattering?"

Lorna told him that it was. It was a strange will. Usual enough in a way. Numerous bequests to institutions, charitable organizations, hospitals, the Museum and King's College.

"Surely, he didn't cut you off?" put in Ross.

"No, of course not. But instead of making Aunt Julia the residuary legatee, as they call it, leaving her the house and everything, he left it all to me—which you can see is very embarrassing."

"And your aunt?"

"Oh, she is provided for, of course. It's all legal enough, but so unlike Uncle Jim, I can't understand it."

"How did she take it?" he asked gently.

"Like the angel she is. She has no relations of her own excepting a couple of elderly cousins somewhere in New England. She wanted Mr. Laimbeer to draw a will at once

leaving all her share to me, too. I couldn't bear it"—
Lorna's lips quivered for a moment. "I—I told her that
the—the house and everything in it was hers, as long as
she lived."

"And now she feels badly?"

"Oh, it upset her a good deal—the whole thing—naturally. But she is resting now. I suppose I shouldn't have
bored you with all this, Professor Ross, but I have been so
miserable and I wanted to—"

Ross took her hand gently and kissed it.

"You did exactly right, dear child, as you always do."

"I suppose I am still a brat," she laughed through her
tears, "masquerading as a grown-up."

"By a judicious estimate," he answered her, "probably
the most delightful brat in the world."

"Gross exaggeration," she smiled returning to her normal mood. "And I am not a brat! But anyway, you can't
know how glad I am you are here to be bored."

Ross smiled and the entrance of Cross with the service
put an end for the time being to intimate conversation.

No sooner were they alone, however, than Lorna eagerly enquired for any new developments in the case. Ross's
invariable practice being to withhold nothing that was
already an established fact, gave her a brief resume of the
discovery of the field-glass in the vacant house opposite
and of Forbes's visit to his rooms the preceding afternoon.
Lorna listened spellbound, and then she looked grave.

"Doesn't that show how little we really know people?"
she said. "Mr. Forbes is the last person I could have asso-
ciated with anything of the sort. Human nature is very
complicated."

"Even truer, Lorna, is to say human nature simply *is*.
Every one of us has besides his workaday public self a
sub-cellar self that makes material for clinics, prisons,
asylums, law-courts, policemen and novelists."

"Oh, and that reminds me," she cried. "I meant to tell you the minute you came. Our nurses are being shadowed!"

"The nurses?" repeated Ross in some perplexity. "Now I wonder whether that is a demarche of my friend Callahan or of the District Attorney's! I would give a good deal to know."

"I don't know, of course," she said, "and I don't suppose they do. But Miss Baker is in what is technically called a state about it. 'Decent people can't call their souls their own. Just because a person has to earn their living, can't cross the street without being watched'—and all that kind of thing. You can imagine."

"I can," he nodded. "And Miss Kelly?"

"She is not absolutely sure. Being followed by men is less of a novelty with her. But she thinks she also is being shadowed. I suggested to both of them that it's a temporary condition and that they'd best say nothing about it."

"Admirably done, Lorna. As always, admirable. My friend Callahan wants all the secrets of my life, but he tells me little in return. However," he added with a sudden abstraction, "I may be doing him an injustice."

"You mean somebody else may be watching them?"

"Who can tell?" he turned to his more reserved manner. "Where there are so many cooks, the broth is bound to be eclectic."

Lorna scrutinized his face closely and asked him no further questions. She only added:

"Of course Miss Kelly's spooky atmosphere is running through the house like a grippe-cold. Everybody is having it. Two of the maids have given me notice. There are times when even I feel the danger of succumbing."

"So much the better," he answered enigmatically.

After this brief excursion into the bearings of the case, the evening became one of those delightful occasions

which these two, notwithstanding their discrepancy in
years, could make by their mere presence together. They
discussed Van Dine and Proust and Dostoievsky; the ethnic peculiarities of the Tuaregs, and the social customs of
the Trobriand Islanders. They capped limericks, remarked
on the sameness of the newspaper columnists and yet their
personal addiction to reading them. Finally they even
recalled poor forgotten Jimmie Trumbull.

"What is so appealing about Jimmie," said Lorna, "is
his enchanting youth."

"I expected that, Lorna," laughed Ross. "Every now and
then you talk as though you were a hundred years old. My
aging proximity is responsible for that."

"There are times," returned Lorna, "when you seem
younger than Jimmie."

"That leaves you the universal mother of us all—the
most ancient instinct in woman. That is the way woman
was worshipped in prehistoric times, as the universal
mother. Even nowadays—I came across a tribe—"

What that tribe was never came to light, for at that
instant the telephone seemed to shatter the welkin and all
discussion, and Lorna was greeting Jimmie.

"Yes, Professor Ross is here," she was saying, "but how
did you guess, Jimmiekins?"

"I have been trying to get him for half an hour," was
the answer, "and against my better judgment I concluded
he must be with you."

"Against your better what, did you say?"

"Against my jealousy, if you really want to know. My
first impulse was to ring your number." With a laugh she
handed over the instrument to Ross.

"Listen, Prof, you've got to come up here tomorrow, see
what I mean?"

"You seem to imply that I ought to come up there, if I
understand you, James."

"No fooling—things are ripening fast. I guess a good time will be had by all."

"I begin to comprehend, Jimmie."

"There is a train gets here at twelve tomorrow, just in time for lunch. Do I meet you?"

"You do indeed, James. But my duties—you know I cannot stay long." Jimmie's laughter in the telephone betrayed an excited state.

"You'll stay just long enough, I promise you. But I hope it won't be raining cats and dogs, the way it is now."

"You really have something to—"

"You don't know the half of it," quickly interrupted Jimmie, mysterious either by compulsion or sheer exuberance of spirit. Then his voice was suddenly intensely serious. "There's no time to lose."

"I shall be there, James."

"Bring—bring—" Jimmie added, then he paused uncertainly.

"Perfectly, James, I shall bring two. Goodbye."

"So long," murmured Jimmie, "if you know what I mean," and hung up.

Lorna gazed at Ross enquiringly, for his face was suddenly expressing a gravity remote from the apparent jocular tone of the conversation.

"What is it poor Jimmie wants you to bring him?" she could not help enquiring. "I thought they supplied everything at the Ali Baba."

"Everything but automatics," murmured Ross, "at least I must assume so."

"He asked you to do that, over the telephone?"

"Not exactly. He could not quite bring himself to utter the word. But I guessed what he meant."

It was now Lorna's turn to look grave.

"If you two are going on an errand as dangerous as that, then I ought to go with you," she said simply.

"On no account, Lorna. We need you here far more than we need you there."

"But suppose—suppose—"

Ross interrupted her:

"Life is full of risks, Lorna. The one way is to meet them smiling. You run risks here every day."

"I?—I have hardly stirred out of the house since Uncle Jim went."

"I know that. Is it your habit to lock your doors at night?" he asked with what struck her as a strange irrelevance. She looked at him steadily for a few moments.

"I have never done that so long as I have lived in this house. And I have never been afraid of spooks. Why do you ask me that, Professor Ross?"

"Because from now on I wish you would do so," he said with quiet distinctness.

"Whom is it I ought to be afraid of?" she all but whispered. A tense silence hung for a moment between them so that the ticking of the tiny platinum watch on Lorna's wrist was distinctly audible. Finally, as though he had carefully chosen the words he meant to say, Ross spoke:

"For the next few days—the Unknown Person who killed your uncle."

"You think he will come back?" she murmured faintly.

"I think it extremely probable."

"But I can't see why you suddenly came to such a conclusion. What gave you the idea?"

"You did yourself." Lorna appeared bewildered. "I am not trying to mystify you, Lorna. But when you first told me the nurses were being watched, my mind ran upon certain lines. Since then, however, I have seen light in another direction. Please don't ask me any reason now, Lorna, only I beg of you, do as I ask."

"I will, of course," she agreed with a return to her usual blitheness, "and I won't talk about it any more."

She joined him at the window, which he approached from the telephone table. He was peering outward at the parted curtain.

"I had best be going," he said.

"I had no idea it was raining so hard. You can't think of going now," said Lorna.

"I fear this isn't going to stop in a moment. It has settled down to a steady downpour. Besides, it's eleven-thirty and I must be keeping Cross up."

"I have a brilliant idea," she cried with sudden animation. "It's such a horrid night, why shouldn't you stay here? Heaven knows there is plenty of room. I'll ring for Cross and he'll steer you to a room. He'll find whatever you need."

"That would be charming." He was wondering whether necessary though it was, his warning had seriously frightened Lorna. "I have that train to make somewhere at about eleven tomorrow."

"I always have breakfast at eight-thirty," she met him. "Besides, Cross will call you at any hour you like." His hesitation was only momentary.

"I shall stay with pleasure, Lorna," he answered quite firmly. "But don't regard me as a watchman. Lock your doors as I advised precisely as though I did not exist."

"I have lived here eleven years," she answered lightly, "and no one ever tried to steal me. I have been disgustingly safe." Her eyes, however, were shining. She suddenly felt her existence in this large mournful house powerfully buttressed, and all at once she was overcome by the vast gulf that lay between being and having in the world of man. Ross was poor as the world counted riches, but in himself he was a well-spring of life.

They chatted for a few minutes longer with the deep intimate confidence that was proving more and more a profound delight to both of them. Then they said good

night and Cross, duly appearing like some carefully con-
structed god of this machine, piloted Ross to a room two
doors farther at the end of the hallway.

"Tell me, Cross," Ross turned to him as he brought the
necessary nightgear, "are you a good sleeper?"

"Exceptionally good, sir. At first, after the tragedy I
was a bit restless. But now I sleep my seven hours like a
top, if I may say so, sir."

"Do you ever hear anyone moving about the house
during the night?"

"Moving about? I can't say I do, sir. I sleep on the
fourth story, almost directly above you, sir."

"And those nights when you were wakeful, did you ever
notice anything of the sort?"

"No, sir. Yes—I did though, come to think of it. I was
a bit nervy then, and I remember hearing someone moving
about below. I opened my door and looked down the well
of the stairs. We keep dim lights in the halls. But I could
see it was only the nurse. So I went to bed again. I lock up
very carefully sir, naturally."

"Naturally," agreed Ross. "I was merely curious. Oh, by
the way, you haven't forgotten a razor for me?"

"No, sir. You will find everything in the bathroom."

"Excellent, Cross, and thank you. If you give my door
a tap at eight o'clock, I shall try to be grateful."

"Very good, sir. Good night, sir."

"Good night to you, Cross. And whatever you and I say
to each other is private, isn't it?"

"Absolutely, sir."

"Good. And if you can avoid mentioning my presence
here, so much the better."

"Everybody is in bed, sir."

Whatever the work Jimmie had in store for him on the
morrow, Ross nevertheless resolved to be a light sleeper
that night. The bit of luck he had hoped for earlier in

the evening had been as good as presented to him upon a platter by the god of autumnal rains. He did not mean to neglect it. Had chance not brought it to him, he would have been obliged to invent it.

"But chance is, in her way, a very courteous little deity," he reflected; "only how she does love to be recognized in a crowd. The little jade!"

There was no transom over his door. He turned the lights on full in his room and stepped out into the hall to see if any sign of the illumination was discernible through chinks or seams. Goold's material house, however, had been better built than his spiritual. For all Ross could discern from the hall, his blazing room might have been filled with the palpable darkness of Egypt. The hall itself now was not so much illumined as barely saved from total darkness by a faint blue bulb of small candle power in a wall socket, beneath which was a switch that lighted two clusters in the ceiling.

"The comforts of the rich," smiled Ross as he re-entered his room and softly closed the door.

The bedside books in the particular guest room occupied by Ross were not many, but those he found there were choice. They appeared to run to intimate philosophies and private journals: Montaigne, Rabelais, Amiel, Bashkirtseff and Barbellion. He looked into various, but finally selected none of them for fear they might put him to sleep. Fortunately there was a copy among them of Stendhal's "Le Rouge et le Noir."

That great novel packed with life he could reread again and again with no diminution of interest, even excitement. The fortunes of Julien kept him absorbed until past two o'clock after which he extinguished his lights and, moving softly in the slippers and dressing gown provided by Cross, he opened his door less than an inch and ensconced himself in a chair in such a position as to be able to

command a survey of a considerable portion of the hallway. That was where he meant to keep his vigil for the
remainder of the night.

The house was still. And the rays of the blue bulb shed
a faint eerie light as in some dim grotto filled with fables
of monsters. A sentence of Stendhal's ran in his head.

"A novel is a mirror walking in the highway; now it
reflects the blue sky to your vision, now the mud of the
puddles on the road." And the same appeared true of this
case—in this house, under this very roof. Upon the one
hand, a creation of grace and beauty, like Lorna, and upon
the other, some foul diabolic thing plotting and boiling
with fiendish criminality, some distorted soul stalking
prey.

He had much ado in keeping himself from going to
sleep. The blue light of the hall was in itself a soporific.
After what seemed to be hours, his acute hearing caught
the sound of a faint rustle.

Presently a figure in white stood outlined in the dim
light.

It paused and listened, then moved forward again and
came to a halt before Lorna's door. The white dress fortunately reflected what little light there was.

It was the traditional nurse's habit of stiff white.

Again the woman listened, then very gently she tried
the knob of Lorna's sitting room! The door was locked.

Overcome apparently by a sudden trepidation, the figure in white, as though propelled by an internal force,
went gliding noiselessly down the hall.

"Then that is that," Ross smiled grimly to himself as he
wiped drops of perspiration from his forehead.

The entire episode, a matter of a few seconds, seemed
to have partaken of the duration of eternity. And yet, once
ended, it had about it a dreamlike quality as though it had
all come to pass somewhere in the chambers of his mind.

"I think I may safely go to bed now," he reflected. "To bed, perchance to sleep—ay, there's the rub. But no matter. It will be a night well spent."

The following morning at eight-thirty, Lorna, who disregarded even Amalie's questioning glances in her pleasure at having Professor Ross to breakfast, remarked that his sleep must have been exceptionally sound since he appeared so fresh and rested.

"I have always slept well," he grinned quizzically, "and especially so last night, because I felt sure you were carrying out my—let us say, imperative advice."

"You mean about the door?" He nodded. "Oh, I shall always sleep under lock and key now until you release me from my promise. What sort of a Watson would I be if I did anything but obey?"

"No sort of a Watson at all," he agreed.

"Or asked questions Sherlock did not want to answer?"

"Unthinkable." Then more gravely he added: "And my last charge is eternal vigilance."

"How long do you expect to stay up there with Jimmie?" she asked.

"Not long, Lorna. I dare not. Jimmie will have to carry on on his own—if that should be necessary. That angle has its importance, but—in any case, I shall be in town tomorrow, I hope in time for my lecture. By the way, before I go would it be possible for me to see the night nurse? I should like to ask her one or two questions."

Cross, however, when summoned declared that Miss Kelly had gone for the day. "But Miss Baker has come in sir," he added.

"I shall not trouble her now," said Ross. "When does Miss Kelly come on again, at seven?"

"At seven o'clock this evening, sir."

Lorna gazed at Ross with a mingled expression of curiosity, apprehension, and excitement. Her eyes were bright with queries but aloud she said nothing.

24
Jimmie Clicks

In the brief train journey to Harrison Ross had at least half an hour to collect his thoughts and to survey briefly the high points in the case.

In swift cinematographic progress the events and the testimony of the various persons passed through his mind, and each separate item seemed to stamp its own relative value on the chain of his deductions.

"Regrettable my having to leave town even for a few hours," he reflected. "There is Forbes and there is—Lorna."

Acutely he saw the possibility of Callahan, Wells and Burton putting their heads together and making some flagrant arrest that might loom sensationally in the newspapers, but thereby radically wrecking the perfect unfoldment of the case. Even that, however, was less dangerous than the peril by which Lorna was encompassed. Her courage and her radiance—a splendid person, Lorna, poised and ageless, the stuff of which greatness is made!

Though a pallid sun illumined the landscape along the right of way, the foliage of trees and shrubs had that stricken air heralding the death of the year. The haze in the atmosphere portended the coming of winter. Ross had lived in all climates and was possessed of an organism singularly adaptable to changes. Nevertheless, the declining season and the previous night of vigil and tension

219

brought a shadow of depression to his spirits. The rhythm of the rumbling train fell into a melancholy accompaniment to his thoughts.

"Idiot!" he exclaimed rousing himself. "There is still plenty to do on this case and here I am allowing my thoughts to wool-gather like a schoolboy's." And silently he laughed to himself.

He leaped from the train as it pulled into the station and scanned the platform for Jimmie. Jimmie had already espied him and was moving rapidly toward him. It was evident Jimmie felt vastly relieved to have Ross in person near him once again.

"I didn't bring a car," began Jimmie in businesslike manner seizing Ross's small suitcase, "because I thought you might like a little exercise after the effete city life, and it's only half a mile walk, and anyway I want more than two minutes to talk to you before you get there."

"Right on all counts, James, but I see no reason why you should carry my bag. I am still able-bodied, however effete the city."

"Oh, that," Jimmie dismissed the suggestion contemptuously. "Let me spill the big news."

"Is it big?"

"Yes—that is, it got big yesterday evening before I phoned you. But let me begin at the beginning."

"Capital place to begin, James."

"Well, you know when I arrived here it was some job to hit on the right personality I wanted to assume in order to get in right with Erzeroff, and with everybody else. To tell you the truth, I thought at first, or not exactly thought, suspected, rather,—that you just sent me up here to get rid of me."

"Unworthy of you, my son, and untrue. Why this painful sense of inferiority?"

"Well, anyway, I don't think so now."

In his excitement Jimmie seemed unaware of the small suitcase in his hands, of the autumnal landscape with its still gorgeous colors, of the carpet of dead leaves underfoot along the country road they had taken.

"I don't think so now," he ran on, "because pretty big stuff seems to be breaking. There was nothing at all doing at first. Erzeroff at the first meal when we sat down at table—there were only seven guests and we looked like a small dinner party—Erzeroff, I say, looked at me as though I might be one of the lower animals. Just an American kid, you know, without any sense, or knowledge or experience—that's what I seemed to him."

Ross managed to conceal a smile at Jimmie's evident chagrin, even in retrospect, to be so misjudged.

"You see, he, this Erzeroff, is quite a fellow. Been everywhere, done everything, lived with all kinds of people—and he's still not so old you know—about your own age"—whereat Ross laughed outright. "I mean quite young," Jimmie amended hastily, but refused to take further notice of his own clumsiness.

"But you see," he went on, "I didn't shove my oar in too far—answered when I was spoken to—as much to the point as I could—you know. Well, it wasn't long, next morning in fact, he suggested a walk. I tried to be on hand whenever he happened to be around. Get me, Prof?"

"Do I not, James! Perfectly admirable."

"Well, we walked. He asked me a lot about American college life and so on, told me about Russian universities and about Oxford and Cambridge—he'd been to both, did you know that? Anyway, take it all in all, he seemed a very square guy, interesting and all that, and I liked him a lot. Somehow I didn't feel like doing much lying to him—went too hard against the grain, see what I mean?"

"Lucidly, James."

"I told him what was pretty darn near the truth, that I have enough to live on, that I've gone back into post-graduate work to give me a chance to make up my mind what I want to do. We got quite confidential. He tried to enter into my point of view. Told me if he was in my place his choice would be between two ways of life—either active or passive, depending upon which he felt most dominant. If he felt himself absolutely called to active life, he'd go into politics and make the best of it. If he thought he wanted to leave action to others, he'd collect books, or pictures, something to keep the mind alive, and enjoy himself all he could. Not bad for a Russian, is it," added Jimmie with unconscious patronage.

"You forget, Jimmie," smiled Ross, "that he was in his time and place a highly placed prince with a great name."

"Oh, I know," retorted Jimmie emphatically. "He's told me a lot about it. What I mean is, he's no mere waster is he, not just a plain damn fool. A very good egg all around.

"Well you told me to look-see if anybody was watching him. I looked my durndest but I couldn't see a thing. Could hardly see anybody at all. You see the place is so damn perfect. You hardly ever see servants round unless you happen to want them. Here and there you see a gardener working or a chauffeur driving up or driving away. Everything seems to move like some wonderfully oiled invisible machine. You don't see the machinery, but only the results."

"This case has been as good as a liberal education for you, James," was Ross's amused comment.

"Yes, hasn't it!" agreed Jimmie readily in his absorption. "Well, as I said, I couldn't detect anybody watching anybody—until yesterday noon. Erzeroff and I were coming back from a walk before lunch—he's no golfer, Erzeroff, and I told him neither was I—we were coming up the porch, when we heard a servant telling the manager, or owner, or whatever he is, Mr. Blaine is his name, that a strange man was hanging about outside the place."

"Did you notice whether that made any impression upon anyone?"

"Sure did. Not on me, though, not then. I was too dumb to think it might have anything to do with any of us. But when I looked at Erzeroff I noticed that he'd gone white to the gills—even his lips turned white. He never batted an eyelid otherwise, but I could see he was all of a sudden a little shaky."

"Then what happened?" prompted Ross in a matter-of-fact tone, though his eyes were now agleam with interest.

"Oh, he went upstairs, chatty as you please. We went to our different rooms. He came down to lunch—handed out some of the best conversation at that lunch since I've been here. Then he and I played a couple of games of Russian bank in the lounge, he joking, telling anecdotes and so on. About half-past three he said he was going up and asked if I cared to come up to his room for a few minutes for a chat. I said that would be great.

"He's got some swell Russian cigarettes and we were palavering up there in his suite—he can't be so poor as he talks—when suddenly he asked me how old I was. Didn't know what he was driving at then, but I got it about five minutes later. Wanted to get an idea whether I was old enough to be trusted."

"And then came the great confidence?"

"Surely did. And believe me, Prof, it was greater than I had any idea, or than you have."

"Shoot, Jimmie—and let us linger as we stroll, for I wish to hear you with mine ears."

"Well, he began about losing everything in the Revolution, palaces, property, everything excepting the money he had on deposit in England and France and what he escaped with. Luckily for him he had taken a few of his best pictures out of their frames and managed to get them away by rolling them up in a metal tube."

"The next step was the disposal of some of the pictures?" prompted Ross.

"Well not right away, but pretty soon. I guess he's a high liver," ran on Jimmie with a laugh. "He tried to be economical, but he spent that ready cash in those banks pronto, in a few months. Then he thought of his pictures and, to make a long story short, he began to sell 'em off. He always tried, he told me, to—what d'you call it— hypothecate them, that is arrange to redeem them after a certain time if he had the money. Sometimes it worked. He tried the same thing with Goold. But I guess there was a misunderstanding somewhere. Anyway, you know the rest of that. That sure is a great picture, The Tartar Chieftain. I don't blame Goold for wanting to own it for keeps."

"Yes, yes, James," interrupted Ross now tensely interested, "but where are we getting to?"

"Oh, excuse me," laughed Jimmie, "I'm blathering. Well, you know Erzeroff was thick with those fellows that killed the monk Rasputin, don't you? Yes—well, there was a Grand Duke in it, Dmitri, and a Congressman—I mean a deputy of the Duma, Purish—Purish—"

"Purishkevitch?"

"That's it—and there was another guy—I forget his name—he's still living somewhere abroad. But those fellows who looked up to Rasputin swore vengeance against the patriots—that's what Erzeroff calls them—the patriots, and he, Erzeroff, says he's proud to call himself one of them."

"Was he the one who killed Rasputin?"

"He didn't say so, Prof, but he let me understand that he was and that he's proud of it."

"By the fellows who looked up to Rasputin you mean the Khlysts?"

"Those are the guys. The Khlysts," repeated Jimmie, lingering on the word. "They have been following him about for years. His life seems to be one long Marathon to keep ahead of them. Anyway they're always on his trail and that's why—"

"That is why he blanched when he overheard that a strange man was following him about?"

"Yes, Prof, that was one reason. But if you think you've got the whole climax of the story, then I'm one up on you, for there's more coming."

"I am now prepared for anything," smiled Ross. "You are marvelous, James. Proceed."

"Well, you know all about the law suit—with Goold, I mean; and how Erzeroff lost out, and believe me, I'm convinced he's telling the truth when he says that when he lost he lost and tried to forget it. For this guy Erzeroff is a good enough sport to take it just like that, get me?"

"I do," murmured Ross in some disappointment. "But is that your climax?"

"No, hell no!" cried Jimmie in his excitement. "I'm coming to that. Yesterday morning when Erzeroff went up after breakfast he found The Tartar Chieftain lying flat on his bed—the Rembrandt he'd sued Goold for! The picture worth about a quarter of a million that Goold was probably murdered for—just lying there flat on his bed!"

Very excusably Jimmie paused for admiration as well as for breath.

"You saw it with your own eyes?" Ross seized hold of his lapel.

"Sure did. It's the Rembrandt all right. And he doesn't know what to do, poor old Erzeroff. He's scared stiff. First he wanted to burn it, he told me. But couldn't bring himself to do it. Loves it too much. May cost him his life, but great art, he says, has cost many lives. That's when he decided to tell me the whole story. Felt he needed a friend badly, and for some reason he picked on me," added Jimmie in a modest tone though he was obviously bursting with pride.

"Be careful, James," exclaimed Ross, "or I may kiss you at any moment. You've done a splendid job. We'll do what we can to help your friend Erzeroff—with gratitude. For our case is nearly complete."

"Hurray!" cried Jimmie. "You really mean I did something useful?"

"Better still—brilliant!"

"But, really, Prof, I didn't exactly do anything. You're just giving me a ride. All that's happened is, a guy has told me something."

"Stop, James, stop belittling yourself. A fellow-mortal of wide experience has chosen you on extremely short acquaintance as confidant in a life-and-death matter. You've clicked, my boy. Can you ask more?"

"Gee! I didn't think of it like that. But he's in trouble, all right, all right, and I wish to Mike we could help him."

"Better and better, James. We shall help him. But I fear there is no time to lose. You did well in calling me urgently."

"What do we do next?"

"First of all, efface from our masks our natural preoccupation. We are simply a pair of friends on pleasure bent. Then circumstances will dictate. But I fear I may not meet my classes tomorrow morning after all. Is that your palace of pleasure we are approaching?"

"Yeh, that's the dump," grinned Jimmie, though his heart was throbbing with excitement. "Are you any good at golf, Prof?"

"Upon occasion I have tried to be even that—but you see I have no clubs," he added in a sudden exuberant loudness. "But perhaps we can borrow a bag of clubs?"

The loudness was for the benefit of a third person Ross had almost by instinct perceived leaning against the bole of a spreading maple.

It was his former shadow, the District Attorney's man! The man's attempt to look blank and remote failed, however, and he broke irresistibly into a broad grin when Ross smiled and nodded in his direction.

"A beautiful morning," cried Ross, "after the storm."

"Sure is great, Professor," answered the detective, but it was obvious he did not dare to continue the conversation.

"I believe it is your important self that is being watched, James," Ross murmured *sotto voce* as they strolled into the graveled gateway of the Ali Baba, "but ignore it so far as you possibly can."

A servant seemed to appear from nowhere in particular, seized Ross's bag from Jimmie's hand and led the way through the exquisitely landscaped grounds to the house which appeared at once peaceful, noble and infinitely inviting.

25

The Shadow of Rasputin

The first thing Ross said when he entered Jimmie's room was:

"You are absolutely convinced, James, that your friend the Prince is no Dr. Jekyll and Mr. Hyde?"

"Absolutely, sir."

"Good! Then we shall act accordingly."

"Gee! This is great, Prof!" cried Jimmie in an ecstasy. "Now, where do we begin? Shall I knock on Erzeroff's door?"

"By no means. The first thing I want is a stroll about the grounds, in the wide open spaces, as though infinite leisure were ours."

"Watch me stroll!" bubbled Jimmie. "I can do it like an expert. I've been strolling with a Prince."

"You know my habit of talking to all and sundry." Jimmie nodded. "Don't seek to hurry me if you see me falling into conversation with the least worthwhile persons we encounter." Jimmie looked blank.

"Who am I to hurry you?" he protested.

"Still over-modest, James. You have the making of a great detective."

"Yes," said Jimmie gloomily, "and I have the making of a Prime Minister, too. But you tell me about as much as the Prime Minister tells the third assistant doorkeeper."

229

"You surprise me, James, after your brilliant work, too. Didn't you accompany me to Ivan Tcherabin's eating house?" Jimmie looked dazed.

"Sure," he laughed. "And I have been in a Child's restaurant, too. But what does that mean?"

"Reason backwards for a bit, my son. Analyze, analyze! It's poor reasoning that doesn't work both ways. You get facts and you obtain a result—but from a result you must also learn how to obtain the contributing facts."

"It's clear as mud to me," grumbled Jimmie.

"Never mind, it will soon be clearer," Ross overrode him impatiently. "But, come, we have no time to lose. Luncheon will be upon us and our matchless leisure will become very much congested." And he led the way out of the room.

It is to Jimmie's credit that he immediately fell into his teacher's humor, endeavored to restore to his features the look of serenity and in matter-of-fact tones as they descended the stairs again remarked that it was too bad Ross had brought no golf-bag with him.

The flower beds were already trimmed away or wholly empty against the winter months. Here and there some late-blooming plants like the chrysanthemum, the zinnia, and the scarlet plant called fire, made splashes of color over the grounds. There was a considerable hothouse to one side and, Sunday though it was, a gardener and two assistants were at work, puttering at the flower beds or raking dead leaves, which the magnificent old maples made gorgeously plentiful.

"Let's see," began Ross pleasantly. "Your room overlooks all this parterre, doesn't it?" Jimmie nodded. "A very pleasant room you have, James. Very pleasant indeed. After lunch I fancy, I shall have to select one myself, for it looks as though I may have to stay all night."

"Sure, you'll stay," grinned Jimmie. "Mine is a double room. You can move in there. This isn't a place people leave in a hurry."

"And where, by the way, are the windows of your friend, Erzeroff?"

"Oh, he has a suite, two rooms, the sitting room facing south toward the green-house, and the bedroom east over a vegetable garden. He's just opposite me. He is a glutton for sunlight, is Erzeroff."

"Wise man. Sunlight is a luxury worth pursuing. Is it proper to have a look at the vegetable garden?"

"This is liberty hall if ever there was one. We can go anywhere as though we owned the place."

They strolled on leisurely. Ross seemed bent upon observing and admiring everything, bending over plants, talking of genera and species, examining seed-pods with a pocket glass, as though gardening and botany were the two sole interests of his life.

"Would these be the windows of your friend?" he cast a glance upward.

"Those on the second floor, yes. He gets the sun all right. I don't care for so much of it early in the morning. I always take north or west rooms."

"Ah, tastes differ. He probably likes the homely vegetable garden, too. Some people do. It's an instinct that goes back to the childhood of the race—man's first essay in agriculture. I notice by the way that the garden comes close up to the house at that point."

"Yes," murmured Jimmie absently. He was watching Ross narrowly.

"And who has the rooms above Erzeroff, do you chance to know?"

"No one, I think. The house is nearly empty just now. Seven guests—you make the eighth."

"I break the mystic number," murmured Ross. Suddenly, with a cautious glance about him, he fell to examining the plants, as it seemed, beneath Erzeroff's windows.

Jimmie glanced up anxiously. If Erzeroff saw this it might look like spying. In a moment, however, Ross had straightened up and in an undertone observed:

"Don't be alarmed, Jimmie. I shall not give ourselves away." They were strolling back toward the front of the house over the graveled path. As they turned a corner they all but collided with a man carrying a heavy wooden flower-box.

"Excuse me," smiled Ross readily. "I am very sorry. Shall we help you?"

"No—no—" the man grinned broadly yet apologetically and stumbled on with his load. Ross looked after him, as he disappeared within the door of the green-house.

"A foreigner," he remarked.

"Yes," answered Jimmie, "all foreigners. Though how could you guess from his just saying no, I can't see."

"Nonsense, Jimmie. A foreigner who speaks little of our language doesn't have to say anything. It's in his eyes."

"His eyes—" repeated Jimmie, puzzled.

"Clearly, you've never earned your living in a foreign country," went on Ross, "or you would know the signs and the unmistakable stigmata."

"I wasn't thinking of that," muttered Jimmie. "But that guy's eyes—they remind me of something—or someone—"

A gleam of interest appeared in Ross's face. "Now, what, for instance?"

"I can't remember. But there's something—a look about them that kind of haunts me."

Ross did not pursue the matter. "Have you talked with any of these men?" he asked.

"The help, you mean? No—only with the indoor servants, when I had to. You see, I concentrated on Erzeroff from the start."

"And well you've done it, James. However, all human beings have their interest—the least among them often the greatest," he added a shade sententiously.

"That man we just met—you are not going to try to connect him up with all this, are you?" Jimmie demanded.

"He interests me," admitted Ross. "I wish you would let me stroll off by myself while you, in the guise of an old inhabitant, make friends with him."

"What do you expect me to find out, Prof?"

"I believe you will find he is a Slav, a Russian, and that his employment here is recent."

Jimmie lifted his eyebrows: "If you can tell all that from just bumping against a man who didn't say excuse me, you are even more of a wow than I thought."

"Try it, James." And Ross strolled off humming to himself. Those well laid out grounds with their not too formal gardens, and their aged trees, offered a delightful terrain for solitary musing. In less than five minutes, however, Jimmie rejoined him and he was laughing.

"I wish I had made a bet with you, Prof."

"I was wrong?"

"He is an Italian from Lombardy, that guy, and he speaks enough English to tell me so."

Ross joined in the laughter against himself and put his hand through Jimmie's arm.

"That just shows you, James, and me, too, that as soon as we get over-confident we can all make more or less egregious asses of ourselves."

"Now where did I slip up?" challenged Jimmie.

"I meant all except you, James," Ross answered solemnly.

"All the same, Prof," Jimmie, ignoring the thrust, put in eagerly, "I begin to get you. You want to look out for some Russian among the help who might be a friend of Erzeroff, eh?"

"Or an enemy," added Ross.

"Yeh, I get you, Prof. Lunch," he glanced at the watch on his wrist, "is in about ten minutes. Suppose you sit down on the porch and twiddle your thumbs, while I improve my knowledge of horticulture?"

"Delighted—though I warn you, Jimmie, it may not necessarily lead anywhere."

"I'll take a chance."

They approached the verandah. Scattered about in comfortable chairs were three or four of the guests absorbed in their Sunday papers, the American's aperitif before the Sabbath-day dinner. Erzeroff, sitting somewhat aloof, seemed absorbed in thought, the newspaper lying idly upon his knees. He glanced up at their approach and greeted Jimmie with a smile of charming urbanity.

"Hello," said Jimmy easily. "I want to introduce my friend, Mr. Ross."

"So delighted!" Erzeroff sprang up, clicked his heels and bowed. "It is a beautiful morning in the country."

"I couldn't resist it," Ross answered pressing the thin fine hand in his. "My friend Jimmie here, made out a good case when he invited me."

Erzeroff's eye perceived at once that Ross was no casual visitor, that doubtless his arrival had a bearing upon his previous day's confidence to Jimmie, of whom he evidently thought well.

"Will you not both sit down?" he invited.

"Thanks a lot," said Jimmy quickly. "I'll join you two in a minute. I've got to—" and without concluding he was off.

Even the desultory conversation of two civilized men of varied and wide experience is bound to be interesting. So swiftly did the minutes fly they glanced up in some surprise when Jimmie, breathing somewhat more rapidly than his leisurely wont, returned to them, a gleam of excitement in his eyes. At the same moment a servant appeared from behind them and announced that luncheon was served.

Excellent as was the meal, prepared with the ulti-
mate touch of the finest continental cooking, and served
accordingly, it is certain that Jimmie consumed it with
less than his customary gusto. His mind more than once
appeared to be adrift, and his manner of savoring the
dishes clearly did them less than justice.

When, after the meal was over, Erzeroff courteously invited them both for a cigarette in his sitting room, Jimmie
almost brusquely said:

"Excuse me just a minute, Prince. I've got something I
want to say to my friend. Then we'll join you." Ross lifted
his eyebrows in imperceptible reproof. Erzeroff, however,
merely said:

"Of course, Monsieur Jimmie. I shall expect you."

"It is obvious how well he thinks of you," murmured
Ross as Jimmie and he moved away. "Now," he began once
they were in Jimmie's room, "what's this great excitement
about?"

"Simply this," almost exploded the boy. "I was an ass!"

"Incredible, James!"

"Yeh, I was. When I went back to talk to that gardener
I got the wrong man. They look a lot alike, and I didn't
get a very good slant at the fellow who bumped into us,
I guess. When I went back I spotted the wrong guy and
began to talk his hind leg off."

"And you've found the right one?"

"Yes, I sure did. It's his eyes I finally identified him
by. He pretends he doesn't understand all I say, but he
understood me all right. Didn't understand when I asked
him about his nationality, or where he comes from. But he
got me all right. But his eyes—know what they've got in
them? The same thing that fellow had we saw playing the
accordion in the Russian eating house! Remember?"

"Perfectly."

"I spoke a few words with that Lombard Italian afterwards," he laughed. "He said that guy understands all right. That he is a Russian—and that he's been on the job only a few days. Doesn't that about cinch it?"

"Cinch what exactly?"

"That he's trying to find Erzeroff."

"That he is trying to find—" Ross repeated thoughtfully—"that is putting it mildly. More likely now he is trying to lose Erzeroff. He has found him some time ago. But I wonder—I wonder."

"Wonder what?"

"Whether your excited search may not precipitate matters. Does he live on the premises?"

"I—forgot to ask," faltered Jimmie.

"We can manage that presently. Let us, however, delay no longer. We are keeping your agreeable friend waiting."

Erzeroff, a man too experienced in life to beat about the bush in approaching what was vitally important, wasted little time in preliminaries when the two friends entered his room. After passing cigarettes, he glanced at Jimmie, understood his nod, and proceeded to relate to Ross substantially what he had already told Jimmie to the point where he found the picture spread out upon his bed.

"You have, as fortune tellers say, plenty of enemies, Prince," commented Ross.

"The woods they are full of them," replied Erzeroff, who could smile in the face of grave danger.

"You do not suppose," he went on, "that the stupid police, they will think I stole the picture, and now I am scared and wish to make, what do you say, restitution?"

"I hardly think so. In any case, you have an alibi, haven't you? You were in the hospital—and then you were here?"

"Yes," he said thoughtfully, "but on the day Goold was shot, I was in New York. I was buying shirts!" he ruefully added, and they all laughed simultaneously.

"My best advice, Prince Erzeroff," counselled Ross, "is that you come into town with us tomorrow morning. We will go straight to the police and you will tell them your entire story. I am somewhat acquainted with them. I believe you will have no serious trouble."

Erzeroff held out his hand. "I thank you both *di cuore*. A stranger and an alien here—you perhaps understand."

"Perfectly," said Ross. "But I wish we could lay hands on the man who wished this on you."

"Ah, it is a bitter enemy, I feel sure."

"And you suspect no one?"

"But—whom can I suspect? There is a man, I have heard, watching this house—could it be he, do you think?"

"No," Ross shook his head and smiled. "I know that man. He is interested in something else."

"Ah, you are very wise," cried Erzeroff. "Perhaps if you stay the night here you will find out?" he added with a sudden inspiration.

"I fear not," laughed Ross. "I am merely a Professor of Criminology at King's College. I take an interest in crime."

"Ah, I knew Jimmie was a man of distinguished relations. I am delighted you will pass the night here. To tell you the truth, this, all this—it shook my nerve a bit."

"I am not surprised," agreed Ross. "May I see the picture?"

"Certainly," and Erzeroff drew forth the famous Rembrandt from a locked closet. As he unrolled it, the aged canvas seemed to shed an aura of beauty, color, harmony and form, stilling all conflict and passion.

"Magnificent thing!" breathed Ross. "I suppose you have handled it a great deal?"

"You mean because of finger-prints?" Ross nodded. "Sorry, I forgot about that. I did handle it, but not much." He smiled. "It rather burned my fingers."

"What we really ought to do," said Ross, "is to telephone to the New York police that the picture has been
found. That would be safest. Unfortunately they would
come up for it at once and that would make a commotion
here that might embarrass you."

"Yes," said Erzeroff. "If we could wait till tomorrow,
that would be better."

As events proved Ross had deep cause to regret his
yielding to such fine consideration in sparing his new
acquaintance embarrassment.

The day passed pleasantly and agreeably. Indeed, there
was not much of it left by the time they quitted Erzeroff's
suite and went out for a stroll. The early dusk of autumn
was already hovering in the air. Shortly after five Erzeroff
excused himself owing to the need of a rest before dinner.

"I am still a valetudinarian," he explained.

Ross took the occasion to saunter out alone to the gateway to pass the time with his old friend the plainclothes
man from Burton's office. To Jimmie he assigned the commission of discovering as unobtrusively as possible, the
traces of the Russian gardener and his present whereabouts.

To his disappointment, however, Ross no longer found
the man at his post. Whether he had been called off duty
or left for some other reason it was impossible to say.

"Poor devil," thought Ross. "I wanted to give him an
opportunity of covering himself with glory."

Some time later Jimmie arrived in his room to report
that he could find no trace of the gardener. But the day
being Sunday, it was his own from midday on. He had left
the grounds of the Ali Baba and had not returned.

"I shall be glad," remarked Ross, "when this night is
over and we take the train for New York."

"Why? I thought you were having a good time, Prof?"

"Somewhat too good, Jimmie. Some of us here are in
imminent danger of our lives." Jimmie stared at him aghast.

"You really mean that?"

"I do indeed. And we will both be well advised not to leave the house again tonight, and, in any case, to keep our eyes and ears open."

"But I don't understand—Erzeroff has the picture. He's told us about it. He's going to turn it in. What else is there?"

"Some diabolical enemy is at work against Erzeroff. He has planted the picture in his room. Now we must wait for the next move. Do not be surprised, Jimmie, if I rise with the sun tomorrow. I could do nothing today for fear of attracting attention. And now it is dark. But shortly after dawn no one will be stirring and yet I shall have daylight to work with. I thought I perceived some footmarks beneath Erzeroff's window that were not without interest."

"Holy mackerel!" exclaimed Jimmie. "Do you think I ought to sleep in Erzeroff's rooms—give him a hand in case of need?"

"I dare not risk your life, Jimmie. If anyone does that, it ought to be myself."

"Oh, heck! Do you think I am afraid?"

"No, but I am. However, let's wait until after dinner and talk it over."

"We all dress here, you know," said Jimmie irrelevantly.

"I surmised as much."

Jimmie was restless. "Shall I unpack your suitcase?" he asked.

"No, thanks. I am used to do without valeting." And Ross proceeded to open his bag himself. "Here, by the way, is the automatic you wanted. You were very wise to ask for it."

"Gee!" exclaimed Jimmie. "I'd completely forgotten about it. I must have been excited when I phoned you. I wonder what made me ask for it?"

"Instinct, probably."

"Hoot! This gives me the willies, Prof. Let's go down and shoot a game of billiards."

"Go, by all means, James. You are restless. I will stay here and try to think some things out."

Jimmie was about to protest, but decided to obey orders. Down in the billiard room he found a Mr. Royce, a middle-aged broker, who was pining for what exercise walking round a billiard table would give him. At sight of Jimmie he offered him enormous odds to lure him into a game.

The crack of the billiard balls deflected Jimmie's mind from its preoccupation far more than high thinking might have done. Besides, he was doing well. With the great odds Royce had given him he was winning and that lent gusto to his play.

"Look here, young fellah," said Royce. "You're too good for the odds I gave you. I'll have to reduce 'em next game."

"I've been kidded by experts," retorted Jimmie in a high state of glee. "But tell you what I'll do—"

Jimmie's offer however never came to light.

A cry, agonized, terrifying, resounded somewhere above stairs. Though muffled by distance and doors it was shrill and nerve-racking like the death cry of a trapped animal.

A quick scuffle of feet was faintly audible and then, stillness. Jimmie, after a frozen second of numbness dropped his cue and flew up the broad staircase.

The door of his room was ajar. Heads were peering wild-eyed out of doorways. A valet was running bewildered along the corridor. Jimmie took one glance at his empty room and literally threw himself upon Erzeroff's door.

The picture that confronted him was horrible, ghastly, yet dimly comforting.

In his bedroom Erzeroff lay upon his back, dying, with a dagger through his heart. Blood was flowing from the wound over a white silk under-vest to the rug, and from his nose and mouth in a bubbling death agony.

Ross, flushed, excited, was kneeling and holding down the prostrate struggling figure of a man—the missing Russian gardener!

"There's a pair of handcuffs in my back pocket—" cried Ross. "Quick, Jimmie, get them out."

Jimmie, suddenly galvanized into life, bent down and in a moment the flat metal rings were snapped upon the wrists of the gardener. Anyway, thought Jimmie, dimly triumphant, Ross was safe!

26
Two Murderers of Goold

The manager of the Ali Baba, Mr. Blaine, refused even to consider calling the New York police first.

"I live in Westchester County." He spoke with some warmth, as though Ross and Jimmie were responsible for the murder. "This is a terrible thing to have happened in this house. I must call the local police at once."

"You will have no objection to my calling the New York police?" enquired Ross.

"You may call whom you like, sir. But I must ask you gentlemen to remain where you are until the Westchester police come. You are important witnesses."

By this time the murderer lay upon the sitting room floor, his ankles bound with cords, his manacled wrists strapped to the front of his body, owing to the violence he had exhibited in the struggle. As, however, he had perceptibly cooled down and asked that his arms be unstrapped so that he could assume a sitting posture, Ross complied, allowing him to sit up, and instructed Jimmie to keep him covered with the automatic.

"I have never before had guests here with pistols," grumbled Blaine, still smarting under the incalculable harm a murder and the attendant publicity were bound to do to his delightful hotel.

"Perhaps there had never before been any need of pistols," Ross answered gently.

"I should certainly hope not," retorted Blaine. The Westchester police were on their way, and Ross took up the telephone upon the late Erzeroff's table and called for Spring 3100 in Manhattan.

The response from the Detective Bureau was that Inspector Callahan was not available, that Sergeant Burke, however, was on duty in the Homicide Bureau.

Briefly, Ross recounted the events leading to his telephoning, Burke injecting dreary monosyllables of sparse comment. But if Ross expected an electric springing to life of all those myrmidons Callahan had repeatedly promised, he was bitterly disappointed.

"Yeh," concluded Burke, "now what d'you want us to do, Professor Ross?"

"Do?—don't you think one of you—Inspector Callahan, yourself, or someone, ought to come out here at once?"

"Why, I can't see as we'd ought," said Burke. "That's a Westchester police matter."

"You misunderstand, Sergeant. This man is certainly the person who stole Goold's picture. Don't you remember Callahan saying if he finds the thief of the picture, he'll find Goold's murderer?" Surely this was a trump card to play!

"Oh, Goold's murderer—we've got him locked up already."

"You—what!" cried Ross in consternation. "And who is that?"

"I can't tell you that over the 'phone. But if you come down and see the Inspector or the Commissioner, maybe they'll tell you." That seemed to take the energy out of Ross far more effectively than his recent struggle with the prisoner.

The Russian, in the meanwhile, upon the floor, was making violent gestures with his manacled hands and crying out: "No—no!—No!" whereat Jimmie ordered him to keep quiet.

"What is it you want to say?" Ross, laying down the instrument, turned to the man. Ross spoke to him in Russian and for a moment, the manacled man was so startled he was speechless. Finally he blurted out:

"I took the picture, but I did not kill Goold."

"Do you also deny that you killed the man in the next room?"

"No, that I do not deny. I surely killed him. But I did not kill Goold."

"Well, you will explain that to the police."

"Yes," he went on, "I killed the man in there and I am proud of the deed. I have squared accounts with him as God decreed."

"You are a Khlyst?" queried Ross. The man appeared astonished, but made no reply.

"The only redemption is through sin?" pressed Ross.

"The only redemption is through sin," murmured the prisoner mechanically, as though his lips long drilled in the formula, were of themselves repeating it. Strange blend of religious mystical diabolism half an hour from Broadway!

The arrival of the Westchester police put an end to the conversation and the formal investigation followed the routine procedure.

The prisoner made no denial as to killing Erzeroff. Through Ross, serving as interpreter, he admitted stealing the Rembrandt, and tracking Erzeroff until he found him. He also admitted planting the picture in his room.

"Why did you do that?" enquired Ross.

"To bring misfortune upon the man," was the simple answer. "We wanted him to suffer the tortures of imprisonment. Death was too easy a fate for him who slew our holy brother. Prison for him would be worse than death."

"Then why did you not leave it at that?"

"Because," was the answer, "that man was very cunning. I saw that he had found friends and I feared that he would wriggle out of it before my people had time to denounce him to the police. In that case my orders were to kill and take no chances. He was an antichrist, the arch enemy of my people. He slew our holy brother, the ruler of Kings!"

"Do you know that the penalty for murder in this state is death?"

"I am in God's hands," mumbled the man with a sudden febrile fervor. "The only redemption is through sin!"

The Westchester police to whom this was translated, looked preternaturally wise.

Ross and Jimmie made their respective depositions and were asked to remain until after the inquest to be held on the following day.

"You better have the man's glands examined," murmured Ross, but the police paid no attention.

Notwithstanding the grisly solemnity of the occasion those Westchester policemen could hardly conceal their exultation. They, as they felt, and they alone, had not only captured a dangerous and unusual criminal, but the murderer of James Goold!

"But he says he didn't kill Goold," Ross explained.

"That's what he says!" sniffed the Chief of Police.

That night, only a few hours of which remained by the time the police had concluded their work, lingered for long in Ross's memory. For some time he lay awake pondering whether it is of any use trying to help society at all, in view of the vast impermeable stupidity of mankind. After a piece of detective work that, by any standard, must be adjudged brilliant, after the capture at great personal risk of a criminal at once unique and violently dangerous, he was now being treated by the New York police as a meddlesome interloper, almost as a criminal himself!

What glaring blunder had they made? Whom were they holding there in New York? Was it Forbes, Sheila, Cross? It might as well be Lorna! Knowing what he knew, he could not but feel bitterly disappointed. He passed at that point some of the most disillusioning hours of his career.

Monday morning's newspapers brought two pieces of startling news with screaming headlines on the front pages.

One, spreading over two columns even in the *Times* was to the effect that Cullen Forbes, well-known millionaire, sportsman and collector, had been "detained as a material witness" in the Goold murder case, the arrest being due to the fact that Forbes, in defiance of police orders, had been about to leave the city on "a business trip."

The quotations, from what was evidently a carefully prepared statement from Police Headquarters, were virtually tantamount to a charge of murder against Forbes.

Startling developments were promised the public almost immediately. And, significantly, it was added that no bail had thus far been fixed and that Gillette, Ward and Ward, attorneys for Forbes, would immediately begin habeas corpus proceedings, unless bail was accepted or their client immediately released. There was some bitter comment and severe strictures upon the chaotic stupidity of the Police Department in a statement from Howard Gillette.

The other big piece of news was the murder of Prince Erzeroff, who had been convalescing at a resort hotel in Westchester, and the allegation of the Westchester police that not only had they recovered the Rembrandt stolen from Goold's gallery at the time of the latter's murder, but that in the slayer of Erzeroff they were convinced they had laid hands upon the Russian fanatic who was also the murderer of Goold! The papers praised extravagantly the outstanding brilliance of the Westchester police.

Ross scanned the two items and turned the paper over to Jimmie.

"Take your choice, James," he smiled. "It costs you absolutely nothing."

"Gee!" exclaimed Jimmie after an eager perusal, and then he uttered a whistle conveying wonder, awe and astonishment. "This is a mix-up, Prof! It does look as though one of these two is the guilty guy, don't you think so?"

"If I thought so, James, I should probably be on the New York police force sitting, as they say, pretty, instead of miserably desiring to get back to New York."

"You think there's still somebody else?"

"If only they'll hurry this damnable inquest!" murmured Ross irrelevantly.

"I wish I could do something," muttered Jimmie.

"You've done your share, my son."

"Yeh," said Jimmie, "I have. Probably hurried poor old Erzeroff to his death."

"Now, listen, my boy: Never allow thoughts like that to lodge in your mind, or all living in this world becomes impossible." Ross was speaking with unusual earnestness, the light touch so characteristic of him, now wholly absent.

"Erzeroff was paying a debt, wholly alien to us, in which neither you nor I had any part or lot. We happened to be present at the discharge of the debt. But neither of us was nearer than four thousand miles from the slaying of the reprobate monk which started all this tragic business. Nor anywhere near the scenes of the monk's crimes and debaucheries which preceded that."

"I didn't think of it that way," breathed Jimmie.

"'No. That is why all scriptures and all codes warn so persistently against vice and crime. They go on breeding endlessly."

"Sure, I see," said Jimmie.

"You and I, James—we are soldiers enlisted against crime," Ross smiled again.

"For the duration of the war," said Jimmie.

"Which is lifelong," supplied Ross.

"That's why we're here," added Jimmie brightening.

"Precisely. Now let them bring on their inquest."

Almost immediately a policeman came to the Chief's office, where Ross and Jimmie were waiting, to announce that a coroner's jury had been collected and that the inquest was about to begin.

To Ross the one point of interest in the proceedings was the startling fact that not a single member of the New York police department was present.

So sure, evidently, were Messrs. Callahan, Wells and Burton that in Forbes they had the murderer of Goold, that they did not even send a man up to watch the proceedings in Westchester.

"Fantastic!" Ross could not help murmuring audibly. "The stupidity of it!" he reflected. "They'll think better of it almost before they know it."

They deserved all the criticism and ridicule the public could shower upon them. In his anger he suddenly determined to show them in as foolish a light as possible.

Then all at once he remembered that to have "detained" Forbes, a man as Callahan and Wells, reiterated, was of such prominence in the city, must have been a decision very costly in effort to those men.

"They are simply blundering," he thought. "Their lights are what they are. I must get back to New York."

For a suburban inquest the proceedings moved swiftly. Blaine and some servants, as well as the gardener, gave brief testimony, and then Jimmie and Ross presented their simple evidence. Jimmie was not asked how he happened to be a guest at the Ali Baba. His presence there was taken wholly for granted. So was Ross's.

Ross had heard a cry and rushed to the neighboring room. He overpowered the assailant and handcuffed him. The prisoner's confession established the crime as one of vengeance going back to Imperial Russia, one of the many involved in the dissolution of a long tottering dynasty.

"How did you happen to have handcuffs in your possession?" enquired the coroner guilelessly of Ross.

"I am a Professor of Criminology at King's," was the answer, "and I use various objects pertaining to crime for purposes of illustration."

That was satisfactory. The police, too exuberantly aware of the service Ross had rendered them, had not even mentioned the automatics.

By the time Ross and Jimmie had reached the city it was after one o'clock. The first thing that greeted them as they emerged from Grand Central Station was the startling cry of the newsboys' calling an extra:

"Mrs. Cullen Forbes Confesses to the Murder of James Goold! Extra!"

Jimmie's face turned a shade pale. Automatically his eyes searched the eyes of his master. Ross, however, merely swore under his breath, his lips assuming a faint inscrutable smile. But almost in the same instant his face abruptly changed to an expression of unusual gravity and concern.

"That, too," he muttered. "The whole bag of tricks."

27

The Lions' Den

Well knowing the things he ought to do, the moves he must immediately make, Ross was for a moment confused as to which he must make first.

There was Sheila—and that adolescent-minded husband of hers. Then there was Lorna—Lorna, the splendid young girl alone in the midst of the danger that encompassed her—both his duty and inclination drew him ineluctably to her.

Since Lorna, however, was worth the pair of Forbeses put together and a whole world besides, he must obviously proceed to help the weaker mortals whose human frailties had landed them in their present grim predicament.

Clearly he must go at once to the assistance of the Forbeses.

"Sheila's confession," he finally broke out, handing the newspaper to Jimmie, "is the climax to a series of stupidities in this case out-topping all stupidity in fact and fiction."

"What—" gasped Jimmie in his bewilderment, "after her own confession—you don't think she did it?"

"Did it! Good Lord, no! But I wasn't thinking of that. I am speaking of the criminal stupidity of Callahan, or Wells, or whoever allowed such a thing to be published in the newspapers. They will see their mistake soon enough. But unfortunately the harm is done."

Jimmie's face suddenly and strangely brightened. "Then our man is the guy! That issky-vodsky we caught is the real murderer, isn't he?"

"There is no time for discussion, Jimmie. Let's get to a telephone booth. I must call up Lorna and then I must get down to the police station."

The imperturbable voice of Cross answering the telephone seemed infinitely soothing and reassuring to Ross as it came over the wire. What it said was merely, "I will see, sir, if Miss Storey is in."

The wait for Lorna to come to the telephone seemed interminably long. Cross returned to say that "Miss Storey was with her aunt and would speak to him directly."

Ross's heart missed a beat, though for no sentimental reasons. That sinister figure he had seen gliding about the hall during the night he had spent at the Goold house! Lorna was surrounded by peril. At last Lorna's voice:

"Hello, Professor Ross—" what infinite relief!—"It's wonderful to have you back in New York," she went on. "It seems as though the whole city was upset since you left it."

"That part of the city I stand in still seems pretty solid, Lorna"—it really didn't matter what he said. His delight in hearing her voice was too great for collected thought. Nevertheless he must think.

"Lorna," he began more quietly, "there is much I want to say to you, but I cannot come now. I must hurry down to see that superlative vaudeville team of egregious asses downtown. I dare say you know whom I mean. In the meanwhile I am sending you Jimmie, our masterful James, who will recount our small adventures of the last twenty-four hours. I say, Lorna, couldn't you and he take a drive or a walk and get some fresh air? Strikes me you have been somewhat shut in of late."

"I don't see how I could, Professor Ross. I am playing nurse today. Miss Baker is away, ill, and Dr. Humphreys hasn't sent over any substitute as yet. He said he would."

"What—!" cried Ross. Then abruptly he checked himself, returning to a more even tone. "I am sorry to hear that, Lorna, I am certain you need the recreation, however. Set one of the maids to nurse your aunt. Let Jimmie take you out to a belated lunch. What, by the way, is wrong, with the substantial Miss Baker?"

"She telephoned this morning that she was quite ill. In fact, someone telephoned for her. So I had to take her place."

"Naturally," agreed Ross. "Jimmie, however will claim his privilege as a friend to tell you in private of our adventures."

"I'll see what I can do"—Loma seemed dubious.

"Jimmie," Ross turned to his faithful acolyte, "I want you to go up to Lorna's house. Take her out to lunch if you possibly can. Insist upon it. If you fail, keep her in sight so far as is humanly possible—tell her about Erzeroff,—tell her anything, so long as you can contrive to keep near her. Use your well-known blandishments and charms, James. Use *force majeur*. Anything."

Jimmie gazed into the stern eyes of Ross and nodded. He was aware that his teacher had never been more in earnest.

"Thank God for you, James!" said Ross. "Now I must to the lions' den."

"I thought you said they were asses."

"Same thing," was the cryptic answer. "I shall accompany you part of the way to Lorna's house."

"But I thought you were going downtown?"

"True, James. Your name should be Thomas. I wish to stop for a moment at Dr. Humphreys' office. It is he who supplies the nurses for Mrs. Goold. Now, any more questions?"

Jimmie laughed. "I thought you wanted us to be curious?"

"I do. And I shall answer even the questions you haven't asked—as soon as the case is ended."

"That may take years," protested Jimmie.

"It will take no longer than about twenty-four hours, my dear Watson—certainly not more than thirty-six."

"What—you mean you already know who murdered Goold?"

"That is precisely what I mean, my son—but say nothing to Lorna about that. Now, au revoir." And with a pat on Jimmie's solid shoulder Ross turned off in the fifties leaving Jimmie to strike up Madison Avenue with a head buzzing like an apiary.

When Ross entered Callahan's office he found the Chief of Detectives behind his desk with an expression at once Rhadamanthine and yet suave, with the solemn suavity of an undertaker.

"Well, Professor," he clutched Ross's hand in his great paw, "a lot has happened since I saw you last, hasn't it?"

"To be sure," agreed Ross. "But relieve my suspense, Inspector. Are you any nearer knowing who murdered Goold?"

"Nearer!" And Callahan forgot himself so far as to utter a blasphemous monosyllable. "Haven't you read the papers?"

"Yes, I have, Inspector. But according to the papers you have not one, but no less than three murderers of Goold. Are you going to try them all?"

"No!" laughed Callahan. "Not by a damn sight. We'll try the one who did it, never fear."

"And who may that be?"

"Who! Forbes of course!"

"Oh!" said Ross and Callahan's face darkened, betraying a conscience somewhat clouded.

"Mean to say," he cried, "you don't believe he's the guy?"

"You haven't asked me my beliefs, Inspector. You are telling me yours. But if you are so certain of these, why did you allow Mrs. Forbes's so-called confession to get into the newspapers?"

"What d'you mean so-called? It was a real confession all right."

"And you believed it to be true?"

"Well, no. To be frank, I didn't and don't. That dame is sure crazy about that husband of hers!"

"Exactly. I am ashamed of you, Inspector. As a man of heart and chivalry, you should have done all that in you lay first to prevent her confession—"

"Who in hell was I to prevent it?" he broke in fiercely.

"—And second," Ross went on calmly, "to prevent its publication."

"I might have prevented it if she'd come to me," Callahan became more conciliatory. "But she went to the D.A.—see? What could I do then?"

"He doesn't believe her confession, does he?"

"Well, no, I don't think so."

"Then why did he allow it to get out?"

"Tell you how it was, Professor. Have a cigar? No? I'll light one myself. It was like this: Between ourselves, it took quite a lot of deciding to arrest Forbes. But once the D.A. and the Commissioner decided to give him the works—why, you see?—that confession of the lady's sort of bolsters them up. Bolsters up the case, too, see? Trying to save her husband and all that."

"And you believe Forbes guilty?"

"Guilty as hell!" asserted Callahan. "And so does everybody else!"

"Is that why you sent nobody to Westchester when I actually caught for you the man who stole the Rembrandt?"

"I been thinking about that," said Callahan with a slow frown. "It's all been happening so quick."

"You had better think more actively, Inspector. And the same applies to the District Attorney. For so far as circumstantial evidence goes, this Russian who killed Erzeroff and stole the Rembrandt can be proven absolutely to be the murderer of James Goold."

"Now listen, Professor," Callahan laid a detaining hand upon his arm. "Nobody has charged Forbes with the murder yet. Don't run away with the idea that it's all settled. This Russian now—he's locked up out there in Westchester. He's not going to get away. Honest, Professor, do you think he is the guy that croaked Goold?"

"What is the use of asking me, Inspector? I told you I shall present you with Goold's murderer by the middle of this week. Meanwhile you lock up Forbes, you publish a hysterical confession of his wife's and generally run amuck. If friends of mine were not involved, I should throw up the case and wash my hands of you all."

"Funny thing," Callahan reflected aloud. "When I go along by myself everything I do seems right and follows the lines I've always worked on. When I hear you talk I get to feeling I'm all wrong and that I missed the whole point of the case."

"The moral is obvious, Inspector," smiled Ross. "However, there is no time to lose in psychological discussion. Get your hat, Inspector and let us go to the District Attorney's office. I think I can convince him that Forbes must be released at once."

"Gee!" gasped Callahan. "You move pretty fast. If we release Forbes, we not only admit we are all wrong, but we've got nothing to show for all our work—not a single arrest!"

"Quite correct. All you have to do is to announce that the sole reason for Forbes's arrest is that he is an important witness and that he attempted to leave town in defiance of the authorities. Now that he has promised to remain, he was instantly released."

"Yeh," said Callahan dully, "but how do we know he will remain?"

"I shall ask him to do so!"

"And he'll listen to you?"

"I guarantee it."

"Then what do we do—wait till the Westchester police get through with that Russian and play second fiddle to them, when the case is all cold?"

"I've told you I shall present you with the murderer."

"When?"

"Tomorrow—if not sooner."

Callahan gazed at him sternly, searchingly, for some seconds, and then his features broke into a crooked grin.

"I guess I told you, Professor, you are like a woman: Can't live with you and can't live without you. Let's go."

28

Forbes Tells What He Saw

Upon the entrance of Callahan and Ross into his office, the District Attorney for New York County frowned and without even courtesy motioned them to chairs near his desk.

"Well, what's this," he growled, "a delegation, or another hunch?"

Callahan, without giving Ross a chance to speak, impressively outlined the latter's request for Forbes's immediate release, the detective's eyes holding that cunning look of double-dealing peculiar to the cheap politician: If the District Attorney was favorable, he was with him; if opposed, those cunning eyes were ready to laugh away Ross's request.

"He's got to learn," retorted Burton with heat, "that just because he's a rich man, he can't defy the authorities. To this office, rich and poor are exactly alike."

It seemed to soothe some vague inferiority in Burton to be appearing as a tribune of the people. Ross listened to him impassively without interrupting.

"I don't mind telling you," Burton was concluding, "that since the arrest of that man in West-Chester, who killed Erzeroff, I made up my mind to release Forbes anyway. But he's got something he won't give up and, by God, he's got to. If he doesn't, this office has no fear of putting a rich man in jail."

"May I suggest, Mr. Burton, that you bring him here? I believe I know what it is he's refusing to tell and I think I can convince him that he'd better tell us."

"Helen Maria!" Burton broke into a famous oath now forgotten. "If you'd played fair with us, none of this would have happened, Ross. Damned if I haven't a great mind to lock you up yourself!"

Ross laughed. "Nothing would be easier, Mr. Burton. You could undoubtedly lock me up, and on quite color-able grounds. However, I advise against it, chiefly for the reason," he added negligently, lighting a cigarette, "that I presume you would prefer to arrest the murderer of James Goold."

Burton glared at him for a long moment, then burst like a volcano.

"Blank! Blank! Blank! You mean you really know and you've been keeping us from knowing? What kind of a man are you? Talk of the police! They may not be professors, but at least they spill all they know."

"That," observed Ross, "with all due respect to the Inspector here, is one reason why their results thus far are, shall we say, a little confused?"

Burton pressed a button. The chief of his detective force entered.

"Healy, bring Forbes across here right away."

"Yes, sir," and the gray-headed functionary vanished.

"Across means the Bridge of Sighs?" smiled Ross.

"You bet it does," snapped Burton viciously.

A few moments and Forbes in charge of Healy and another appeared in the doorway. Burton with a gesture dismissed the attendants and gruffly invited Forbes to sit down.

"How are you, Professor Ross," Forbes greeted him pleasantly and Ross held out his cigarette case. Though pale and somewhat excited, Forbes appeared as meticulously dressed as ever, and quite as jaunty in demeanor, with that something of the adolescent that is at once touching and humorous and, in a mature man, just a shade grotesque.

"I brought you here, Mr. Forbes," began Burton, "because Professor Ross says he can convince you that you'd better come across with anything you've got in the Goold case and not obstruct justice any longer."

"The devil he can!" retorted Forbes with characteristic vehemence. "I've told you all I am going to tell you. I'm not a policeman. And I'll tell you this: I'll do my best to get square with you for persecuting an innocent man. Just because you're a blunderer is no reason why I should suffer."

Burton turned livid. He was about to cry out in all his wrath when Ross, laying a hand on his arm, checked the torrent and then he addressed Forbes.

"Mr. Forbes, I've heard a good deal about what is called southern chivalry and I am a little that way given myself, but I have never known it carried quite so far as this."

"What the hell d'you mean, sir!"

"I mean this, Mr. Forbes: The man who saw what you saw, who refuses to tell what he saw, *and yet employs detectives to shadow the nurses* in the Goold house, has, to say the least, a very confused sense both of his principles and of his moral obligations."

"The nurses!" cried Burton, all but leaping from his chair. "What did I tell you, Callahan?" Callahan stirred uneasily in his chair. Forbes's face darkened in hot anger.

"A fine friend you are," he flung at Ross, "if you'd been spying on me to that extent."

"Perhaps some day you'll know how much of a friend of yours I've been, Mr. Forbes."

"If he hasn't been a friend of yours, Mr. Forbes," Burton himself couldn't help putting in truculently, "then you've never had any. He's almost in jail himself on your account." Forbes was about to speak, but suddenly with a curious expression of shamefacedness he fell silent—precisely like a boy in too great confusion.

"Excuse us for a moment, Mr. Burton. I only want to say one word to Mr. Forbes which I think may make a difference to him." And with a gesture he asked Forbes to step away with him to the far end of the room. Forbes somewhat dubiously, yet with an air of defiance, too, obeyed.

"Mr. Forbes," murmured Ross in a tone audible to him alone, "for Sheila's sake, for your own, tell them the truth—tell them that on the afternoon Goold was murdered you were from motives of jealousy spying upon him through field-glasses from the empty house you own opposite the gallery and that you saw a woman shoot Goold from behind and kill him. You needn't mention that you thought at first the woman was Sheila. But that by now you are convinced it was one of the nurses. That is why you are having them shadowed."

Forbes gazed in speechless consternation at Ross. Then his jaw snapped against his upper teeth.

"And serve him damn well right," he muttered. "But why should I tell on a woman? It's their job to find out. I'm not a damned policeman!"

"No," murmured Ross patiently, "you are not. But Sheila's interests will be better served by your telling than by your present attitude."

A shadow passed over Forbes's features, an expression conveying at once pain, jealousy, regret, love—and abruptly he grasped Ross's hand.

"Damned if I don't think after all you're the best friend we've got!" he exploded, gripping Ross's hand. And his hot eyes were suddenly clouded by a film of mist.

"Very well," he turned and in quite another tone addressed Callahan and Burton. "Professor Ross has convinced me. I'll tell you all I know."

"One moment," put in Ross raising his hand. "Before Mr. Forbes makes his statement I want to ask one favor of the District Attorney. I am sure he will grant it to us. There is somewhere a bundle of letters from Mrs. Forbes written to Goold before she really knew her present husband whom she loves devotedly, as you know. There is nothing disgraceful in that. It takes most of us some time to find where our hearts are. I undertake that the case will be complete without those letters. Assuming that you come to agree with us, have I your promise, Mr. Burton that we may have those letters, unread, when they are found?"

"Well—" Burton looked from one to the other, "if as you say, the case is complete without them—why, let's hear the testimony."

"Agreed, then," said Ross.

Brief as the statement was, it held both Burton and Callahan spellbound. Forbes's forceful personality by its very force and obstinacy, carried conviction in every word he uttered. He spoke of his jealousy precisely as a confused schoolboy might have done. Very shamefacedly he admitted his spying upon Goold that fateful afternoon, because he had learned of Sheila's anxiety to retrieve the letters. He was wrong, however, as to the hour of her call, and in any case, he had been too long detained by Gillette at the Varsity Club. His wife's alibi was proven to a certainty. He was now, he reluctantly admitted, sure it was one of the nurses.

"Could you discern the face and figure of the nurse so that you could recognize her?" broke in Burton, wiping perspiration from his forehead.

"No. I couldn't. That's why—"

"Why you had them both watched?"

"Yes."

"You didn't want either of them to get away, is that it?"

"Yes—that is, in case—" he stammered miserably.

"You're a better citizen than I gave you credit for, Mr. Forbes," conceded Burton handsomely, "and I apologize." He held out his hand which Forbes accepted with a curious wry grin.

"Now, Inspector," Burton turned to Callahan, "nothing left for you to do but to bring in both of those nurses. I don't know that I'd call the case complete, Professor, until we pick the right one, but that ought not to be difficult now. Our agreement as to the letters stands." And Ross also was favored with the handshake of the tribune of the people.

Callahan, not to be outdone, joined quickly in the handshaking.

"This is great!" he cried. "Now I'd better go after those sisters of mercy."

"No need for you to go alone," said Ross quietly. "We can all go together. That is except you, Mr. Forbes. You will doubtless want to hurry to Sheila."

"Just what do you mean?" demanded Burton.

"I mean if you and the Inspector will favor me with your presence, you can make the arrest this afternoon without a posse comitatus of Central Office men and District Attorney's men, Guelphs and Ghibellines, Cardinal's men or musketeers. The case might as well culminate now as tomorrow." Lorna's safety decided him to instant action.

"Now's where you are trying to drive woozy again," grinned Callahan in high good humor.

Forbes laughed, waved his hand and left the room with the speed of a schoolboy who had been kept after school.

29
Murderous Fury

"What is all this," demanded Wells bustling into the Goold gallery, whither Ross had telephoned him to come, "what's all this, a directors' meeting?"

Cross, who had admitted the Commissioner a few moments after the others, was about to withdraw when Ross checked him.

"Will you," he said, "ask Miss Storey if she would kindly see me for a few moments—here?"

"Yes, sir. I believe she is in, sir."

"You needn't mention the presence of anyone else."

"No, sir—that is, unless she should ask me."

"She will not ask you—but even if she should, I would rather you would convey that I am alone."

"Yes, sir," almost sighed the butler. His world was again becoming confused. He did not wish to lie to Miss Storey.

In the gallery the group whom Wells had joined consisted of three men besides Ross—Callahan, Sergeant Burke and Burton. They surveyed the place with the melancholy air with which we inevitably view a spot where we have seen death.

"That picture is going back into its place, anyway," observed Callahan, "thanks to the Professor here."

"Damn the picture," muttered Burton. "I want that nurse."

"Is that what we five men are here for?" demanded Wells, "to question one of the nurses?"

"We are here," said Ross, "to arrest the slayer of James Goold."

"Power to you," almost giggled Wells in his sudden excitement. "We are certainly with you to the hilt."

Lorna entering the gallery paused abruptly and her color changed to a momentary pallor and then to a deep flush.

"Oh—I thought—" she stammered. "I didn't know you gentlemen were here, too. I thought it was only Professor Ross."

"My fault, Lorna," Ross spoke up quickly, "but I did not want explanations to go to you by messenger. It's all right. We shan't detain you a minute, Lorna. Is Miss Baker still on the sick list?"

"Yes. But she telephoned that she is feeling so much better, she'll be here tomorrow. Dr. Humphreys called up saying he would send a substitute tomorrow, but I told him it wasn't necessary. I simply took Miss Baker's place today."

"And has Miss Kelly come in?"

"Not yet, but she is due any minute. She will be earlier tonight because I phoned her Miss Baker was ill."

"Good," said Ross. "Now here is what I want you to do, Lorna: When she comes in, give orders for someone to ask her to come in here directly—not to go to your aunt's room, or to the upper floor at all. Do you, by the way, ever smoke in your aunt's sick room?"

"Oh, yes," she smiled. "Aunt Julia is not at all old-fashioned. She doesn't smoke herself, but she doesn't mind my doing it."

"Excellent. In that case, will you resume your nursing of your aunt without mentioning the presence of anyone else in the house—"

"Jimmie is up there talking to her now," interrupted Lorna. "I took him in—I thought it would brighten her. And she's quite taken to him. You know what a little sunshine he is—"

"Better still!" laughed Ross. "Keep Jimmie there, too. Only in about five minutes after you return, I ask you, Lorna, to do this: Now please mark carefully: Ask Jimmie for a cigarette, but on no account let him light it for you. Light it yourself. And so contrive by your incredible clumsiness that before putting out the match or the lighter, you ignite the window curtain. Is that clear?"

"Why—yes—but Professor Ross—" she stared at him in amazement—"but why—the danger ?"

"Have no fear. We shall have an extinguisher ready. Don't be afraid. Only please do as I ask—Watson."

The last word seemed to have its effect. The other men gazed at Ross as though they suddenly perceived in him a candidate for the lunatic asylum or some fakir from a Hindu bazaar. Lorna, however, at the mention of "Watson," smiled and nodded.

"Five minutes after you leave this room," repeated Ross with emphasis. Lorna glanced at the watch on her wrist.

"Then I'd better go and give that order about Miss Kelly."

"Precisely," said Ross. "And the hour now is five fifty-five."

Cross, summoned, was ordered to take a fire extinguisher and to accompany them as quietly as possible to the main bedroom floor where the sickroom was situated.

"Now," whispered Ross rapidly, "you, Commissioner, and you, Mr. Burton, please wait in the hall here for a few moments. Don't come in until you are called, for there is some danger. You, Inspector, come with me. Cross, please lead us, on tiptoe into the room adjoining Mrs. Goold's, where the nurses stay, when they are not beside her. You, Sergeant Burke, stay quietly outside the door of the sick-room and don't open it until you hear a cry or a scuffle or both. Discourage anyone's loitering in this hallway."

"I get you, Professor," answered Burke wearily.

"What's it all about?" demanded Wells in a tense whisper. "Why the mystery?"

"A minute or two, and all will be revealed," breathed Ross. "Inspector, have your automatic ready and your best bracelets. Now, Cross, lead the way."

Carrying his barrel-shaped copper extinguisher, the miserable Cross tiptoed into the room where the psychic Miss Kelly had been accustomed to doze through the night, to dream her dreams and feel the vibrations of oppressive and circumambient hatred. It was comfortably, but simply furnished.

Through the partly closed door leading into the sick-room they could hear Lorna and Jimmie talking.

"Never mind, Jimmie," Lorna was saying. "I like to light my own cigarette." The listeners held their breath.

Then a shrill terrified scream seemed to tear the very ear-drums of the men in the adjoining room. The eldritch scream was followed by a second, a stifled cry.

Ross rushed in, the others following. What they saw, against a background of flame, was a slender middle-aged woman in a trailing blue silk negligee standing erect beside the bed, her hands quivering at her sides.

The bed was empty. In her blazing eyes, the first instinctive terror snapped like a mechanism into a look of livid venomous hatred at Lorna, at Jimmie, at the new intruders. The lace curtains were already rioting in dancing flames.

"Secure her, Callahan!—quick, your handcuffs, on that woman by the bed!—Cross, hurry put that fire out! Lorna!

Lorna"—he made a movement toward the girl, who was swaying almost stupefied, too close to the curtains.

Cross alone responded promptly, his extinguisher filling the room with a thick smoke.

An instant of dazed hesitation upon Callahan's part, and it was too late! The woman in blue, now turned to a fury of insane ferocity, reached swiftly to the head of the bed, drew out a pistol and fired point blank at Lorna.

Lorna, staggering and groping for a chair, fell into a heap upon the floor.

With a swift movement Ross pinioned the woman's arms from behind and Callahan, with an oath, snapped the handcuffs, at some risk to himself, upon her quivering wrists. Simultaneously his automatic went off—toward his prisoner.

She managed to fire another shot before she, still a struggling maniac, was finally disarmed by Ross and Burke, who had rushed in as directed, stood for some instants with his back to the door watching the scene in amazed stupefaction. To do him justice, it was all happening with a too lightning-like rapidity for thought.

The handcuffed woman, bleeding from the right side, now sank down upon her own bed.

Her second shot, however, had grazed the front of Callahan's thigh and a spot of blood was spreading over the gray of his trousers.

"Who is this—who is she?" Callahan finally blurted out.

"It's Mrs. Goold. She's a maniac. She's wounded, but hold her fast," shouted Ross bending, with a ravaged face, over Lorna. "Good God! Lorna!—Lorna! What have I done to you? I asked too much—too much!" he was repeating to himself as he sought with trembling fingers for a pulse in her temple.

"Thank God! She's alive!" he cried out in a sudden exultation. "Get a doctor somebody—Jimmie—quick!"

Lorna at this point opened her eyes and smiled pallidly.

"I—I must have—how stupid of me," she murmured faintly. "But—but—"

"I know—I know, my dear," Ross was soothing her. "But you'll be all right now. Were—were you hit?"

"I felt a sting in my shoulder—" she sighed, "it hurts." And again her eyes closed.

Frantically, Ross seized and lifted her in his arms. The shoulder of her dress and the chair against which it had been leaning were wet and crimson with blood.

Suddenly the manacled woman, notwithstanding her ebbing strength and though held up between Callahan and Burke, made a desperate movement toward the limp figure of Lorna. Callahan appeared dazed. Burke, however, held fast and jerked the woman backward. Then he thrust her into the chair vacated by Lorna.

Ross, placing Lorna upon the bed, laid bare her shoulder, tore a portion of the sheet from the bed and was applying a bandage to the wound. Cross was still busily extinguishing the flames.

The door from the hall suddenly opened to admit the ghost-like figures of Wells and Burton into the smoke-clouded apartment.

"That Mrs. Goold?" demanded Burton, pointing at the quivering woman held down by Burke.

"Yes, sir," nodded Callahan. "Shot me, the damned wild-cat," he glanced down at the crimson hand and stain upon his thigh. "Shot the young lady, too," he jerked his head toward the bed.

"Yes, shot the young lady, too," muttered the prisoned woman with a strange fading venom. "And shot Jim Goold, too," her voice trembled with a last dying fury. "He'll never go to that vile Sheila creature again. Too bad I couldn't lay my hands on her."

The men gazed at one another in awed amazement. Jealousy and hatred had turned a well-bred though neurotic woman into a rabid animal, had brought a whirlwind of death and disaster in their train! Poor Miss Kelly had not been so far wrong, after all.

Jimmie, still bewildered and terrified, reappeared to announce that Dr. Humphreys would arrive directly.

He uttered a cry of unrestrained distress. The sight of Lorna upon the bed, of blood flowing, shattered for a moment even the steady nerve of Jimmie.

30
Finale

Ross refused any explanations until the arrival of Dr. Humphreys. Mrs. Goold, still guarded by Burke had meanwhile been removed to the nurses' room. Her strength was visibly ebbing. Callahan's accidental bullet had perforated her internal organs. Her time was brief. To all of them this seemed better news than would have been the promise of her recovery.

With tense emotional absorption Ross hung near the bedside the while Dr. Humphreys, pale and greatly perturbed by the scene that greeted his eyes in the bedroom of his former patient, proceeded to make the examination of Lorna's wound.

"It is not serious," he finally pronounced. "The bone has only been slightly chipped. The flesh will heal quickly. You may feel twinges occasionally for a time, Lorna, but eventually even that will pass."

Burton, Wells and Jimmie, who had left the room, were called back by Ross and Callahan was taken to a neighboring room to have his own wound treated. Fortunately it was exceedingly slight, having merely grazed the flesh of his thigh.

"It's very extraordinary, very strange," murmured Dr. Humphreys shaking his head as he came back with Callahan, the latter limping slightly. "I suppose you gentlemen will hold me to blame as the medical authority that pronounced that woman a paralytic, but I assure you—"

"You need say no more," broke in Ross, with his old smile now he knew Lorna was not seriously harmed. "You diagnosed the case correctly as hysterical paralysis."

"No one can tell exactly how such cases begin," Dr. Humphreys looked up grateful for this ray of sympathetic understanding.

"Or how they end—or why," added Ross with a nod.

"But how do you—did you tell me you were a doctor? I forget."

"No. I didn't, Dr. Humphreys. I am not a doctor. I've never had time for such highly specialized knowledge. But your own record of the case confirmed my suspicion regarding Mrs. Goold."

"My—own—record?" He repeated in slow amazement. "That no one has seen but myself—and my substitute when I was away—"

"And myself, Dr. Humphreys. I'm very sorry, but I had to see that record and—I knew you would not show it— nor could you under your Æsculapian oath as a physician."

"Then how in the name of—"

"Very simply. When I came to see you in your office early this afternoon, to talk to you about Mrs. Goold's nurses, those nurses in effect interested me little. It was Mrs. Goold I desired to talk about. Unfortunately, and you must forgive me, doctor, your manner was not inviting. Then a piece of luck came my way."

Dr. Humphreys stared at him blankly.

"You were called out for a minute—it wasn't longer, I know—I was alone in your consulting room—"

"And you looked into my records?" the physician muttered aghast.

"Precisely. I am sorry, and I apologize. But it was a life and death matter. I had to. Hysterical paralysis you have already pronounced, yourself, here in our hearing. You have said nothing of the little medical Latin phrase standing on a line by itself on the card: 'Femina frigida.'"

"Outrageous, sir," cried Dr. Humphreys. "Outrageous!"

"But the truth," added Ross, "and that is what I absolutely had to know. Remember, doctor, this is a very grave matter. She was an hysterical paralytic and a frigid woman. The paralysis, as you agree, can come and go no man knoweth whence, whither or how. But the femina frigida has certain well-known psychological characteristics. Because of her own anaesthetic disability, because she cannot tolerate the love of her husband, she is often furiously, even insanely, jealous if that love strays elsewhere."

The men glanced in the direction of Lorna, and Dr. Humphreys sternly observed:

"Hardly a discussion before a young lady."

"Before that young lady virtually all things may be discussed," Ross answered warmly. "She has a better brain than most of us and, besides, I shall take that phase of psychology up in the class of which she is a member. Frigidity often leads to criminality. Much cleptomania has its origin in frigidity, and other and graver crimes as well."

"I have never dabbled in Freudism and all that sort of filth," announced Dr. Humphreys almost with arrogance.

"More's the pity, Doctor," answered Ross quietly. "If you had paid some attention to modern psychology, of which Freud is the discoverer, to be sure, but only one exponent, much of these tragic occurrences might have been avoided."

"Sir, how dare you!" cried the physician purpling.

"Never mind now," put in Burton heavily. "What we want to know now is how you reached your singular conclusion to this case—true as it seems to be."

"Air-tight, I'd call it," put in Callahan truculently, as though his own work was assailed.

"By the only process an investigation can successfully employ, Mr. Burton," proceeded Ross, "I eliminated the impossible. And, however, improbable the remaining factor, that factor fixed the line of investigation. It is simple to the point of being elementary. My earliest conviction was that it was not only an inside job, but one executed by someone long an inmate of the house, who knew all its ways, who knew that Goold kept a pistol and where; who knew the peculiarity of a switch disconnecting the doorbell, whose appearance would set Goold's facial muscles into amazed stupefaction; and, lastly, a later detail, who knew Miss Baker's weaknesses and habits sufficiently well to count upon them. It all culminated in my succeeding in frightening the woman in there into leaping out of bed, thus proving that she's no paralytic."

"But I thought you were all excited about the nurses? And didn't you make a man who shall be nameless confess in my office that he actually saw a nurse doing the shooting?"

"Yes, certainly. My call at the doctor's office, that confirmation of Forbes's and one other fact completed the chain of logic that the so-called nurse who shot James Goold and the woman handcuffed in there, his widow, were one and the same person. Incidentally, she should throw light on the gland theory of crime."

"I don't get you there, Professor," grinned Callahan weakly. His remark was ignored and Burton nodded emphatically. He understood.

"What was the third fact?" he pressed.

"My suspicions, as I implied, were early turned toward Mrs. Goold. I had been waiting and asking for an opportunity to put my theory to the test. Now as it happens, last Saturday evening I was dining with Miss Storey. As luck would have it—the Inspector will tell you how great a part luck plays in the detective's calling—as luck would have it, the rain poured in torrents when the time came for

me to leave. I could have got a taxi, of course, but when
Miss Storey courteously suggested that I stay the night, I
jumped at the chance. A night in this house was what I
needed more than anything else. I managed to keep awake
far enough into the small hours to watch for any night
prowlers about the house.

"I sat at a crack in the door till nearly three watching in
the dark. But my vigil was rewarded. A woman in nurses'
costume came stealing along the corridor and trying Miss
Storey's door. The door was locked. She failed and slunk
back. But the face which I could see only dimly was neither Miss Kelly's nor Miss Baker's. Nor was the carriage or
the figure. I recognized these again in Mrs. Goold. In fact
I had been certain she was Mrs. Goold."

"Why was she trying Miss Storey's door?" broke in
Wells. Lorna was gazing wide-eyed at Ross.

"Oh, I forgot to tell you that earlier in the evening Miss
Storey had happened to mention that her uncle's lawyer,
Laimbeer, had that morning read the will to her aunt and
herself; and how sorry Miss Storey was that though she
had intended to take care of her aunt for the rest of her
days, the testator had left his niece the bulk of his residuary
estate, and contrary to usage, the house and all its contents.
That is almost invariably left to the wife. James Goold,
you see, knew his wife better than we might suppose.

"If my theory was correct, that was about the time the
woman in there might attempt to make a murderous attack
upon Miss Storey. Miss Storey will confirm me that then
and there I begged her to lock her doors and to lock them
every night for the few days until the case was settled—in
any event, until I came back from Westchester."

"And by that, you saved my life, Professor Ross," Lorna
murmured faintly from the bed and she put out her hand.
Her eyes were bright with tears.

"Thank Heaven for that," Ross pressed her hand gently.

"If you were so sure of all that," Burton came back in stubborn protest, "then why on earth did you go to West-chester at all?"

"Because my young friend Jimmie, whom I had sent out there, called for me, and because that matter had to be cleared up."

"That's what beats me," muttered Callahan as if to himself. He was like a child who will remain obtuse to a jewel, but will covet a jack-knife. "How did you hit on that Hunky glazier going out there when all the police in America couldn't find him?"

"I don't know—I don't know—" Ross answered half-ab-sently, as though considering something else. "Or, rather, I do know. I can only say that was a bit of special knowledge which as you and I know, Inspector, the detective can use in quantity. I happened to know that the men who killed the Russian monk, Rasputin, had made implacable ene-mies of Rasputin's old sect, the Khlysts. They are a fana-tical bunch, almost like the Thugs of India. And since their slogan is, 'There is no redemption save through sin,' murder stands in their way not at all. On the very night of the crime I came across some bits of evidence that led me to believe the man who stole the picture was either an Eastern European or an Asiatic."

"You mean the seeds?" all but whispered Lorna.

"Yes, the seeds. Here they are, by the way," he brought forth an envelope from his pocket. "Datura seeds. Asiatics, gypsies and eastern European criminals, often scatter a few of them at the scene of their crime that their deed may remain unpunished—lucky, you know."

"Yes," cried Burton. "All right, I follow you. But how could you tell he didn't murder Goold?"

"To begin with, the seeds were under the picture, not at the desk. But leaving that as a trifle, you, Commis-sioner, and you, Inspector, recall our observing that there were no signs of struggle in the gallery. Yet Goold was no weakling. He was a powerful man. Can you imagine him offering no resistance to an assailant?

"But suppose the man had stolen in and shot him from behind? I did not think so. Goold had been shot with a bullet from his own package in his desk. That was established by your fire-arm expert at Headquarters, Commissioner."

"Yeh, sure was," nodded Callahan, like a confirming consultant.

"Then what was the alternative? That Goold sat disinterestedly watching the assailant taking Goold's own pistol from his desk and quietly shooting him? Nonsense, obviously. The shooting was done by someone in the house, someone who knew well Goold's ways, someone who could walk with a catlike softness, someone who had stolen Goold's pistol on some other occasion and shot him with it—on that fatal afternoon. The expression in Goold's dead face amounted to chill horror. He knew his wife to be a paralytic. Yet he had caught a glimpse of his wife's face in the mirror of the radio console the instant before she shot him."

"Very fine-spun," Wells shook his head. "Seems to work out, but very fine-spun I call it. And she opened the doors, and she also disconnected the bell?"

"Certainly! I admit," Ross went on with a laugh, "that this was the weak link in my chain of reasoning. That was the chief reason I wanted to catch the picture thief—whom Jimmie Trumbull really caught, by the way. I wanted to hear from the thief's own lips that he had not shot Goold—that he had found him dead. That he was prepared to kill if necessary, but by a strange turn of events, possible in life but improbable in fiction, Goold had been killed a few moments earlier by a more implacable enemy."

"And when this Russian up there in Westchester told you that, you believed him?" Burton threw out half-contemptuously.

"Why not? It confirmed my own theory. The man himself, who was clever enough to play glazier, to throw a golf-ball, break a pane and be called in, clever enough to steal the Rembrandt in an attempt to saddle the theft upon Erzeroff, in order to cause that poor roving spirit the frightful torture of long imprisonment, that man was clever enough to know that his life is already forfeit, and that it could not be more so no matter how many men he had killed. I believed him and the results have justified that belief. The woman who killed Goold confessed it in your hearing."

"One thing I wish to know—how you got track of that glazier," sighed Callahan with a look of pain. His wounded thigh was evidently hurting him.

"Nothing extraordinary in that," Ross answered quietly. "Jimmie Trumbull and I took a little trip on the East Side, the real Bagdad of this city. All I wanted was to find if there were any Khlysts about. I happened to know something of them during my Siberian experiences. I was lucky. After that all we needed was to watch poor Erzeroff. I am only sorry we could not save his life. But—the wages of sin—" he smiled sadly, reminiscently, "few people escape the penalty, one way or another."

"Now, if it's a fair question," Callahan spoke up more energetically, professional curiosity winning over physical pain, "what first gave you the idea where to look for the right person? That is, isn't it, the thing we all want to know?"

"A number of small details," smiled Ross, "and one of them was what you considered perhaps the most trivial and absurd: The psychic Miss Kelly's testimony of a pervasive feeling of hatred surrounding her. May sound funny, but some people have the gift of feeling atmosphere even when they are asleep. Indeed, more so then, for they feel with their subconscious. I have a knack that way myself—but that would take us into mysticism. Miss Kelly, I gathered, often slept, and Mrs. Goold saw to it that she did. It was then Mrs. Goold donned the nurses' costume and prowled like an evil spirit about the house. Somewhere in an unopened closet that nurse's costume will be found."

"Oughtn't we to look into those nurses as accessories?" speculated Burton.

"Possibly Miss Baker—as an unconscious accessory, but not Miss Kelly. However, Miss Baker was probably sufficiently poisoned by Mrs. Goold to make her ill for a day or two, so the fiendish woman could do away with Miss Storey. Thank Heaven, she failed. My best advice now would be to leave all that alone. Sufficient unto the day is the evil thereof."

Callahan had telephoned for two more men and for two matrons from Central Office, the latter to dress Mrs. Goold before removal.

Cross was ordered to disperse the huddling servants with their eager frightened faces from the hallways and Ross and Jimmie led Lorna, who laughingly refused to be carried, to her own sitting room. Wells and Burton went down into the gallery to await the removal of the prisoner to the criminal section of Bellevue. Callahan felt called upon to remain where he was and await the arrival of the central office people.

The central office men, however, and the matrons as well, arrived too late. When Dr. Humphreys returned to her, Burke, her guardian, informed him that, "she'd kind of sighed and gone off to sleep." Dr. Humphreys bent down and made a hurried examination.

"Sleep," he repeated somberly, straightening up. "No. It's not sleep. She'll never wake again in this world. And perhaps that's best for her."

This news, for the present, it was deemed advisable to withhold from Lorna.

Lorna, however, though having both friends in close proximity, seemed restless and ill at ease.

"Sheila's letters!" she suddenly exclaimed, thinking of the cause of all this train of ills.

"Don't worry about those, child," Ross reassured her. "They were under the mattress where Mrs. Goold got the pistol. They are in my pocket now, however, and I shall give them to Sheila tonight."

But still Lorna appeared uneasy. Finally, upon a pretext, she sent Jimmie out of the sitting room.

"What is the matter, Lorna," Ross asked her gently. "Is the pain too acute?"

"Oh, that's nothing," she sighed. "But it is all so terrible. Poor Aunt Julia! It's her mind, of course. What will they do to her?" Ross knowing what he knew urged her to turn her thoughts away so far as possible from that subject.

"There is the charming Eastern doctrine," he reminded her, "that each one of us has to live out his own peculiar karma."

"Oh, I suppose so," she breathed. "And now, that the 'case' is over, I shall be left all alone,"—she smiled, but her lips quivered—"and see you only in class—if I ever come back to class?"

Ross gazed at her for an instant before replying.

"Lorna," he took her hand in both his own, "if I were a few years younger, or you a few years older and not so ridiculously rich, I would propose an arrangement vastly superior to the one you outline."

"What difference," whispered Lorna, "do years and money make if two people are—are fond of each other?"

"Fond of each other!" Ross laughed. Then he grew suddenly grave. This was his temptation in the wilderness.

"We shall be fond of each other to our dying day my dear," he went on. "Of that I am certain. But in the meanwhile I know a young man who loves you as you should be loved, a young man incidentally, whose heart is pure gold. I mean our own Jimmie," he added with a misty smile of almost paternal kindness and tenderness in his eyes. "I will send him in to you this minute."

And softly, with the whimsical gesture of a blithe comradely gayety, he tiptoed out of the room.

THE EDINGTONS
THE HOUSE OF THE
VANISHING
GOBLETS

THE
SLEEPING CAT

Isabel Ostrander

THE SEVEN BLACK
CHESSMEN
John Huntingdon

DEAD
WEIGHT
ADDISON
SIMMONS

Coachwhip Publications
CoachwhipBooks.com

SINISTER CARGO

STANLEY HART PAGE

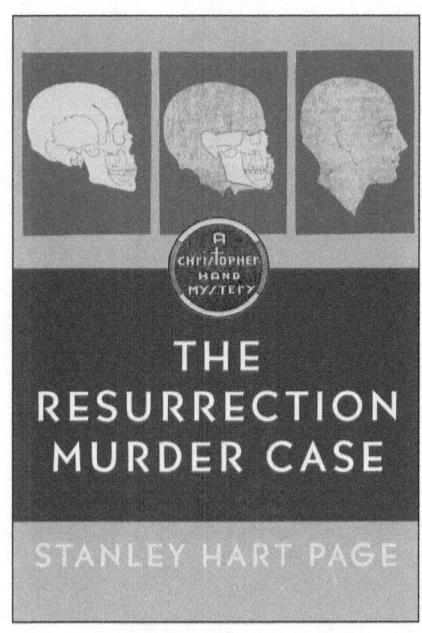

THE RESURRECTION MURDER CASE

STANLEY HART PAGE

FOOL'S GOLD

STANLEY HART PAGE

TRAGIC CURTAIN

STANLEY HART PAGE

Coachwhip Publications

CoachwhipBooks.com

THE
MYSTERY
OF THE
FOLDED
PAPER

HULBERT
FOOTNER

The
Hollow Tree
Mystery

MADELON ST. DENIS

VIRGINIA RATH

FERRYMAN,
TAKE HIM ACROSS!

No Face to
Murder
EDITH HOWIE

Coachwhip Publications

CoachwhipBooks.com

THE QUINNY HITE
MYSTERIES
CHINESE RED · HERE LIES THE BODY

RICHARD BURKE

THE MAY DAY MYSTERY

OCTAVUS ROY COHEN

MURDER'S COMING

GRAVE WITHOUT GRASS

BY
DONALD CLOUGH CAMERON

MURDER IN
MALAYA

FATAL SHADOWS

DEATH OVER
HER SHOULDER

DOROTHY
COLE
MEADE

Coachwhip Publications

CoachwhipBooks.com

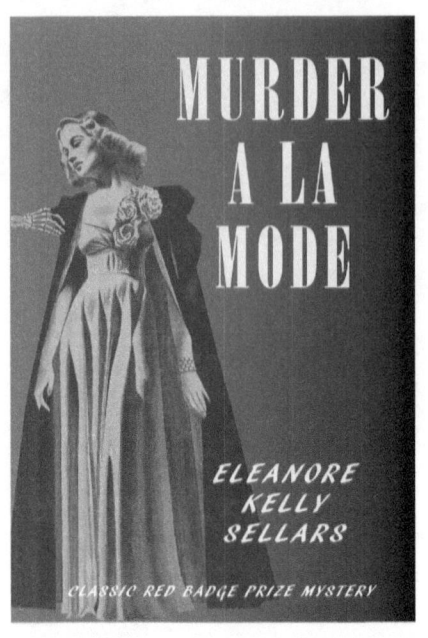

MURDER A LA MODE

ELEANORE KELLY SELLARS

CLASSIC RED BADGE PRIZE MYSTERY

MURDER ON THE BLUFF

ESTHER TYLER

MURDER BY JURY

MURDER ON THE APHRODITE

RUTH BURR SANBORN

THE 5.18 MYSTERY

J. Jefferson Farjeon

Coachwhip Publications

CoachwhipBooks.com

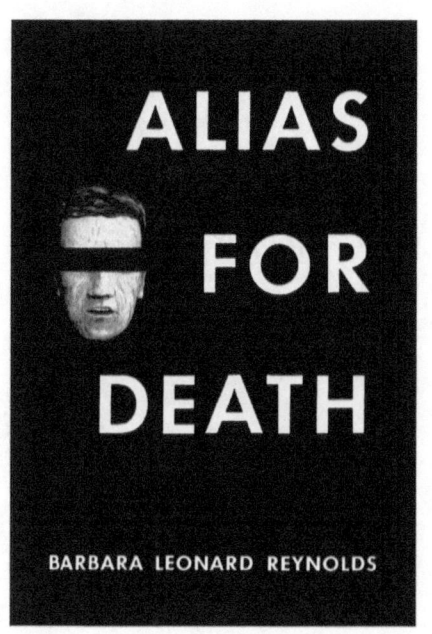

ALIAS FOR DEATH

BARBARA LEONARD REYNOLDS

THERE IS NO RETURN

THE ADELAIDE ADAMS MYSTERIES

ANITA BLACKMON

Jack Dolph

MURDER MAKES THE MARE GO

FEAR CAME FIRST

VERA KELSEY

Coachwhip Publications

CoachwhipBooks.com

MURDER AT DRAKE'S ANCHORAGE

E. LEE WADDELL

MURDER AT THE KENTUCKY DERBY

CHARLES PARMER

MURDER ENDS THE SONG

ALFRED MEYERS

3 DETECTIVES
MURDER ON THE RAILS
WHITECHURCH • THORNE • TORGERSON

Coachwhip Publications

CoachwhipBooks.com

THOMAS KINDON

MURDER
IN THE
MOOR

DRESSED
TO KILL

Emma Lou Fetta

GRIMM
DEATH

THE
GROUSE
MOOR
MURDER

JOHN FERGUSON

Coachwhip Publications

CoachwhipBooks.com

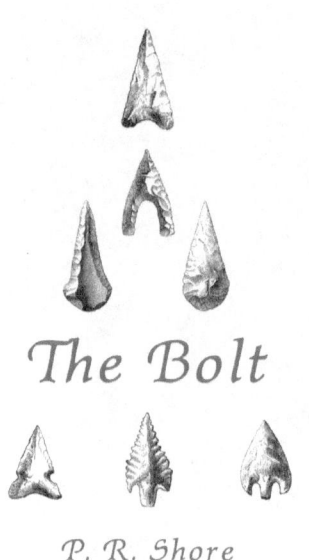

The Bolt

P. R. Shore

MURDER
IN A WALLED TOWN
KATHERINE WOODS

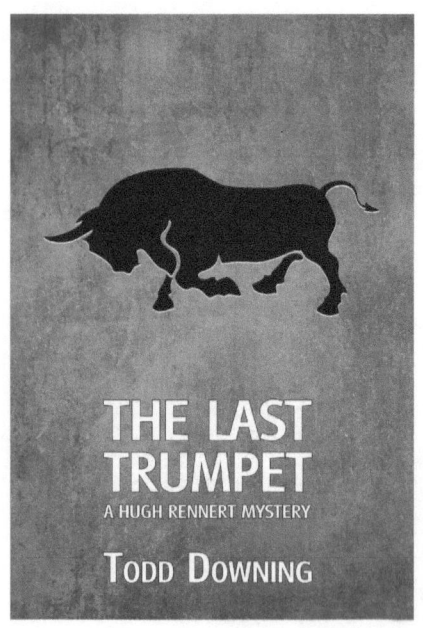

THE LAST
TRUMPET
A HUGH RENNERT MYSTERY

TODD DOWNING

DEATH SAILS
THE NILE
F. BURKS MCKINLEY

Coachwhip Publications

CoachwhipBooks.com

FEAR OF FEAR

FLORENCE RYERSON
COLIN CLEMENTS

MURDER IN THE FAMILY

NICE PEOPLE MURDER

Mary Hastings Bradley

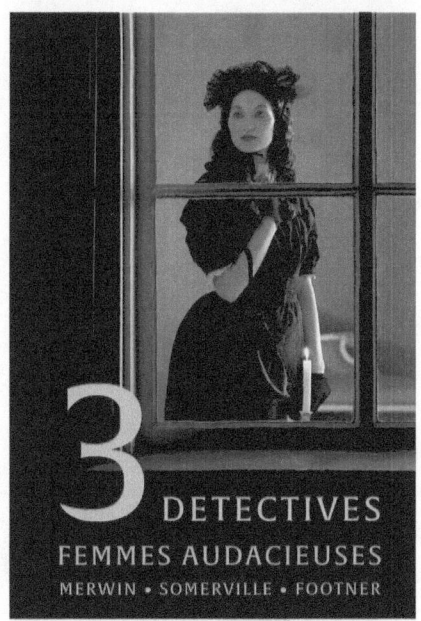

3 DETECTIVES
FEMMES AUDACIEUSES
MERWIN • SOMERVILLE • FOOTNER

DEATH DOWN EAST

Eleanor Blake

Coachwhip Publications

CoachwhipBooks.com